FORECASTING THE FORWARD

MILE HIGH SPORTS SERIES
BOOK 1

JENNIFER J WILLIAMS

JJW PRODUCTIONS LLC

This book is dedicated to all the self-proclaimed nerds. The girls who love STEM, technology, and above all else, weather. Keep on doing you, ladies.

Becca

CHAPTER 1

"You're a great friend, Dani, but I think I might die if I have another blind date. Even if it's one set up by you."

"Come on."

"No. They keep getting worse," I moan to my co-worker, Danica.

If I have one more well-meaning friend, or co-worker, attempt to set me up, I may lose my mind. Here lies Rebecca Stephens, meteorologist extraordinaire, killed by too much small-talk, overuse of Axe Body Spray, and way too many dick pics.

May she finally rest in peace.

Alone, but in peace.

"Okay, but seriously, this is the one for you. I promise!" Danica says, gripping my hand between her ridiculously cold ones. Goodness, how are her hands this cold? We are sitting outside in August, where the temperature topped out at a balmy ninety-nine degrees at Denver International Airport today. Courtesy of our studio being surrounded by concrete buildings shooting up dozens of stories, I'm sure our downtown temp is into the triple digits.

"No more dates, Dani. Really. I can't go on one more bad first date," I moan.

"They couldn't have all been bad," she says hesitantly. "You're the hottest meteorologist on Denver TV. Hell, maybe even in the entire state of Colorado. And you're regularly featured on national shows. How could these guys perform so badly? Do you think they're all nervous because you're famous?"

"I'm not famous," I murmur.

Danica scoffs. "In Denver we are. The only people who count as bigger celebrities here are the sports stars."

I find myself grimacing. "And those are the guys I definitely avoid. They think they're above everyone else, all cocky and self-absorbed. I have no desire to experience that day in and day out."

Danica laughs, her pitch higher than normal, and I notice her face reddens slightly. I chalk it up to the warm temperatures and move on. "Should I give you a list of why every blind date has gone badly?"

"Uh, okay," she says, avoiding eye contact. "Sure."

I slap my hands together, rubbing them against one another as I excitedly launch into what should be a very bad list. Somehow, it's become a code for me, and it's almost as if it's gotten so bad that I don't think a man can give me a good first date. "I had the guy who told me his mother kept all of his hair clippings."

"Like … as a kid?" Danica asks hesitantly.

"No. His entire life," I say smugly. Her face screws up in disgust, and I soldier on. "There was the forty-year-old man who lived at home with his parents. And before you talk about the economy, prices of everything, and saving up for a house, just know, he'd never moved out."

"Never?" Danica whispers.

"Never. He doesn't even give money toward rent or food, and bragged that if 'things got serious with us,'" I use air quotes, "It would be totally cool for me to move in with him. In his parents' basement."

"Oh, dear," Danica says.

"One guy asked if I'd be a third for him and his wife. Another asked for him and his husband. They were curious, he said. They both liked my voice on television, and said I had nice calves."

"Both? The husband showed up?"

"Yup. Then they did the dine-and-dash, leaving me to cover the entire bill."

"It's a pity the network wouldn't consider a new piece called 'Becca Dates in Denver.' You wouldn't need to do any research," Dani muses.

"Which is why I can't do any more dates. I've come to the realization that I'm not meant to have a relationship."

"I promise I'll leave you alone, but only if you let me fix you up this one last time," she says hopefully. I sigh in frustration.

"Can I think about it?" I hate hurting her feelings, but I'm so over blind dates.

"You know what?" she says as she stands, "I'll take it. That's better than a flat-out refusal. I'll see you back at the station."

After Danica scurries off, I tilt my head back, closing my eyes, and enjoy the warmth of this beautiful day. I know I'll miss the heat when we're dealing with hurricane-force winds, and blizzard-like conditions, during the winter months. Colorado loves to advertise three hundred days of sunshine per year, but they neglect to inform visitors and newcomers that the remainder of the year is filled with cold, snow, thunderstorms, and fog … sometimes all in the same day. I thought I knew what chaotic weather was like when I moved here for my job at the ABC affiliate. Growing up in Indiana, I was used to severe weather, snowstorms, and the kind of humid cold that could freeze the snot in my nose as soon as I stepped outside. Once I graduated from Valparaiso University with my degree in meteorology , I grabbed the first broadcast position I could find, serving the tiny market of Gulfport, Mississippi. Coming from the Midwest, I was thrilled to be on the coast, and assumed — incorrectly as it turned out — that I'd get to cover hurricanes every year. In my three years there, only one hurricane came close to Gulfport, and it happened the week I was back in Indiana for my grandfather's funeral.

After Gulfport, I moved up to Knoxville, Tennessee. After two years there, I took a morning position with a station in Cincinnati, then moved again, to Kansas City. When the morning meteorologist position opened up in Denver, I was thrilled to apply. I'd always been fascinated by the Rocky Mountains, especially how the topography and elevation impact weather. I've been blissfully happy in my position here for five years, and finally accepted the chief meteorologist position a year ago. They're going to have to forcibly remove me to get me out of here.

I was meant to be a Coloradan. I find joy in every season, and I never miss an opportunity to gape at the mountains. Great food, shopping, and outdoor activities. The dating market, however, was drier than a La Niña summer in Colorado. Any man I do meet shows his true colors within two dates: he's either married, a compulsive liar, talks about having an open relationship on the first date, or, like I explained to Danica, lives at home with his mom.

"He's as windy as a sack full of farts," Grammy used to say. My grandmother, God rest her sassy soul, was from southern Kentucky, near the Tennessee border. She grew up dirt poor. I thought that was just a phrase, until she explained that the house where she spent her first five years literally didn't have flooring. It was just a dirt floor. One of nine siblings, Grammy fondly remembered her momma reading to them every night by candlelight, and all the fun she and her sisters could have with only the outside as a toy. "We played a lot of pretend. On the rare chance we got a new toy, oh my, we'd be happier than a dead pig in the sunshine."

Translation: they had fun.

Grammy taught me to find joy in the little things. Don't focus on trivial matters. Look at the big picture before writing something — or someone — off.

Which is why I'll let Danica set me up one last time. Her heart is in the right place, but I think I need a dating moratorium. A man sabbatical. A no-sex semester.

Besides, it's not like men can really help me out sexually. When was the last time I had a male-led orgasm? Goodness. It's been years. Why is finding the clit so hard for men? Are they really that dense, or do they actually not care about a woman's pleasure? At this point, I'm beginning to think it's the latter.

Sighing, I grab my bag from under the table and stand up to push in my chair. As I look down to see a new text message, I hit something solid. Gasping, I let go of my phone, throwing my arms out to balance myself. I already envision slamming into the pavement, and hope I avoid scraping my face. No matter what I tell viewers, they'll assume the worst. Or, they'll think I'm doing it for attention. I can never win, and usually get at least one hateful email per week about something. My skirt was too tight. Too pink. Too loose. Too bland. Someone didn't like my hair. Thought it looked like a hooker's hair. Asked if I owned a hairbrush. Have I gained weight? How far along am I in the pregnancy? Do I ever eat? I need to see a physician to treat my undiagnosed bulimia. Oh, and I mispronounced the name of a town in southern France while showing a video of a flash flood there. How dare I.

Before gravity takes over, a warm arm clamps around my waist, yanking me into the solid surface I'd bounced off. Another arm lashes out, grabbing my phone with alarmingly quick reflexes.

"Are you okay?" Wow. That deep voice, a baritone that I feel in my bones, seems smooth, yet gritty, at the same time. I have an immediate thought of that voice talking me through an orgasm, and I instinctively shudder. For fuck's sake. It's been way too long since I've had sex, and my lady bits are taking notice. My nipples are diamond peaks smushed into his thick chest, and it's the most action I've gotten in forever.

Men may not know where the clit is, but I still enjoy the process.

As I gather my wits about me, my eyes take in the body from the neck down. Athletic shorts snugly cover incredibly thick thighs, while black and white slides sit on his sturdy feet. How can I be thinking of feet as sturdy? I don't know, but this guy has them.

A loose University of Michigan T-shirt adorns a thick chest. It's a well-loved shirt, the large M faded in the middle, but the fabric feels soft under my fingertips. That's right, I'm now fingering his shirt.

"Oh! I'm so sorry, I wasn't looking," I stammer, pushing against his chest to step away. It's only then that I get a view of his face. And holy hell, what a face. I should know, as he's featured on the news almost daily.

Jacob Mitchell.

Star forward for the NHL Denver Wolves.

Jacob is known more by his nickname of Jax, but I've never thought the name suited him. Jax sounds like a pompous name of someone my father would bring around the house for me to date. A man who wears a sweater over his shoulders and boat shoes all year. Jacob, however, explains the testosterone and man still holding me.

It explains the athletic slides, as well as the tree-trunk sized thighs that could probably crack a coconut if he tried hard enough. A backwards hat covers dark blond curls that always look perfectly out of control, and I hate knowing I've thought about what it might feel like to run my fingers through them. I just know his hair is soft.

"You okay, darlin'?" he asks again, his stupid southern twang hitting all the right places in my body. When his grin widens, I realize he knows he's affecting me, and that really pisses me off.

I hate athletes. Loathe. Detest.

That's not entirely true, as almost every long-term boyfriend I've had in my life has been an athlete in one way or another.

Professional athletes? Not enough words to express my disdain for them.

"Do I know you from somewhere?" he says, and I laugh sarcastically.

"That's the best you can come up with?"

His brow furrows as he studies me. "That wasn't a line. You look really familiar."

"I get that a lot." I'm not going to explain myself. He probably only watches the sports report on my channel, undoubtedly ignoring anything else newsworthy.

"Me too."

I roll my eyes as I push away from him. Yeah, he's still holding onto my waist, and I'm clueless as to why I've stood stationary this entire time. Jeez, Becs. Get it together. "Okay. Great. Thanks for — well. You know. Saving me and all. Gotta go."

I step back, and the warmth of his arm drops from me. Beautiful baby blue eyes peer down at me in confusion, I'm sure due to me not falling at his feet like women undoubtedly do. He reaches up to twist his ball cap around, giving me a glimpse at his tousled curls pointing in every direction, before he slides the cap down onto his forehead. It's like his hat, when backwards, allows an open dialogue with Jacob. Once he turns it around, however, I can see the invisible wall slamming down as he schools his expression.

"You sure you're okay?" he asks again.

"Yup. Totally fine," I respond, slapping my hands together for an unknown reason. Am I okay? Hard to tell. Physically, yes. Emotionally, I'm a complete mess. This man has rattled me, which is something that rarely happens to me. "Thanks again."

"Hey!" Jacob calls out.

I shake my head, choosing to walk swiftly in the opposite direction from where I need to go, but I don't notice it until my arm is grabbed and I'm spun around.

"What?" I snap.

Jacob chuckles, and I feel the sound like the lightest of touches wafting across my skin. "You want your phone back, or is it mine now?"

I look at his bemused expression, one hand extended as he holds my phone toward me. "Oh. Yeah. Uh, sorry."

"Also, Spitfire, I think you were walking that way," he says, gesturing with his head behind us. "Although it's nice knowing I rattled you."

"I'm not rattled," I lie. "I forgot where I was going for a second."

"Uh huh. Keep telling yourself that," he says with a wicked grin.

"I just got turned around when I ran into you. Maybe I have a concussion from hitting your massive body." Blood drains from my face as my eyes widen, and Jacob's grin gets even bigger. "I mean you're like a brick wall, and I probably hit those amazing pecs. At least I didn't hit your dick, and oh my God, I need to stop talking now."

Jacob throws his head back in laughter, and mortification covers me. Growing up, I had trouble with not recognizing when I needed a filter. It took years of working on communication, as well as a very long-standing relationship with my therapist, to teach me the social skills I lacked. One interaction with Jacob Mitchell has me reeling, and I'm spiraling as I think back to a tumultuous childhood where I never felt I got the support and unconditional love I craved.

"I have to go," I mumble, ducking my head as I dash toward the station. I hear Jacob call after me, but I'm too embarrassed to stop. I pop into the building next to our station, knowing there's a connecting hallway, uneasy Jacob might follow me and do ... something. I don't know what.

Dashing into the first women's bathroom I can find, I collapse into the last stall, locking the door with shaky hands. A whirlwind of memories takes over as my breathing quickens.

How embarrassing can you be, Rebecca?

You have to apologize to the Miltons. You humiliated us.

I can't take you there! You'll say something stupid.

Such a disgrace, Rebecca.

Shut your mouth before you say something ridiculous.

God, my sister is so re —

No. I will not think of that word, and any of the other vile things my brother said to me growing up.

As the spiral threatens to take over, I hear a very distant voice reminding me that I control my own thoughts. My therapist, Simone, has been a light in the darkness for over a decade. She taught me years ago to focus on the present, looking at everything around me to ensure the past doesn't overwhelm me. *You've got this, Becca. They don't define you.*

I breathe raggedly as I take in my surroundings. It's been quite some time since someone, especially a man, threw me off my game so soundly. Simone is probably going to have all kinds of thoughts on this interaction.

Ten minutes later, my breathing under control and my skin no longer flushed, I make my way back to my cubicle at the station. I'm fortunate to have a desk by west-facing windows, giving me a breathtaking view of the Rocky Mountains. Cumulus clouds build above the mountain peaks, sure to bring some late summer thunderstorms to someone along the front range of Colorado. I sigh, shaking my head in awestruck wonder that I get to live here.

My usual gig is working the morning shift, but today I'm also covering the afternoon time slot for another meteorologist. I've been up since just after two in the morning, and I won't get home until around dinnertime. My phone chimes with a text from my ChatBook app, and I find myself smiling as I look forward to whatever my online friend has sent me.

I hate dating apps. Loathe them. The percentage of men who use them as a way to cheat on their partners, send unsolicited dick pics, blatantly lie about their lives, and treat women abysmally just makes me lean into the expectation I'll be living alone with my cats for the rest of my life. I'm only on ChatBook because it's more about conversation and connection than it is about 'matching' with someone. It started for me as a joke, and has never moved past messages. Maybe it's the fact that I'm completely anonymous on this app, using a stock photo of a bouquet of my favorite flower, a hyacinth, as my profile pic, and never using my name. My username is NerdGirl1025. I'm careful about giving out any personal details, and have yet to tell StickUM92 what state I live in. The only reason I know StickUM is male is because his profile pic is of his feet at the edge of what I think is the ocean. Well, I assume they're his feet. Maybe they aren't. Maybe I'm talking to a sixty-seven-year-old dog-hating woman who never leaves her dingy apartment in

Queens. Whatever the case, StickUM makes me laugh whenever I read his — or her — messages.

StickUM92: I cannot stand olives. How they look, taste, and even smell. I honestly can't understand how anyone can cook with them, let alone eat a handful. I've always hated them, which sucked as a kid because my mom thought they were a food group, and put them on everything. Because we were a "you sit here until you clean your plate" family, I was forced to finish them. A few times, I got away with telling her I had to go to the bathroom, then spitting a mouthful out. She caught onto that real quick, and then she checked my mouth before I was allowed to leave the table. Mom knows I don't like olives, but just sent me a big box of various olives for my birthday.

NerdGirl1025: It's your birthday? Oh wow! Happy birthday! Sorry about the olives, though. I hate them as well. I can't even eat anything with olive juice on it. They taint the entire meal. There are so many other vegetables I prefer! I can dump broccoli sprouts on everything, and eat a cucumber right off the vine.

StickUM92: Right? Tainted. And my birthday was in May. Never had broccoli sprouts, though.

NerdGirl1025: You're missing out on broccoli sprouts. Under-represented.

NerdGirl1025: But about your birthday ... seriously? And your own mother screwed it up?

StickUM92: I know. My mom either forgot to send them in May, or she doesn't remember when my birthday is. Honestly, I'm not surprised by any of it.

NerdGirl1025: I'm sorry. That sucks.

StickUM92: It is what it is. I've never had the best relationship with her.

NerdGirl1025: What about your dad? Can't he help?

StickUM92: They divorced when I was five, and my dad died a few years later. He had initiated the divorce, and my mom was really salty about it. She's been hunting for the elusive happily ever after ending since. She just married husband number five.

NerdGirl1025: Wow. Five?

StickUM92: Yup. That doesn't even count the revolving door of men while I was living at home. We moved a lot as she chased one guy or another. I think I saw every small town in east Texas by the time I was a teenager.

Ah. He lives in Texas. Probably why he seems so nice. I have yet to meet a southerner who hasn't been cheerful and fun to talk to.

NerdGirl1025: Well I say you slowly give the olives back to her, or donate them to a food kitchen. Might as well make some people happy with the disgusting little fake grapes.

StickUM92: Fake grapes. HA! I'll think about what to do with them. Sorry for being a little down-in-the-dumps. Any interaction with my mom makes me grumpy.

NerdGirl1025: I understand. That's how I am with my parents, so I get it.

When StickUM doesn't respond, I turn off my phone screen. Honestly, I get grumpy thinking of any of my family members. My father and older brother were the worst to me growing up, but I've held a lot of animosity toward my mother for turning a blind eye and allowing it to happen.

I haven't been home in quite some time, and I'm not sure how long it's been since I've spoken to any of them. As far as I'm concerned, I'm the last remaining Stephens family member.

Jacob

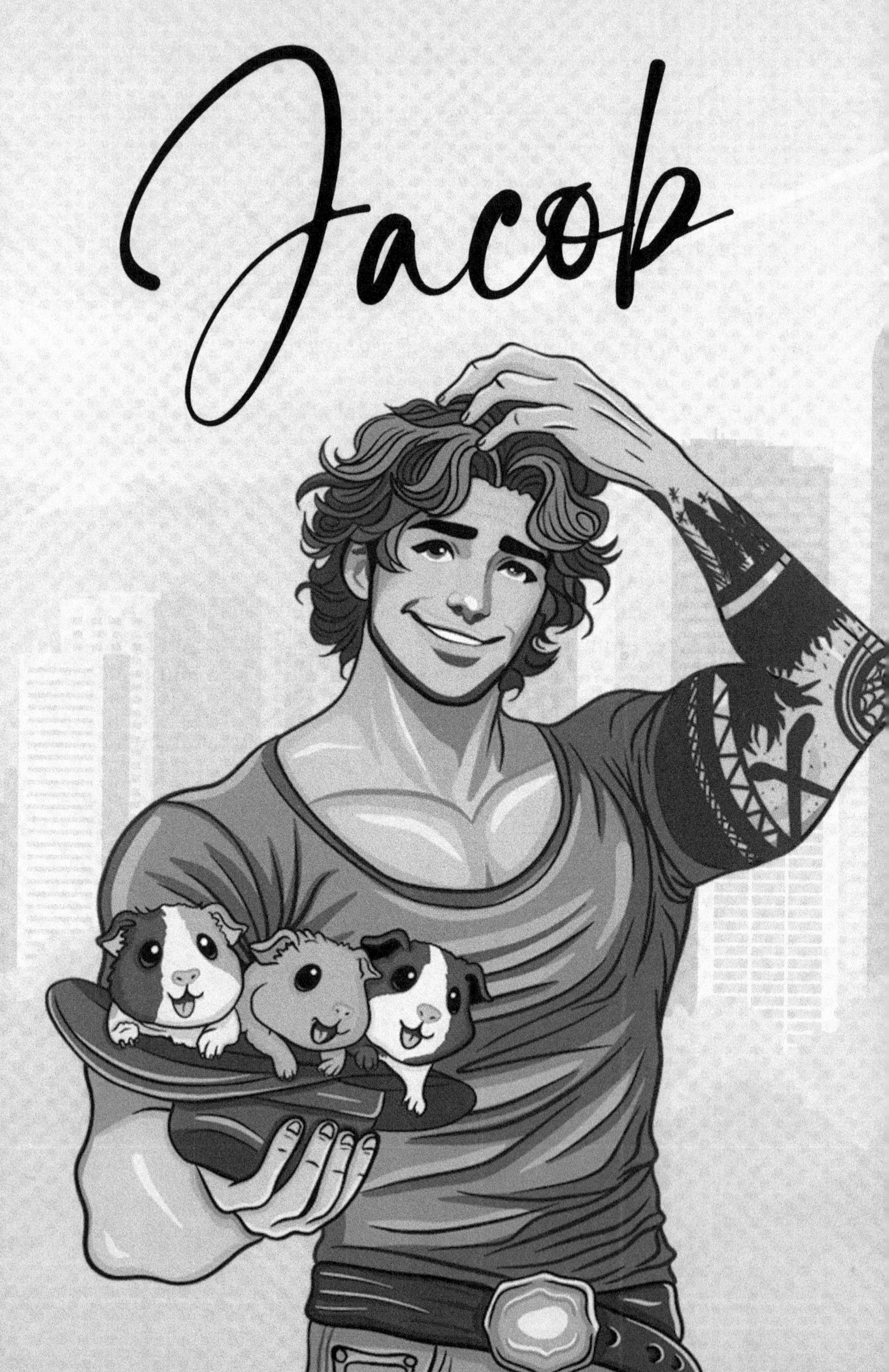

CHAPTER 2

I'M AN EASY-GOING GUY. I DON'T NEED MUCH. AS LONG AS I CAN BE around my buddies on the ice, my guinea pigs are healthy and waiting for me at home, and I have access to a grocery store and the library, I won't complain. I could do away with Internet and television. You won't find me burning the midnight oil at a club or bar. Hell, I rarely leave my downtown apartment building. Why bother? We've got a gym, a small convenience store, and I'm one block from the arena where I play with my team, the Denver Wolves. Adding in my phenomenal balcony overlooking the Rocky Mountains to the northwest, and I'm one hell of a happy man.

So explain to me why I'm watching a beautiful woman, with tears in her eyes, run away from me, and I'm tempted to run after her.

I have no problem getting pussy. I'm a fucking NHL forward. Women flock to me. I'm not bragging, just stating a fact. On the rare occasion I'm out with more than one of my teammates, we're surrounded within minutes. I've lost track of how many phone numbers, and hotel keys, have been snuck into my pockets. Yeah, I've taken advantage a time or two. But that shit gets old after a while. No one wants to get to know *me*. The real me. The me without hockey.

Who am I? I'm Jacob Mitchell, first line forward on the Wolves. I'm thirty four, and I'm no longer the young and hungry guy I was when I started in the league over a decade ago. Don't get me wrong, I'm still in excellent shape. But I'm slowing down. I can feel it, and my team sure as fuck sees it. I wasn't surprised to get called in to speak with the coach and GM today, the only reason I'm out of my apartment. It's the off-season. Training camp will start soon, but for now I'm enjoying sleeping in and doing nothing all day.

A lot of the guys move home during the summer, but not me. I happen to love Denver. Growing up in Texas, I dealt with heat and humidity. Then when I played college hockey at the University of Michigan, I dealt with cold and humidity. Here in Denver, humidity is a figment of my imagination. It's cold as balls in the winter, and we routinely get around one hundred degrees in the summer. But the dry climate is amazing, and I love being able to open my windows and sliding door overnight. I'm on the twenty-fifth floor, so it's not like anyone is going to break in.

As I head into the arena, I find it odd that we're meeting here. Our practice facility, located just outside of downtown, is much nicer, and each coach has better offices there. Here, we share the arena with the basketball team, and other times there are concerts and functions. It's still a nice setup, but I much prefer the practice facility.

Knocking on Coach's door, I hear him yelling for me to come in. I'm surprised to find he's not alone. Our general manager, one assistant coach, and the owner are also in attendance. As Coach's office is fairly small, it's cramped and awkward as I greet everyone individually.

"Alright, let's get this over with," Coach says. "I've got lunch plans with my wife, and I'm not making her wait again."

Coach Davenport married his girl only a few months ago, with the entire team in attendance. It was quite the story when he finally got with her, as she was a physical therapist for the team, and he was an assistant coach. She's also a decade younger than him. In any case, the grumpy coach calmed down quite a bit once she tamed him, and it's nice to see him smile every once in a while.

"Jax, do you know why we called you in?" The GM asks.

"Uh, not really, but I assume it has to do with my play at the end of last year," I answer sheepishly. We won the Cup a couple years ago, and then last year, it was like none of us knew how to skate. We barely made it into the playoffs, losing in the first round. My buddy Luca Santo retired when we won the Cup, and our other good friend Levi Quinn has nonchalantly said he's thinking about retiring this year. While I have no plans in place, I wonder if I'll be the resident old guy on the team, grasping at his youth and praying for survival, while the teenagers skate circles around me.

"Two things bring you here today," Coach says, clearing his throat as he tosses something at me. I catch it easily, looking down to find the captain's patch in my hand.

"What?" I breathe. Santzy was our captain two years ago, then Boone took it on last year before he asked for a trade to be closer to family, and it honestly never occurred to me that I'd be considered for captain in his absence.

"You're surprised?" Coach asks, chuckling.

"Well, yeah. I thought you'd give it to Levi." Levi is a powerful force on the ice, and I'd never want to be paired against him.

"We thought about it, but Levi would hate being captain. The team vote was tied between you, so it came to us as a tiebreaker. A captain is someone the young guys can go to for advice, or when they need help. No shot in hell our new draftees would feel comfortable going to him," Coach explains.

"That is true. Sometimes he even scares me," I admit. I love the guy, and I know he'd do anything for me, but he's so stoic — to the point of looking pissed off and gruff a lot of the time — and introverted that I really don't know that much about his youth. I only know about his hockey nickname because he got drunk one night and confessed the whole sordid debacle.

I'm not even sure I've ever seen Levi with a woman. He's a

handful of years younger than me, but we meshed as soon as he joined the team.

"We think you'd be a great example for the team, and you will have no problem reining them in when needed. You've got a calm way of explaining things, whereas we think Levi would scare the shit out of a few guys."

"That's true," I chuckle.

"You can absolutely decline, if you want."

"Oh. Uh, no, I'd be honored to be your captain," I say quietly. I've never been a team captain.

"Great. We'll issue a statement for the media, and we'll let the equipment team know to add the C to your stuff," Coach says, gesturing for me to give him back the C in my hands. "No, you don't get to keep it."

"I've never been a captain before," I tell him. "Just thought it would be cool to have on my desk at home."

Coach sighs. "Fine."

Elated, I shove the patch into my shorts pocket. "So what's the other thing?"

The four men look at one another before the GM speaks up. "We're thinking of moving some positions around. Playing with some dynamics on the lines."

"Okay?"

"Well," GM says, his eyes darting to Coach's, "We're going to move you to the second line. See how you do there."

"You're separating me and Levi?" I ask incredulously, focusing on that detail instead of the doubt churning in my gut about being demoted from first to second line.

"Like I said, we're trying some things out. We want to pair you with Shears and Billings at the beginning of camp. We feel their tenacity will blend well with yours."

"You should just call it like it is. I'm fucking being demoted," I say bitterly. I've been on the first line for years. I shouldn't be this pissed off, but I am. I knew this was coming. I'm not as fast as I was. I got beaten to the puck more often than not in the second half of last year.

"It's not a demotion. You know each line is as important as the last. We can't pack all of our talent on the first line. We're damn lucky to have the defensemen we have, and you'd never hear us saying one is better than the other. It's the same with the rest of you. Yeah, you might not start the games all the time, but you're still an asset to the team. We just made you captain for fuck's sake," Coach says exasperatedly.

"I know," I sigh. "I think I knew this was the reason why you wanted to see me, but it still didn't prepare me for actually hearing the words. I can't compete with these kids coming right from high school hockey. My legs are too old."

"You aren't going anywhere," the owner pipes up. "You still have two years on your contract, and we have no desire to send you elsewhere. I want to see you retire as a Wolves captain. This is absolutely not a demotion, Jax. It has nothing to do with speed or ability. We want you to lead. As Captain, you're responsible for teaching and leading the younger guys. You can't do that with Levi."

Hopefully I won't be retiring anytime soon.

Heading back to my apartment building, I'm flagged by our concierge, motioning to a large box by his desk. I don't remember ordering anything, and only when I see the familiar chicken scratch of my mother's handwriting do I pick up the package. Oddly heavy, I shake the contents as the elevator climbs to my floor. God only knows what she sent.

I don't have a close relationship with my mom. She was never much of the mothering type, and I found out only a few years ago that she got pregnant with me to trap my father into marriage. She lived the high life for five years, until he'd finally had enough, divorcing her and leaving her mostly penniless, courtesy of an iron-clad prenup she claimed she had no memory of signing. A judge split custody for them, but it didn't matter. Dad died of a heart attack a few years later, and I was stuck with my mom. The only thing that saved me was a trust he'd left to me, specifically to continue with hockey.

Dad and I bonded over hockey. I was enamored with it from the first moment I saw a game. I'm sure it had something to do with it being on ice, as growing up in east Texas meant I rarely got to see anything wintry. Dad had a booming voice, and his presence took over every room. But when he'd get down on the floor with me, quietly pointing out everything happening on the television screen, it was like we were the same person. Our joy was palpable. Only one week before he passed away, he took me to my first NHL game. I vowed from the moment the puck dropped that I would end up in the NHL someday.

When Dad's will was read, my mom was furious. She demanded the trust money, claiming she'd make sure I stayed in hockey. The attorneys refused, explaining the law, and introduced me to one of Dad's business associates. I'd met the guy before, and I knew he was as big a hockey fan as Dad was. Drew O'Connor was the trustee in charge of paying for anything I needed for hockey. His secretary, Jackie, drove me to every practice and game until I graduated from high school. No matter where my mom moved us, Drew and Jackie found me. The longest I went without playing was a month.

Ice hockey in Texas is hard to come by, so I spent a lot of time in the car with Jackie, driving hours for practices and games.. She became the mom I'd wished I had, quizzing me on algebra, teaching me the difference between adjectives and adverbs, and giving me advice on girls. I spent more time at their house, and my neighbor's farm next door, than I did at my own house. In fact, Jackie and Drew were at my senior night as my parents, not my own mother. I never told her about the event.

In the fifteen years since I graduated high school, I've only seen my mother four times. I was expected at each of her weddings, and it was demanded that I bring a gift to show my station. In other words, I better bring something nice and expensive. Mom knows that's the only way to get any money out of me. The day after I signed my rookie contract, she came calling. I shut her down and told her never to contact me asking for money again.

Drew and Jackie, however, are a constant presence in my life. We speak weekly, and I have a great relationship with their kids as well.

As I unlock my apartment door and place the heavy package on my kitchen island, I wait to open it, instead choosing to slide open the curtains at my balcony. Seeing the mountains reminds me that I'm here. I'm no longer the lonely little boy from east Texas, craving a connection with his mother. I'm a fucking big deal, and she has no power over me.

Once I open the package, I stare in shock.

Fifteen glass containers of olives? Seriously?

She knows I hate olives. I swear, she put them on everything out of spite throughout my childhood, then watched as I tearfully choked them down.

Seeing an envelope in between the jars, I snatch it up, hoping there will be a joke or something inside that explains this box. Instead, I find an awkwardly scrawled "happy birthday" without a signature. I guess that is the joke, considering my birthday was three months ago. I can't stand this passive aggressive bullshit. This is her way of letting me know she's mad at me for not giving her more money.

With a loud sigh, I sit down on my well-loved dark brown leather sofa. I want to talk to someone, but I don't know who. My teammates all have their own shit going on. I could call my buddy Jamie, the current quarterback for the Colorado Coyotes NFL team here, and ask him to meet for dinner. He's already in the preseason for the NFL, but he might be able to swing a quick meal. I know he won't drink at all during the season, so I can't ask him to meet at a bar. Jameson Wahlberg is football royalty, and having only two

Lombardi trophies under his belt is bad in his family. His younger brother has three, and their dad has four. At thirty six years old, Jamie is pushing to get another before he retires.

Instead, I pull out my phone and message my online friend. NerdGirl insisted early on that we don't give out many personal details, if any, and I wholeheartedly agreed. I get used by people all the time. It's nice to talk to someone who has no idea that I make millions a year swatting at a little piece of rubber while balancing on razor blades.

NerdGirl always makes me feel better. Calling olives fake grapes? I cackled. But when she insinuated that she empathized with my relationship with my mom because of her dad, I didn't know how to respond. We said nothing personal. Should I have asked if she wanted to elaborate? Could I have provided any insight into her experiences?

I chuckle when my phone rings, and I see it's Jamie calling.

"I was just about to call you," I tell him upon answering.

"Oh yeah? Wanted to see if you had plans for dinner," he responds.

"No. Meet at our usual spot?" Jamie found this ridiculous hole-in-the-wall taco place that makes the best carne asada tacos I've ever had. Rarely does anyone recognize us there, and with terrible overhead lighting, I'm sure we could make up a story anyway. I'm already salivating thinking about the tacos.

"Yeah. You cool if I bring a friend?"

"Uh, like a *friend* friend, or a friend?"

He laughs. "My new coach. He's had difficulty getting settled here, and the press hounds him nonstop. He mentioned wanting tacos, and that got me thinking that I haven't seen your miserable face in a while."

"Nice. Yeah, that's fine. The press are fucking vultures. Almost as bad as the paparazzi."

"Yep. Meet you around six."

"Sounds good."

A few hours later, I'm seated at a tiny table across from two massive men who dwarf the space. I'm six-three, Jamie is just a tad taller than me, and Coach Silas Youngstown is at least six-five. Hunched over our plates like rabid and semi-feral dogs, we're silent as we inhale the street tacos.

"Jesus, these things are good," Silas mutters through a mouthful. "No good taco places in Seattle."

"Oh?" I ask. It might sound conceited, but I spend a good chunk of my time focused on hockey, and I don't have time to pay attention to other sports. I follow Jamie's career, and I can rattle off if the Coyotes won or lost that week, but I'm not a follower of coaching or trade news. I vaguely remember hearing something about a new coach, but I didn't pay any more attention to who was hired. Not a chance I could remember where the new coach had been last.

"Had family in south Texas," he explains. "My ma dragged us there every summer. I learned what a good street taco looks like."

"Oh yeah? I'm from Texas, and street tacos are a pretty integral part of my off-season diet," I muse, stifling a loud groan as I stuff almost an entire taco into my mouth.

"What part of Texas are you from?" Silas asks as he dumps salsa over his remaining tacos.

"Nowhere you'd know. Small town in east Texas."

"Shouldn't you be back there right now? Your training shouldn't start for a few more weeks," Silas says.

"I don't go home," I state clearly.

"Why?" Silas asks.

"I just … don't." I'm not about to delve into my complicated parental relationship with an NFL coach I just met. I have been known to lose my filter from time to time, but even I'm smart enough to recognize this isn't the time or place. "How're the Coyotes looking this year? Playoff potential?"

Jamie chuckles. "Nice redirection there, Jax. But since it involves talking about myself, I'll allow it. I think we're looking good. Playoffs? Maybe. Depends on how the lines grow. Whether they become a cohesive bunch or not. I'm liking the group we have right now, and it's the most optimistic I've been since I got here."

I look at Silas with my eyebrows raised, waiting for his input. He shrugs before saying, "I never make any preseason predictions. Jamie will tell you, I'm all about a week-by-week outlook. Worry about what's right in front of you. I can't think about January when I need to get these guys through four grueling months first."

"And he's scared as fuck about the fans here," Jamie pipes up.

"Dude, I had barely moved in before a neighbor threatened to remove my intestines through my asshole," Silas says in exasperation..

"I mean, I'd be a little concerned too. But the fans here are hardcore. They can be completely brutal, but their passion is contagious. I even find myself rooting for the dogs every now and again," I tease.

Jamie rolls his eyes. "We've talked about this, dick. Coyotes are no more dogs than wolves."

I shrug, knowing it pisses Jamie off. "Eh. Wolves are cooler."

"Whatever. Oh, I have to go drop off some donations at the adoption center. Can you take Coach home? He's renting in your building." As if Jamie wasn't already a huge football star with tons of adoring fans, he has to up the ante a little by being an all-around good human. When his schedule allows, he volunteers at an animal adoption center, regularly drops off donations and supplies at the humane society, and anonymously helps out a couple of animal related charities in Denver. He's never gone into detail about why he does these things, but I also haven't asked. I assumed it was personal.

He's one of only a few people who know about my own animal haven.

"You should show Coach your shrine for your fucking guinea pigs."

"The fuck? You got some pigs, Jax?" Coach asks with a grin.

Well, shit. That select few who know about my guineas has now grown by one.

Becca

CHAPTER 3

After an incredibly long day, I'm relieved to step foot in my apartment as the sun begins to set behind the Rocky Mountains. I'm greeted by my frantic golden retriever, Thunder, who acts like he's been alone for years. Maybe that's how long it feels like to him. Honestly, the mathematical concept of dog years doesn't make much sense to me.

"I missed you too, buddy," I whisper into his fluff as he peppers me with kisses. Thunder is the epitome of a golden retriever: there are no strangers, he's always beyond excited for everything, and he's possibly missing a few brain cells. He makes me laugh every day.

I quickly change into comfortable clothes, grabbing Thunder's leash, harness, and a ball as I walk past the kitchen. My small one-bedroom apartment is convenient for work, but expensive as hell. I've been debating on moving further into the suburbs, hoping I might be able to save some money, but I can't find anything within the budget I'm willing to shell out toward housing.

Thankful to have daylight for a little while longer, I jog to a small dog park on the edge of downtown so Thunder can get a little off-leash exercise. Dog zoomies in an apartment are not enjoyable for anyone, and the neighbor below me already hates me. I have no idea what I did to offend her, but our interactions have only gotten colder the longer we've both lived in the building. I've never had good luck with female friendships. My analytical brain seems to compute differently than a typical woman. I think the only reason Danica still puts up with me is because of our common bond of work. Usually, if I meet another woman with a job that could be called nerdy, I fall all over myself trying to make a good impression. Poised I am not.

After throwing the ball for fifteen minutes, I call Thunder back so we can begin the walk home. Excessive panting tells me Thunder enjoyed the time to stretch his legs, and I mentally cross my fingers that he's burned enough energy so he'll sleep well tonight.

As we're getting into the elevator back at my building, my phone vibrates with a message.

StickUM92: Am I allowed to ask something personal?

NerdGirl1025: I guess you can ask, but I don't know if I'll answer.

StickUM92: That's fair.

StickUM92: I've been thinking about you all day. You gave me a little piece of information about your past, and your family, but I left you hanging. I didn't mean to. I just wasn't sure if I was allowed to ask anything, or provide you with an opportunity for you to talk if you needed to.

NerdGirl1025: Honestly, at that moment, I probably would have shut you down. But after a really long day, I'm open to it. I don't really have a relationship with any of my family. Any time we talk, it's usually because of something they think I've done wrong, or something they need from me.

StickUM92: All of them?

NerdGirl1025: Yup. I had a pretty rough childhood, I guess, with a lot of verbal abuse. As soon as I could get out of there, I did.

StickUM92: Verbal abuse?

*NerdGirl1025: Yeah. I asked a lot of questions as a kid. I wanted to know why everything worked the way it did, or why people were a certain way. I never really learned how to filter what I said, and my parents felt embarrassed by me a lot. It just kind of snowballed from *there, with my sibling getting in on the verbal beatdowns as well. Once I became the family punching bag, I was a very easy target for everything.*

StickUM92: Fuck. I'm so sorry.

StickUM92: Want me to go beat 'em up?

A bark of laughter breaks from my lips as I usher Thunder into my apartment. Removing his leash, I feed Thunder his dinner and toe off my shoes. I head to my favorite spot on my couch, where I have a perfect view of the mountains between two buildings. I curl into the plush blanket I keep on the back of the couch as I settle into the conversation.

NerdGirl1025: Tempting, but no. I paid my way through college with multiple jobs, and a loan I'll be paying off for years, and I've only been home twice in the last decade when the only family members who I did have a good relationship with each passed away. My parents and sibling are basically dead to me. It sounds harsh, but I had to cut the toxicity out of my life.

StickUM92: I should probably do that with my mom. I only hear from her when she needs money, or when something dumb happens like a box of olives shows up.

NerdGirl1025: I'm not sure what is worse: having no relationship with a family member, or having one where it's clear you're an afterthought and not important at all. I'm sorry you've had the latter.

StickUM92: Eh. It is what it is. It's taught me a lot about who I want to be as a person. For that, I'm grateful.

NerdGirl1025: You're a glass-half-full kind of guy, aren't you?

StickUM92: Who says I'm a guy? Maybe I'm Norma. I'm seventy, and a grandmother to fifteen. My entire personality is my grandchildren. Oh, and knitting.

NerdGirl1025: As long as it's knitting. I can't stand crocheting.

*StickUM92: *adds learn to knit to to-do list**

NerdGirl1025: Are you trying to impress me, Norma?

StickUM92: What man — I mean, grandmother — wouldn't want to impress a pretty girl?

NerdGirl1025: How do you know I'm pretty? I could be a middle-

aged man with a horrible receding hairline and a beer belly that sticks out of my shirt along the waistline, no matter how hard I try to tuck it in.

StickUM92: Are you tucking your shirt in, or your belly in? Because that is incredibly important information.

NerdGirl1025: My belly, obviously. Duh.

StickUM92: YES. It's going to go so well with my gout when I shove my old feet in your lap.

NerdGirl1025: You can't. I have to go take out my teeth to soak them for the night.

StickUM92: Watch it, baby. A toothless mouth may not be a bad thing.

NerdGirl1025: But you're a grandmother, not some guy looking for a place to shove his wiener. Which I very much am, by the way. A dude. Shoving my wiener into you.

StickUM92: Oh, I plan to roll up my boob and shove it in your gummy mouth. Side note: don't call it a wiener. Dick, cock, length, whatever. Never a wiener.

NerdGirl1025: I'll call my middle-aged wiener whatever I want.

StickUM92: Does that mean I get to call my titties whatever I want?

NerdGirl1025: By all means.

StickUM92: I'll get back to you on that. I need to think about it.

NerdGirl1025: I get it. Took me a while to name mine.

StickUM92: Yours have names?

NerdGirl1025: Of course.

StickUM92: Don't hold back on me now, NerdGirl. I need to know.

NerdGirl1025: Thelma and Louise.

StickUM92: 100% nowhere close to what I thought you'd say.

NerdGirl1025: What did you think I'd say?

StickUM92: Something cute or sweet. Like Vanilla Cupcake and Frosting.

NerdGirl1025: You know, I had thought about Cupcake and Frosting, but went with Thelma and Louise instead. Bummer.

StickUM92: Missed opportunity, NerdGirl. Such a missed opportunity.

NerdGirl1025: I'll consider applying to the boob administration and ask for a name change whenever you tell me what your dick's name is.

StickUM92: Thank you for not calling it a wiener.

NerdGirl1025: If you don't tell me its name, I'll revert back to wiener.

StickUM92: Noted.

Laughing, I drop the phone next to me on the couch, leaning my head back to rest on a cushion. That conversation was exactly what I needed. StickUM always has a way to make me laugh, helping me to look past my troubles ,and focus on the positives in life.

Thunder sighs heavily, and when I lift my head to look at him, I find his deep brown eyes staring intently at me. "You know, I bet StickUM has your energy in real life. I bet he's the quintessential golden retriever. You'd probably like him more than me."

As if recognizing my comment as a cry for help, he slowly gets up, ambling over to me, laying his head on my knees. When I scratch the edge of his snout, he attempts to lick me twice, as if to say he'd never choose someone else over me. Sliding down so he's beside my feet, Thunder lets out a long exhale as he gets comfortable. I close my eyes and rest my head back again, thinking about what I can throw together for a quick meal before I pass out on the couch.

My alarm jars me awake. I immediately notice I have a sore neck, and I realize I never left my spot, sleeping in an upright position on my couch, with Thunder at my feet. It's just after three in the morning, and I need to quickly get Thunder out and fed before I report to work. Two to three times a week, Thunder attends a doggie daycare, so I need extra time today to get him to that building … in the opposite direction from where I live and work.

Dressing in my standard outfit of workout leggings and an oversized t-shirt, I carefully roll up a dress and slide it into my backpack. About a year ago, I had a very scary experience with a homeless man who followed me, making lewd comments and threatening to harm me. According to him, I was "dressed like a slut," and he'd make sure I'd "take what he wants to give me." The clothing I was wearing happened to be a very modest dress, but fit my body snugly. I reported him to the police, and the station, and I never saw him again. As a precaution, however, I began dressing casually, then changing at work. This also allows me to wear sneakers in case I need to run from someone. As much as I love Thunder, he doesn't think anyone is a stranger.

After dropping Thunder off at his doggie daycare, I start the trek back across town. Denver has a great train system from the suburbs into downtown, but in the area of the daycare, there are no nearby stations. Sometimes I'll splurge on an Uber, but today I'm walking back. It's a beautiful morning, and as the sky begins to lighten slightly, I take a deep breath of gratitude as I take in the scenery. Sometimes I can catch glimpses of the peaks of the Rocky Mountains, many west of Denver climbing to fourteen thousand feet. This morning, however, clouds dot the sky. A rare humidity is evident in the air, and I know we're due for some thunderstorms this afternoon. If storms get going, as I assume they will, I'll end up with another long day. I make a mental note to order lunch from my favorite Italian restaurant in town. If I'm going to have an exhausting day, I might as well enjoy some good food while I'm at it.

Two blocks from work, in the heart of downtown Denver, my eyes drift toward a figure stretching next to a large brick half-wall. Almost unconsciously, my hand finds my keyring, fingers wrapping around the small bottle of pepper spray I've carried since my college days. My steps slow as I wonder if I should make a run across the street, but one look at this man's calves tell me he'd easily catch me if he wanted to. His stance is oddly familiar, as I take in the shorts, tank top, and cap-covered hair. When he removes the cap to run one hand through his tousled curls, I realize who it is a mere moment before he turns around. I'd question his motives, but even I recognize the surprise on his face. Does that mean he lives downtown like me?

"Well, well, well," Jacob drawls, a beautiful smile covering his perfect face. "If it isn't my favorite little Spitfire."

"Favorite?" I ask. "You have more than one? You know what? Don't answer that. I really don't want to know." I hurry past him, not surprised when he falls into step beside me.

"I wouldn't say I have a ton of women who deserve the nickname. You're definitely in a league of your own. Sure would help if I knew your first name so I could call you something else, darlin'," he says, and when I look out of the corner of my eye at him, he winks. I stifle a laugh.

"It's too early for you to be this happy," I murmur, keeping my voice even-keeled.

"Life is too short to worry about stupid shit, Spitfire. It's a beautiful day. Hockey season is about to ramp back up. Going up to Red Rocks for a concert this afternoon with my buddies. Not much to be that unhappy about."

"Watch it today. There's a forecast for storms," I say absentmindedly.

"Really? Huh," he muses. "I don't really pay attention to the weather. They're never right anyway."

"Excuse me?" I shout, my hackles rising. Of *course* Jacob would inaccurately judge meteorologists. "We're right often, you jerk. Do you have any idea how difficult it is to forecast the weather? We're trying to predict the future, and if a storm way out in the Pacific Ocean deviates even fifty miles, it changes everything. Then you add in the mountains and the Palmer Divide, and it's like dropping a penny from one hundred feet above a bullseye and hoping it hits somewhere on the target."

Jacob stops, staring at me incredulously. His eyes light up as he snaps his fingers. "That's where I recognize you from! You're that weather girl. Becca something or other."

I growl at him. Legitimately growl. "I am not a weather girl, asshole. I'm a certified meteorologist. Chief meteorologist, to be exact. I actually studied in college, which is probably more than I can say for you."

He lifts his eyebrows in challenge. "You think so?"

I shrug. "Probably. You sports guys are all the same. Coasting by because you happen to hit a puck well."

He smiles proudly. "So you do know who I am."

"I work in news. Yes, I know who you are." Realizing I stopped when he did, I continue on. "I have to get to work."

"Why this early? Not a good time for a lady to be roaming around by herself," Jacob comments.

"It's either this shift or the evening shift. I prefer this one."

"You got a concealed carry permit?"

"What? Why?"

"Gotta protect yourself, Spitfire."

I shiver. The thought of carrying a gun makes me queasy. It's why I have pepper spray, and why I've taken more than one self-defense course. Even my keychain has a pointy end where, if all else is lost, I can channel my inner prisoner and shank someone. "I can protect myself."

Jacob hums noncommittally. "Good to know. Guess I'll see you tomorrow morning, then."

As he jogs away, I stop walking. He'll see me tomorrow morning? What the hell does that even mean?

The following morning, already planning a new route to walk in hopes of avoiding Jacob, I stop dead in my tracks when I find him standing in front of my building, a gleeful grin on his face. Stubble covers his chin, but his perfect white teeth gleam under the baseball cap pulled tightly across his forehead. I can't help but wonder if his teeth are real. Aren't most hockey players missing at least one tooth? His look too perfect to be real.

He is at my apartment. It's basically the middle of the night, and he's waiting for me. This brings back some incredibly bad memories, and I need to nip this in the bud — whatever Jacob thinks is happening here.

"Fancy meeting you here —" he begins, but I cut him off.

"Are your teeth real?" I blurt out.

"What?" Jacob asks, chuckling lightly.

"Your teeth. Are they real? Or do you have one of those things that people put in there? What's it called, a porpoise? A dolphin?" I know it's called a flipper, but I want to aggravate him.

"A flipper," he murmurs, the smile sliding off his face. "I don't have one of those. I've been lucky."

"Eh. Why are you here? You know this is stalking, right?" I routinely search my own name to make sure my address doesn't appear anywhere. Female meteorologists have to be way too careful. I'm a little apprehensive about Jacob finding my address, but assume he has connections somehow.

"A friend of a friend works at your station," he says hesitantly.

"I need a name, please." Crossing my arms over my chest, I wait. There isn't much light at this time of morning, but I can still see a faint red blush creep up his neck.

Jacob reaches up to scratch absentmindedly against the back of his neck. "I'm not revealing my sources."

"Whatever. I'll find out on my own then," I say cheerfully, walking around Jacob. He falls into step beside me, holding a disposable coffee cup from one of my favorite small coffee shops a block away. I hadn't even noticed he was holding two cups in one hand. His hands are big enough to do that, which makes me think of — *get your mind out of the gutter, Becca.*

"The friend of a friend also told me your favorite coffee order, and I'm hoping this small token of appreciation convinces you *not* to look into the friend of a friend, because they only did it to help me. I'd feel awful if they got fired," Jacob says quietly.

"How would you feel if I managed to get your home address?" I ask softly. "I can only assume you know what it's like for people to show up at your home uninvited. Why would you think it would be okay to do that to me?"

"Fuck," he breathes, his face paling noticeably. "I swear I didn't even think about it like that. I didn't intend to make you feel threatened or anything."

We continue walking silently, and as I'm about to turn to speak to him, Jacob grabs my elbow carefully. "I'm sorry, Becca. I wasn't thinking."

I'm not used to a man so confidently admitting their own fault, and my mouth drops open in shock. Jacob looks down quickly, but his eyes pop back up to mine, his gaze never wavering as he waits for my response.

"I've had a stalker before," I whisper. "It was bad. You showing up at my apartment hit too close to home."

His face falls as he processes my words. "Here? In Denver?"

I shake my head. "No. It was when I first started out. I had to move twice, and it sucked. I was already a private person, but that just exacerbated it. I don't like finding men I don't know outside my building."

He nods, looking down at his feet. "It, uh, won't happen again."

"Thank you," I say politely, turning away from him again. After walking a few steps, I look back, finding Jacob staring intently at me. "This coffee shop isn't open for another hour. How'd you get it?"

He shrugs. "Friend of a friend."

I shake my head, a light giggle bursting from my mouth. "Is that your answer for everything?"

"No, just for things concerning you."

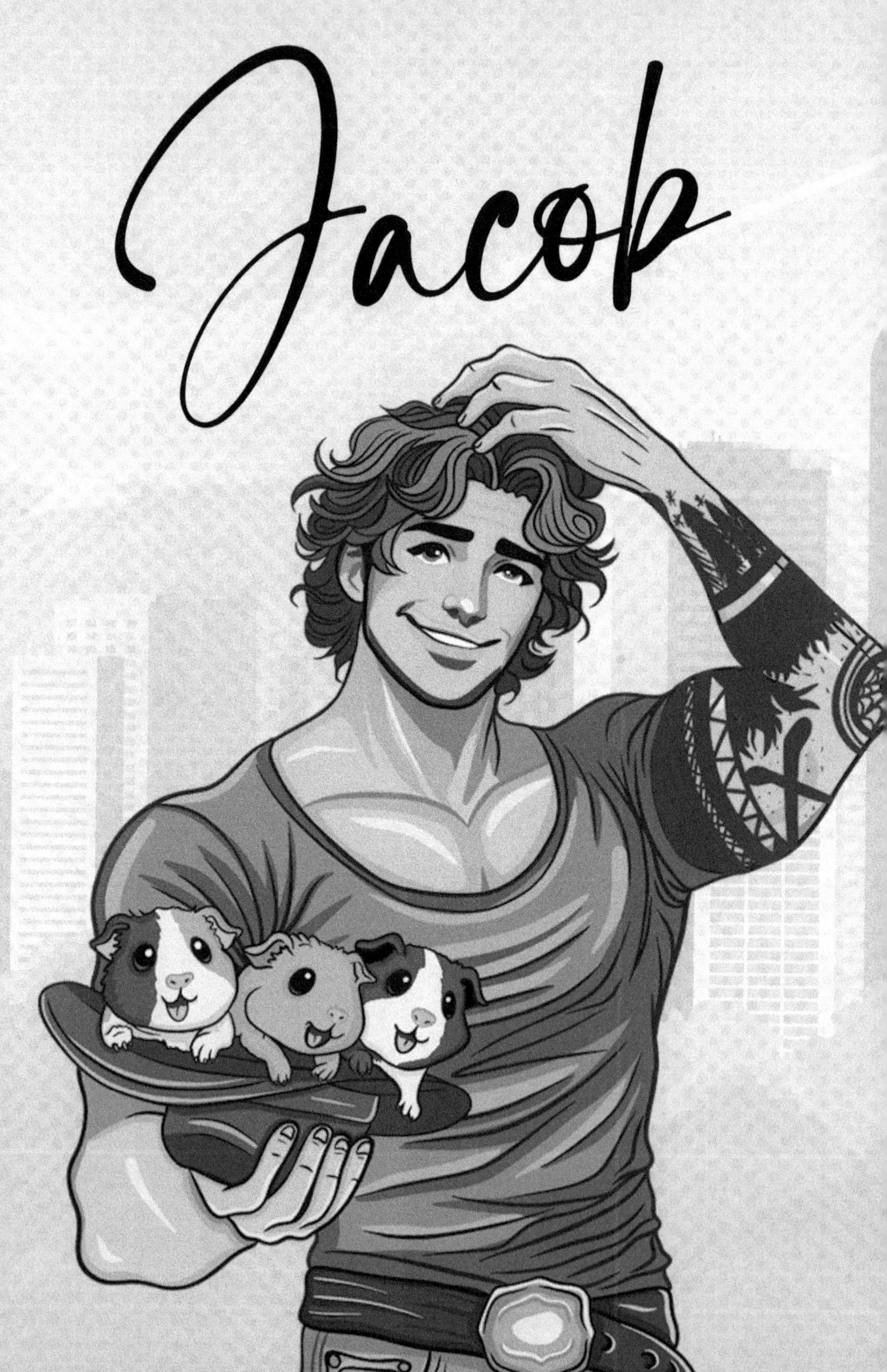
Jacob

CHAPTER 4

It's rare that I feel like a complete douche. Yeah, I make some dumb decisions, but I've never felt worse than I do right now. To know that I may have made Becca feel threatened? Fucking hell.

"You alright, Jax? You're looking like you want to take that treadmill out back and beat the shit out of it," Gabe Dawson, my teammate, comments. While we aren't in training camp just yet, those of us who live in Denver all year round still meet up to work out and get some ice time a couple times a week. Our other buddies, Grant McNally and Levi Quinn look on with interest.

I sigh. "It's nothing. Well, mostly nothing."

"Ah shit," Grant says as he jumps off the elliptical, coming over to rest his hands on the edge of the treadmill. "What did you do?"

I look around the cardio room at the Sports Facility Zone, where every state-of-the-art machine known to man resides for the professional athletes of Denver to use. Just to the west of downtown, all kinds of practice facilities are available for us. We share an arena downtown with the NBA for our games, but the majority of our time is spent at SFZ. The football team occasionally works out here, but they have their own private space next to the massive stadium north of here.

"Earth to Jax," Levi says, snapping his fingers in front of my face. "Seriously, what did you do?"

"Nothing major," I start, and Grant rolls his eyes.

"Famous last words."

"No, really. I just accidentally made a girl feel threatened. Like she wasn't safe. With me. I don't think she exactly felt threatened by me, but she definitely didn't feel safe with me."

"That really doesn't make much sense," Gabe says.

I let out a loud exhale, looking up to the ceiling. "There's this girl."

"Obviously," Grant says dryly.

"And we've had a couple of run-ins."

"Is that code for you've fucked her a couple of times?" Levi asks.

"No, I literally mean run-ins. She actually ran into me once, and the other time I was on a run when we crossed paths."

"Okay? So what's the issue?" Gabe asks.

I squeeze my eyes closed and blurt out, "I recognized her, and so I asked a friend of a friend who works with her to give me her address. I showed up there this morning, because I knew what time she had to be at work, and all I wanted to do was offer to walk with her, but it freaked her out, because she'd had a stalker in the past. And now I feel like such a fucking dumbass."

Silence.

Opening my eyes, I see all three of my friends staring at me in disbelief.

Levi's mouth opens and closes multiple times before he shakes his head. Grant reaches up to rub the bridge of his nose, and Gabe finally lets out a loud guffaw of laughter.

"This is so fucking perfect. Oh my God, just perfect. Jax, the one who doesn't even have to lift a finger to get a group of women falling at his feet, has made a fool out of himself in front of a woman who has no interest in him. Jesus. I can't wait to tell Cassie," he says, laughing. Gabe's wife, Cassie, also happens to be Grant's sister, and originally signed on to nanny Gabe's daughter.

Unbeknownst to everyone, Gabe and Cassie had already met. They couldn't fight their connection for too much longer, and now they're a happy little family of three.

I don't respond to Gabe, because he's not wrong. Frankly, no professional hockey player has to try to score a woman. Hell, puck bunnies are everywhere. I know some players have a rotation of women in every city that they go through while we're playing away games. What's even more fucked up is that the women are okay with it. I've overheard bunnies talking about who gets what guy from the team that night.

I'm not like that, exactly. I don't do repeat performances at away games. Frankly, I rarely hook up out of town, because I have a pretty specific routine that I need to keep. I'm not about to screw up my game by fucking some random woman. If we have a full day off between games, I'll download a dating app and make it clear it's a one-time thing.

"In his defense, none of us ever have to lift a finger," Grant points out.

"He gets more attention, and you know it. Don't even lie," Gabe says with a laugh. "It's the fucking curls. Women are nuts for curly hair."

I pull my hat down further onto my head. I hated my hair growing up. My mom never knew how to care for it, so a lot of the time I looked like I'd stuck my finger into an electrical outlet. Once I was old enough to access the internet, a whole world opened up to me about styling products, sulfates, and the 'curly girl' routine. Once I'd figured out the hair, my confidence grew.

"I think it's because he rarely talks to women. You ever notice that? As outgoing as he is, he's mute with the ladies," Levi says.

Gabe snorts. "I've never heard any complaints from women who have been with Jax, so clearly he makes up for it when he gets them alone."

"Am I even here?" I wonder aloud, waving my hand in front of Gabe's face. "Y'all are talking about me like I've left the gym."

"Do you talk when you get a woman alone?" Levi asks.

I pause to think. "Actually … no."

Grant lets out a loud bark of laughter. "I don't know why I'm surprised. The curls with those baby blues? All you need to do is smile, and the panties drop."

"So literally, no talking? At all?" Gabe asks. I raise an eyebrow at him, and he shrugs. "What? I'm intrigued by this. You never shut up with us. Not even a little dirty talk?"

"No need for that. My mouth is usually busy."

"Damn. Cassie loves when I start talking. Last night she did this backbend on the bed, and then I told her all the things I was gonna do in return, and she —" Grant's hand slams over Gabe's mouth.

"Sister, Gabe. For fuck's sake. That's my fucking sister," Grant growls. "Talk like that again, and I guarantee you won't be doing any talking whatsoever for the foreseeable future."

Gabe looks over at me and winks. He loves antagonizing Grant.

"Asshole, did you just lick me? Fucking disgusting," Grant says as he whips his hand away from Gabe's mouth.

"Serves you right. Learn your lesson, dipshit. Besides, you've told all of us all kinds of stories about your ex. What's her name again?" Gabe asks.

Grant points a finger at Gabe menacingly. "Don't you say another word." Turning quickly, Grant stomps out of the gym.

"Well, that escalated quickly," I murmur.

"He's a ticking time bomb. Whatever happened with his ex really fucked him up. I'm determined to break him so he'll talk to me," Gabe says quietly. "He's got a different puck bunny every night, and I think he's drinking again. I've gotta get through to him."

Grant had a long-term girlfriend that seemed to be his endgame. Suddenly, she disappeared, and Grant's personality shifted. He'd been sober for years, after feeling like he was developing a problem in his early years in the NHL. For Gabe to suggest Grant may be drinking again is a huge concern.

"I'm glad you said something," Levi pipes up. "I thought I saw him with a bourbon a few weeks ago. We met for dinner, and he was there when I arrived. As soon as he saw me, he pushed the glass away. I didn't bring it up, because I figured it was all in my head."

"Now we know, so we can keep an eye on him, right?" I say, watching as my two friends nod. "Camp starts soon, and then the season. We'll be around him a ton, and we can make sure he steers clear of alcohol."

I just hope we're enough to keep him away from his demons.

"Thanks for doing this, man," Levi says as he slaps me on the shoulder. I agreed to some kind of group date, and I'm only going because Levi is the one who needs help. He's a complete bruiser on the ice, but in person, he's quiet and introverted. I may choose to stay silent, mostly because I don't want to play all the stupid dating games, but Levi has a general fear of communication.

"Who are we meeting again?" I ask as we walk toward the bar at a large restaurant in central Denver.

"My friend Danica and one of her friends," he answers.

"And you like this Danica person?"

Levi sighs. "I don't know. Maybe. She's pretty, and she seems like she has a nice personality, but something is … off. And I can't put my finger on it."

"So am I here to watch her, pump you up, flirt with her, or what?"

His eyes widen. "Shit, no. Don't flirt with her. Maybe just tell me later what your first impression is. She told me she has a friend who would be perfect for you."

"How the fuck would she know that? I would remember a name like Danica. Pretty sure I've never met her."

"Maybe just from social media? Anyway, just tell me what you think of her."

"Alright. I can do that."

The server comes to tell us our table is ready, and I take the seat with my back to the entrance. I want to watch *his* face when she arrives. I see the moment the ladies arrive, because his eyes dim slightly. I study Levi, and notice no positive reactions to this woman. That can't be good.

"Hey, Levi," a woman gushes as we both stand up. "Oh, and hi to *you*. I'm Danica."

I'm fucked, because I see Danica's eyes looking at me. Not Levi.

Three reasons why this is the worst case scenario of monumental proportions.

First, I realize Danica possibly set Levi up so she could actually meet me.

Secondly, she very clearly has crazy eyes.

But most importantly, her friend is someone I'd much rather get to know.

Her friend is Becca.

"You can't be serious," Becca says with a glare. The lowlight in the bar makes her chestnut locks appear darker, but I can still see the animosity deep in her eyes. I put up my hands in surrender.

"I swear, this was not me. I didn't know anything. I'm just here to support my buddy." I look over to Levi, hoping he'll back me up, and I breathe a sigh of relief when he nods emphatically.

"It's true. I asked him to come because Danica said she had a friend who would be perfect for him. I never knew your name," Levi says hastily.

"That's not — well, that isn't exactly what I said," Danica says, irritation evident in her tone. I already don't like this twit. She's fucking with my friend, for one. Plus, her hair is so bleached it's white as snow. I don't trust anyone who does that to their hair by choice. Then you add in the crazy eyes, and Danica is a hard pass.

I'm trying to come up with a valid excuse for why I need to leave. Something that won't make Levi pissed, but also a believable lie. Could I — could I get Becca out of this too? She crosses her arms under her breasts, pushing them up ever so slightly, and my tongue almost falls out of my mouth. I can't tear my eyes away from her chest. I can already tell they'd be a perfect teardrop in my palm. Much to my surprise, stiff peaks erupt beneath the royal blue dress she's wearing, and my eyes pop up to hers. Becca's eyes are dilated. She might hate me, but she still wants to fuck me.

I can work with that.

Now I'm not leaving. It's time to figure out a way to get Becca to give me a chance. A second chance. Jesus, it might be a third chance by now.

As I move to pull out a chair for her, disaster strikes. A fire erupts at the edge of the kitchen, and a big ball of flames pushes up into the seating area. I fucking hate these open concepts that new restaurants have adopted lately, with the kitchen being much more visible to guests. The fire kicks off the automatic sprinkler system inside, and everyone panics.

Instinctively, I grab Becca. I don't miss how Danica attempts to get to me, and I'm even more pissed at her than I was before. Not only for what I view as an unforgivable offense of fucking with one of my best friends, but also for pulling Becca into the lie.

I quickly slide my suit jacket off and put it over Becca's head, then wrap my arm around her upper back. I'd love to have a hand on her waist. Better yet, her ass. But I think she'd jam a stiletto heel into my shoe, and my feet are pretty important for my career. Unfortunately, the thought of her heels makes me envision fucking her in just those beautiful black stilettos, and now I'm hard as a rock.

When was the last time I got laid?

Jesus. It's been a few months. No wonder I'm salivating over this woman.

Maybe that's what it is. Maybe I just need to get laid. Then I won't think about this bombshell all the time.

Once outside in the warm air, Becca carefully removes my jacket from her head. "Um. Thanks."

I nod slightly. "You're welcome."

"That was actually pretty decent of you. I guess you aren't a complete miscreant," she says wryly.

I let out a chuckle. "I'll take it. What's the next step up from miscreant?"

"Asshat."

"Ah. How many steps until I get to being just a nice guy?"

"You have a long way to go," she says with a breathy laugh.

"Becca!" I hear wailed from behind us, only to find Levi carrying Danica. Mascara drips down her face, and her white hair sticks up in every direction. "I slipped, and I think I broke my ankle!"

"Oh no!" Becca cries.

"I'm going to take her to the hospital," Levi says, resolution evident in his tone. He looks at me and rolls his eyes. I'm taking that as a sign that he's not too torn up about Danica's obvious interest in me.

"Do you guys want to come?" Danica asks hopefully, her eyes solely on me.

"No," I retort. I'm shutting this bitch down.

Danica noticeably pales. "I don't know what I've done to offend you, but —"

"I think you know exactly what you've done, which is try to use my friend to get to me. Me and you? Never gonna happen. Levi, text me later. You wanted my opinion, and I definitely have one."

"Pretty sure I know what you're going to say, but sure. I'll text you. Our Uber is here," Levi says as he walks past us.

Turning, I look at Becca. "You want a slice of pizza? My favorite joint is around the corner, and I'm starving."

She begins to shake her head, but pauses. "Actually, pizza sounds really good. I don't remember the last time I had a slice of pizza. I'd like to talk about what just happened in there, though."

I point in the direction we're going, and we set off. "She didn't look at Levi once after you both got here. He's an amazing guy, and she wasn't going to give him a chance. I've seen it happen with more than one friend, where they're trying to get around someone to get to who they really want. So tell me why don't you eat pizza?"

"I watch what I eat. I get a lot of nasty emails and messages about my body. I didn't notice her looking at you. How did you see that? You were watching me."

"Damn. That's ridiculous. Your body is phenomenal," I blurt out, then wince. "I mean you look nice. What do people say? I have really great peripheral vision. That's how I saw her watching me."

Becca sighs. "I'm not surprised about Danica. She's nice, but I could totally see her stair-stepping her way up in all areas. Viewers critique my clothing. If my heels are too high or too low. Too much makeup, and not enough makeup. The hem of my dress is too high. Color is wrong. They don't like a stitching pattern, or they think I should wear sleeveless dresses all the time. On the off chance I retain a little water, I get tons of emails asking if I'm pregnant, or telling me to lay off the sweets."

"Seriously?" I ask incredulously.

"Seriously."

"So you watch what you eat because of these assholes?"

"Somewhat, but I've always been pretty conscious about what I put in my body. I try not to eat anything over-processed, or filled with artificial colors. Eating whole foods is my goal. I know pizza will probably make me puff out a little bit, but I'm finding it hard to care right now. I'm ready for cheese," she says bashfully, and I look over to find a hesitant smile on her face. I can't help but smile in return.

"Well, let's get you some cheese, Spitfire."

Becca

CHAPTER 5

It's possible that I've misjudged multiple people this week.

Danica clearly isn't the person I thought she was. From the moment we stepped foot in the restaurant, I knew things felt off. She'd told me we were meeting a man named Levi and his friend, but immediately I knew she wasn't there for Levi. Jacob looked equally as confused as me, and poor Levi was caught in the middle.

I'll admit, seeing Dani like a drowned rat moments ago was comical. Danica is always at her best. She never arrives at the station without her hair and makeup done. Lipstick always at the ready, just in case a camera catches her off-guard. Heaven forbid she be in the background of a picture looking less than perfect. At this moment, I'm sure I don't look much better, but I don't care. Watching Jacob defend his friend while simultaneously putting Danica in her place was refreshing.

Now I'm wondering how I majorly misjudged Jacob as well.

Is it possible he did all of that to impress me? Maybe.

"Alright. I'll only have dinner with you on one condition," Jacob says, stopping suddenly in front of a doorway. He turns to me with a smirk. "What's your favorite style of pizza?"

"Style?" I ask, confused. "I already told you I like cheese?"

He sighs and shakes his head dramatically. "Not what I meant, Spitfire. Style. You've got Detroit-style. Chicago deep-dish. New York. California. I only found out about a Saint Louis style pizza my first year in the league because we played there, and the team bet me I couldn't eat a whole pie. They were wrong, by the way."

"Good to know," I murmur, completely fascinated at how his eyes sparkle with mirth. Goodness gracious. The man has a dimple. He's too attractive for his own good.

"I'm determined to get over to Italy one of these days and get Neapolitan pizza right from the source. Did you know there's also a Greek style of pizza?"

"Can honestly say I didn't know that. You're pretty passionate about pizza," I comment.

He lifts one shoulder, giving me a crooked grin. "It's the base of my food pyramid."

"I thought athletes all ate pretty healthy."

"I eat healthy as often as possible. Pizza is my exception. Besides, I can add a bunch of vegetables to the pizza, get a side salad with it, and it's almost healthy."

"Unless you're eating an entire pizza because someone dared you," I point out, surprised at my own back-and-forth with this man. I'm usually never so outspoken with the opposite sex. I'm sure my therapist will have all kinds of thoughts about a connection to my relationships with my dad and brother when we meet next week.

"I've only been dared to eat an entire pizza twice." He pauses. "Maybe three times. Once the team realizes I'll win, they stop making bets. So. What's your favorite style of pizza?"

"I don't know what my favorite is. I can only say I really don't like deep dish pizza."

Jacob throws a fist into the air. "Yes! I could never eat with you if you liked that crap. Who wants a mouthful of dough? Not me. Come on. We can go in now. Just had to be sure you were on the right team."

"What would you have done had I said it was my favorite?" I ask, intrigued.

"I would have thanked you for walking with me, ordered you an Uber, and sent you on your way. I cannot be seen with the enemy in here," he says, leaning toward me and lowering his voice. "I'm basically family."

Holding the door open, he motions for me to walk in. As soon as he steps beside me by the hostess's podium, I feel his hand on the small of my back, and I inhale sharply. Sure, he put his arm around me as we ran from the sprinklers, but that seemed protective in nature, instead of an attempt to cop a feel. I've had countless first dates over the past six months, yet none have touched me, other than a handshake in greeting. I've kept my body as far away as possible from every man, and they all clearly got the message. One did suggest we go back to his place for sex, and assured me his parents wouldn't mind. I hightailed it out of there before he could attempt anything. Yet feeling the heat of Jacob's palm against my back, even with the fabric of my dress providing a barrier, is like electricity coursing through my veins. I hadn't realized how much I needed to be touched, even in such a simple way.

"Hey, Jax," a woman says with a smile. "Dining in tonight?"

"Yes, ma'am," he says with a drawl. I imagine if he'd been wearing a cowboy hat, he'd have tipped it at the lovely woman in front of us. "Had to introduce this lovely lady to your pizza. She didn't know there were styles of pizza, Mrs. Fratelli."

"How many times have I told you to call me Mary?" the woman says, popping one fist on her hip in faux aggravation.

"I'm sorry, ma'am. I'm Texan. We take a while to learn," Jacob jokes.

"I find that hard to believe. Come on. I'll seat you in the back so you won't be bothered on your date," she says with a wink.

I'm about to argue, but Jacob beats me to it. "Oh, we aren't on a date. I know my place. This beauty would never give me the time of day. We just got rained out on a double date, and we both craved pizza."

"I wondered why you both appeared wet," she says with a laugh. "Is it raining?"

"No," I interject. "A fire at another place caused the indoor sprinkler system to go off."

"Yet the two people you were on dates with didn't come with you?" she inquires. I stifle the laugh that fights to come out. If I had to bet, I'd say this is a family owned establishment, and Mary Fratelli is part of a large Italian family. My friend Natalie just married into an Italian family, and the stories she's told me about how they're all up in each other's business make me laugh all the time. I thought maybe she was embellishing, but it appears Mrs. Fratelli is cut from the same cloth.

Natalie was one of my only local friends, and while I was happy she'd found her man Alex, I'm sad she lives up in Eternity Springs now, because I never see her.

"Well," Jacob says, scratching his scruffy chin as he tries to explain, "I thought I was there to meet *this* beautiful woman, and the other gal was there for my buddy, Levi. But the other gal wanted me, and thought to set Levi up with Becca here. I had no interest in the other woman, but I'm also not about to take a girl from my friend."

"Of course not. You're a good boy. You'd never do that." Mrs. Fratelli looks fondly at Jacob. Almost like a mom would look at her son.

Exactly as my parents look at my brother.

And how they never looked at me.

As Mrs. Fratelli sets menus down at a booth in the back of the restaurant, I slide in one side. The red leather is well-worn and soft. A family photo hangs on the wall, showcasing a large brood of people.

"The two in the chairs are Mary's grandparents," Jacob explains, pointing to the couple in the middle of the photo. "From what I've been told, they moved out here from New York City in the 1950s to start Fratelli's Pizza. Mary has been working here since she was a teenager. She married another Italian guy who was all too willing to continue on with Fratelli's Pizza. Now their kids work here, too."

"I love stories like that," I say softly. "How amazing it must be to be part of a family like that."

"You don't have a large family?" Jacob asks quietly.

I shake my head. "No. My family is small. I don't really have a relationship with any of them, so the size is moot."

"None of them?"

"No."

"May I ask why?"

"It's a long story, and I'd rather not talk about it."

"Okay." My eyes whip to his, surprised at how easily he acquiesced. "What? I'm not gonna force you to talk about your history, darlin'. Mine isn't the best either. How about we just keep it to small talk, then enjoy our pizza? Doesn't have to be deeper than that."

"Unless it's deep dish pizza," I quip, making Jacob chuckle.

"I draw the line at talking about that crap."

After ordering, Jacob regales me with tales of his hockey team. If I didn't think men were gross before, I certainly do now. Stories of jockstrap tampering, smelly socks, and the weirdest superstitions I've ever heard of. A prior teammate had some kind of abused Barbie doll he took with him to all of his games? That can't be right. One guy is convinced if he doesn't poop an hour before a game, he won't play well. Another refuses to wash his underwear for an entire season. *An entire season.*

And yet women line up to sleep with these neanderthals.

"Boys are disgusting," I mutter after Jacob tells me about an awful superstition involving two of the guys and sex. With one girl. At the same time.

"Technically, that wasn't disgusting. Well, I guess it depends on how they're fucking," Jacob muses. "DP wouldn't be as gross."

"DP?"

I notice a very faint pink creep onto his neck. "Um, double penetration."

"Well, I assumed they'd both be penetrating in order for it to count as sex, but I just assumed one was in the …" I trail off. Oh my word. My face heats as embarrassment sinks in.

Jacob cocks his head to the side. "What, Spitfire? What did you assume?"

"Nothing," I answer hurriedly.

"Oh, I don't think it was nothing. Come on, now. Don't be shy. I promise I won't make fun of you."

That's not what I'm afraid of. I'm more worried he'll realize just how sheltered I am, with virtually no experience whatsoever. I don't know why I want Jacob to think highly of me, since I know nothing will happen between us. I'm me, and he's him. Apples and oranges.

"Becca," he says quietly. "Look at me."

When my eyes meet his, I'm taken aback at the intensity. His blue eyes are deeper somehow.

"Tell me what you thought," he commands.

"I thought one was oral," I blurt out, then cover my face with my hands. "I just thought it meant penetrating anywhere, but then I realized you probably meant in her butt."

"That can be true, but these guys liked to find a woman who would take both of them in her pussy," Jacob says matter-of-factly.

My hands drop from my face as I stare at him in shock. "Seriously? That's a possibility? I don't think I've ever even seen that come up when I search for porn. How does that work? That can't feel comfortable for any of them. Logistically speaking, are they laying down? Standing? Who chooses who gets to face the girl and who is behind her? I have too many questions."

As I watch Jacob's grin get wider and wider, I realize what I said. "I mean —"

"Oh no, darlin', you said what you said. And you ain't taking it back now. My sweet, little Becca, searching for porn. You really are a spitfire, aren't you? You got a favorite website? I bet you even have a favorite porn star, don't you?"

"Is there a hole I can crawl into and die?" I moan, laying my head on the table.

"I can ask my friends. Seems like their DP buddies might have holes big enough for that," Jacob jokes.

"I swear, if you tell anyone about this, I will find someone to mess with your hockey crap, Jacob Mitchell," I warn.

"Uh oh, you almost full-named me," he says with a chuckle. "Thank fuck you don't know my middle name."

"I can find it," I mutter. I'm sure there are fan websites out there for him that'll tell me his middle name, shoe size, and probably the shape of his penis. I'm about to say that when I feel his hand coast across the top of my head, gently moving a lock of my hair from my face. The movement sends a shiver down my spine.

"You have nothing to be embarrassed about, Becca," he says softly. "Anyone who says they don't look at porn is a liar. Better lift your head, our food is coming out."

I raise my head, but keep my gaze averted as Mrs. Fratelli places our enormous pizza in the middle of the table. Only after we've both taken a slice do I speak. "Can we never speak of this again?"

"You got it."

After an evening of excellent pizza and remarkably easy going conversation, I begin to freak out when Jacob insists on walking me back to my apartment. The sun has set behind the mountains, casting an eerie glow across the city, but the tall buildings block any remaining sunlight from large portions of downtown. I'd have no problem walking earlier in the evening, but I wasn't kidding about having a stalker. I'm still checking my surroundings wherever I go.

But right now, I'm more aware of Jacob's presence beside me.

Casting a quick glance out of the corner of my eye, I take in his profile. Head held high, he walks with a cocky assuredness that all professional athletes seem to have. I'm not too proud to admit that I may have cyber stalked him a little bit earlier in the day, and I'm fairly certain this suit isn't in his game day rotation. It makes me wonder if he just bought it, or if it's a suit that he brings out for first dates. How many women have seen this suit? Better yet, how many women have taken this suit off of him?

"You're thinking pretty hard over there," he comments, pulling me out of my weird spiral.

"I was thinking about your suit," I blurt out. "Do you normally wear a suit to a blind date?"

"No," he chuckles. "Levi made me. I'd rather be in jeans and boots."

"Cowboy boots?" I ask.

"Once a Texan, always a Texan," he says with a grin.

"Can I ask you a few stereotypical questions about Texas?"

"Sure."

"Do you have a cowboy hat?"

His lips twitch as he nods. "I do. Quite a few, actually."

"Is it true that if you wear a man's cowboy hat, it means you're theirs?" I ask.

"Some view it that way, yes."

"Some?"

"Well, if a man has a favorite hat, and he gives it to a woman, that has meaning behind it. He's not only saying he's interested in her, but also that he trusts her, and values their connection."

"Have —" I stop, clearing my throat.

"You want to know if I've ever given my cowboy hat to a woman?" Jacob asks, already sensing exactly where my mind is heading. "No, darlin'. I've never done that."

"Oh," I whisper. Heat dances across my cheeks as I look anywhere but at him. "Does everyone know how to ride a horse in Texas?"

"Not everyone, but I do. We didn't own any horses, but the people next door did. They knew I didn't get along the best with my mom, and they taught me how to care for their horses. They'd pay me an allowance as if they were my real parents, and that's how I managed to get extra hockey gear when I needed it. My dad left a small stipend for anything hockey related, but sometimes things broke, or I outgrew things too quickly. Mom certainly wasn't going to pay for them herself," he says with a shake of his head.

Assuming he doesn't want to talk about his mom anymore, I soldier on. "Have you ever seen a tornado in person? I know the meteorologists and storm chasers in Oklahoma and Texas are all over the place during storm season, so you've undoubtedly seen some on television."

"I have seen one, yeah. Big one came through town when I was about ten. Scared the hell out of me. We didn't have a shelter, but the neighbors with the horses did. It was one of those outdoor underground ones. There were so many fucking spiders in that thing, but what scared me the most was the roar of the tornado. Never heard anything like it," Jacob says quietly.

"I've done some chasing here," I confess. "One of the most picturesque tornadoes I've ever seen. It was fully white from the base of the wall cloud all the way to the ground. I got within a half mile, and the roar is something I'll never forget."

"Was that your first tornado?" he asks.

I shake my head. "No. I grew up in the Midwest, and I saw one from a few miles away when I was a kid. Then I did a couple years working in Mississippi, and they'd get tornadoes pretty much any month of the year. But the white tornado here is always the one I remember."

"Did you always want to be a meteorologist?"

"I did," I say with a smile. "I've had a love affair with the weather since a meteorologist came to talk to my second grade class. I can sit and watch clouds roll down the mountains for hours, or the lightning from a storm passing by. It just never gets old."

"That's how I feel about hockey. It's the only thing I've ever truly loved in my life," Jacob says, smiling fondly.

"How long is a hockey career normally?" I ask.

"It depends. Some guys can skate into their late thirties. Most don't. I've been in the league for twelve years. I don't figure I have but a couple more years left."

"How old are you?" I ask, wracking my brain on what has come up when I've Googled him.

"Thirty four. How old are you?"

"Thirty three."

"For some reason, I thought you were a lot younger than me," he muses.

"Why?"

"For one, I have more wrinkles than you."

"Is that really due to age, or the lack of a good skincare regimen?" I tease.

"Are you saying I'm supposed to use something other than a bar of soap on my face?"

I gasp in horror. "Please tell me you're joking. I can't tell if this is you being a smart ass, or if you really use the same bar of soap to clean your face and your butt."

"Relax," he laughs. "I have soap for my face. I promise it's not the same bar."

"Good," I say with relief, then turn toward him. "But it's still a bar of soap? Like an actual bar of soap?"

"Yeah?"

"What kind?" I ask hesitantly.

He shrugs. "Dial, I think? I don't know. Whatever catches my eye at the store, I guess."

"You need to use a cleanser, not a bar of soap. Your skin on your face is much thinner than the rest of your body, and due to exposure to the elements, it dries out faster. Especially here. Seriously, Jacob. I can give you some suggestions, if you want. Nothing too girlie. I'd hate to ruin your street cred."

A slow smile blooms across his face. "I like that."

"Me suggesting you have a street cred?"

"No." He pauses, before reaching over and running a finger from my elbow to my wrist. "You calling me Jacob."

Oh.

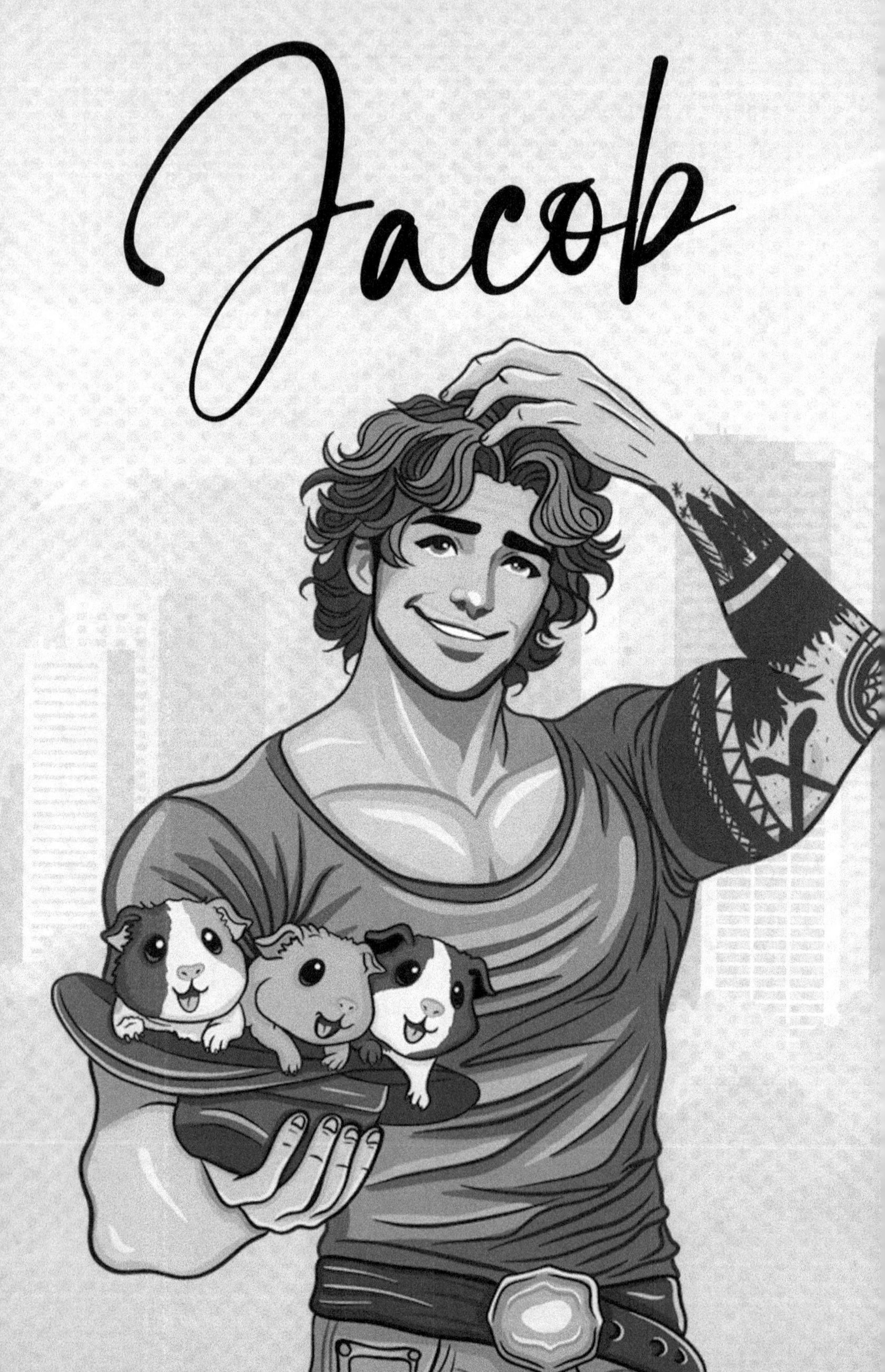
Jacob

CHAPTER 6

I can see it. *I can feel it.*

The chemistry between us is like static electricity, bouncing back and forth just waiting to be ignited. That simple touch on her arm had her pupils dilating, and goosebumps erupted in the wake of my finger.

I want to push her up against whatever building this is and feel her body wrapped around me. Learn how she tastes, and the sounds she makes.

But I know she isn't ready for that.

Becca's mind is at war with her body, and I'm not going to interfere with that. If anything occurs between us, it goes at her pace, not mine.

"Doesn't anyone call you Jacob?" she whispers, her gaze dropping to the sidewalk pavement as she tentatively steps forward.

"Not really, no. Nicknames are a big deal in hockey. Most people call me Jax, or my last name. Only a few people call me Jacob."

"I can call you Jax," Becca says softly.

"No," I tell her, taking her hand in mine before I have a chance to think about it. "I like you calling me Jacob. I like that you treat me differently, Spitfire."

"How so?" she asks, and I silently celebrate when her hand closes around mine.

"My teammates are one thing. But almost everyone else I meet sees me as a commodity. Either they want something from me, or they want to fuck me. You didn't fall into either of those categories, and it was a refreshing change."

"Do you automatically have to assume that someone isn't being completely honest with you? I think I'd never want to meet new people. I'd think the worst of them immediately."

I think for a moment before I answer. "Yeah. It's probably why I only hang out with my teammates, or other friends in sports. I'm good friends with the quarterback for the Coyotes, and he obviously understands because he goes through it too. I can't tell you the last time I had a real date. It's been years since I had a girlfriend."

"It's been a while since I've been on a real date too. Well, a date where I didn't want to run screaming from the restaurant," she says with a giggle. "I have been on too many first dates this year, and all of them ended horribly."

"Oh yeah?" I force myself to say, while bitterness fills my veins. It honestly pisses me off that she's been on dates. Becca is actively trying to find someone, yet I know she won't ever think to give me a chance. "What's the worst date you've been on? You can only pick one."

"Only one? Dang. Give me a minute," she says, tapping her finger to her lips. Her perfect, plump, rosy lips that I stared at so many times tonight. She snaps her fingers and says, "I've got it! A guy met me for dinner, then asked if I'd be okay running to grab his dog from the vet."

"Seems somewhat normal," I comment.

"Just wait. I'm sure you figured it was a dog having a procedure or something at the vet, right?" When I nod, she continues. "Nope. The dog died, and he was picking up the remains. And not the cremated remains, Jacob. The actual remains. He said the cremating process was too expensive. Then, without telling me what we were doing, he drove to a public park, where he proceeded to grab a shovel out of the trunk and start digging a hole for his dead dog."

"What the fuck?" I breathe, completely shocked at her story.

"Yeah. I was pretty freaked out, seeing as how we were alone in a park and he had a shovel, so I bolted and called the police. He was arrested for a bunch of things. The DA wanted me to testify at the trial, but fortunately it was all settled out of court. I never heard from him again."

"That is so fucked up. What was his reasoning for burying the dog there?"

Becca sighs. "He said he thought the dog would like it. It wasn't even a park they went to. It was just the park closest to the vet's office. The entire debacle was so bizarre."

"Wow. My bad dates pale in comparison," I comment.

"Oh please, make me feel better. Tell me a good one," Becca says with a laugh. I'm tempted to make one up on the spot just to keep her happy, and to keep her hand enclosed in mine, but then I remember the worst date I've ever had.

"In college, we did a lot of group dates. Some of the guys weren't as outgoing as me, and they liked the group concept better. I was cool with it, because I can have fun anywhere. Didn't matter to me if it was me and a girl or fifteen of us hanging out."

"You, extroverted? Shocking," Becca says dryly, making me squeeze her hand.

"I know. I'm as surprised as you. One night, there were five guys and seven girls. We'd driven over to Lake Michigan with a ton of beer. I honestly can't remember how we got the beer, because we were all underage, but Ann Arbor is a big sports town, so we prob- ably just got it without being carded. By dinnertime, we were all pretty toasted. One of the girls suggested truth or dare, and brought out a couple bottles of whiskey."

Becca's face screws up in disgust. "Twenty-year-olds drinking straight whiskey? And after all that beer? This is going to end badly."

"You are correct. Anyway, it started off with stupid dares, but everyone had to take a shot of whiskey, no matter if they chose truth or dare. After a couple rounds, we all got a little more … daring."

"Is there any online evidence of this night? If I Google your name and Michigan, am I going to find a picture of your bare ass or something?" Becca asks.

"No." I pause. "At least I don't think so. But if you want to see my bare ass, I'm more than happy to show it to you." I reach for my belt dramatically, but Becca bats my hand away. "Damn. I do enjoy a good mooning."

"In this city, you will make it onto the news if you show your butt on a major downtown road," Becca says. She's probably right. I've been on the news, and on trashy websites, for much smaller offenses.

"Well, the girl next to me dared me to strip down with her, then go stand on a couple of old wooden pilings from a broken pier and sing some stupid song she liked, but don't ask me what song, because I didn't even know what it was then. So off we go, dropping clothes along the way. About twenty feet from the pilings, I realize I really don't feel well. I'm not even looking at her. I'm thinking about how the two pilings we're supposed to climb onto have morphed into six, and they seem to be swaying."

"Uh-oh."

"Yeah. Somehow I climb up on the stupid thing, but she can't get up on hers. She wants up on mine. These damn things were like six inches across, and I have big feet. I tell her I'll help her up onto hers. I reach down and grab her arm, hauling her up and basically tossing her over to the other piling. I still don't know how she managed to land on it, but she did."

"I doubt I could do that sober," Becca murmurs. "So then you sang?"

"Nope. I took one look at her and projectile vomited all over her."

"You didn't!" Becca shouts, then slaps a hand over her mouth. "That is not where I thought the story was going!"

"What did you think I would say?"

"I guess that one of you fell and injured something, so a trip to the hospital ended the evening. I never thought you'd vomit on her."

"It's not like I did it on purpose," I say, defending myself. "Does it make you feel better to know that she then puked on me?"

"Actually, it does."

"You'll probably also enjoy knowing that everyone forced us to sit in the back of a pickup truck for the ride home, because even with the lake there and attempting to wash off the puke, we both still stunk."

"That's really not that bad of a thing."

"Do you know how far Ann Arbor is from Lake Michigan?" I ask.

"Isn't Ann Arbor pretty close to Detroit?" Becca asks.

"Yes."

"Why didn't you go to Lake Erie? That would have been so much closer."

"I'm aware of that. I suggested it. The girl I puked on was the one who complained about how 'disgusting' the beaches near us were, and suggested we traipse two and a half hours across the state to go to Lake Michigan."

"I'm not sure which one of us had the worst date. Me or her," Becca says with a breathy laugh.

"Hey! What about me?" I ask with fake anger.

"You were twenty years old, you got drunk on a beach, and got to see some boobs. You had the best date out of the three of us," Becca points out.

"You're right," I sigh. "She did have a nice rack."

I'm honestly surprised when Becca throws her head back in a loud shout of laughter, and the sound is like music to my soul.

Holy hell does she have an incredible laugh. It's then that I notice we've arrived at her apartment building, and I'm disappointed the evening has to end.

"I was worried tonight would end horribly, but it didn't at all," Becca says shyly. "Thank you, Jacob. I had a really great time."

"I did too," I answer honestly. "It's been a long time since I had such a fun night. What would you say to having a meal again sometime soon? As friends, of course."

Becca stares thoughtfully at me. "A few hours ago, I would have told you no. But now, I think I'd like that. You're not at all who I thought you'd be."

"Likewise. What's your number?" I ask. When she rattles it off, I immediately send her a text. "There. Now you have mine. If you ever want an early morning bodyguard, you let me know. I'm excellent at before dawn small talk."

"Wait! That coffee. Was that Danica? Did she give you my favorite order?" Becca asks.

"No. Maybe? I'm not sure. Levi told me he knew someone at the station, but didn't say who. He's the kind of guy who has contacts everywhere, so it may have been someone else. I promise I've never met Danica."

Becca waves her hand in the air. "I don't care about that. I can't find fault in something that would have happened before we really met. It just bugged me how you figured that out."

"It bugged you?" I inquire.

"I'm a pretty private person. I don't like that someone is out there possibly gossiping about me."

"Is it considered gossip if it's just a coffee order? I mean, clearly getting your address was a huge red flag, but I never thought the coffee order would be crossing a line too."

She shrugs, a wave of hair falling in front of her shoulder. Her green eyes appear guarded. Reserved. We've spent the entire evening having a good time, but the moment we begin talking about her, she throws walls up. Not that I blame her. I'm in the public eye, but I think Becca has it worse.

"I have no idea if other things were discussed. What other information did you ask for? Did the person supply anything without you asking?"

"Do you want me to ask Levi? I'm betting it's one of the sportscasters. Levi's an odd bird, though. He might know the owner of the whole damn station."

"I don't even know the owner. I've only seen him twice," Becca says, irritation evident in her tone. I whip out my phone and text Levi quickly.

ME

Who did you ask at Becca's station for info on her?

LEVI

Rick Marshall

ME

You still with your girl?

LEVI

Definitely not my girl after tonight. And as soon as you walked away, she miraculously could walk. Tell YOUR girl to be careful. I don't trust Danica at all.

ME

I'll let her know.

"He spoke to the evening sports guy. Rick Marshall."

"Oh," Becca whispers. "I rarely see Rick. I don't know how he'd know my coffee order. Did you ask anything else?"

"I asked for your favorite flower, and if you liked hockey," I admit.

"What answers did you receive?"

"Hyacinth, and a resounding no."

"I have no idea how he found out about my love of hyacinths, but me disliking hockey is absolutely correct," Becca says with a laugh.

"How can you not like hockey? It's the greatest sport out there!" I exclaim.

She grimaces. "It's violent, some of the rules make no sense, and you guys celebrate losing your teeth. The puck moves so fast I can't keep track of it, and hockey stuff smells awful."

"I wouldn't say we *celebrate* losing teeth — wait. How do you know whether or not hockey equipment smells?"

She tilts her head to the side, a smile tugging at her lips. "I don't live under a rock, Jacob. I've been to hockey games. Being with the station means I've gotten some behind-the-scenes sights for most of the sports teams here. The locker room after a hockey game smells the worst out of all of them."

"You've been in our locker room? Right after a game?"

"Not immediately after, but yes. Typically most of you were gone. I didn't want to see anything I wasn't supposed to see," she murmurs.

"When was this?" I ask.

Becca looks lost in thought as she wracks her brain. "Within my first couple of months on the job here. The station likes to take newcomers out and show them the sights, and since it was winter, we hit up a hockey game for our introduction into Denver sports. Danica dragged me again once last season, but we stayed outside the actual locker room."

"Did you ever see me?" I ask quietly, and she nods. "What was I doing?"

"You were walking to the shower, I think. In a towel. I left because ..." she trails off.

"Because why?" I pry.

She sighs. "The towel loosened and I saw your butt."

I can't help the loud laughter that booms from my mouth. "Well, I'll be damned. I tried to moon you tonight, and it turns out, I already did."

Becca giggles as she rolls her eyes. "Like I said, I didn't want to see anything like that. I hightailed it right on outta there."

I lean in closer, lowering my voice. "Well, what did you think, darlin'? Did you like what you saw?"

Her cheeks heat with a lovely pink blush. "I barely saw anything."

A wide grin breaks across my face. "Liar."

Becca snorts as she turns away, walking into her building. I don't move, watching her beautiful form. If she turns to look at me, I'll know that she's interested.

Turn, Spitfire. Turn around.

As she opens the door, Becca turns. A small smile touches her lips as she waves awkwardly at me, before going into her building. I watch until she's out of sight.

Game fucking on, Becca Stephens.

One way or another, you're going to be mine.

As I walk away whistling, I pull out my phone. After a quick search of local florists, I'm ready to order a bouquet of hyacinths, when a thought occurs to me.

Why do I think I know someone else who loves the same flower? I've seen it recently, but where?

Stopping dead in my tracks, I almost drop my phone when I remember.

NerdGirl has a hyacinth as her profile picture.

Becca

CHAPTER 7

IT'S SAFE TO SAY THAT I'M IN TROUBLE, BECAUSE I LIKE JACOB.

Like him, like him.

But is he being real with me? Or am I just a challenge? He held my hand almost the entire walk back to my apartment, but never made any other moves. I don't know what to think.

Nor do I know how to react when a beautiful bouquet of white hyacinths arrives at the station the following day. He didn't sign his name, but the only reason I know the flowers are from him is because he wrote "it's not a white tornado, but it'll do" on the card.

I acted nonplussed, but internally, I squealed.

"Who are the flowers from?" I jolt as Danica loudly asks from behind me.

"Oh. I'm not sure. No name," I tell her hastily. Her eyes narrow as she studies me, and I take the opportunity to change the subject. "How's your ankle?"

She sighs. "It's okay. I guess I just strained it. As soon as we got in the Uber, I realized I could move it better. I had Levi drop me off at home instead of going to the hospital."

"I'm glad you're okay," I say sincerely. "I can't believe the sprinkler system went off. That was insane."

"It really was! I researched restaurant sprinkler systems last night. I'm gonna do an entire series on what Denver restaurants do to prepare for fires. It got pretty chaotic in there last night, and the staff didn't seem to know what to do. As Levi carried me out, I watched everyone freak out, running around with no idea of how they should act. I'm making it an exposé on the restaurant industry."

"That's very cool," I say. "Did the restaurant have any major damage?"

"Not really. Smoke damage in the kitchen and water damage everywhere else. Brad said they're hoping to reopen in a couple weeks." Brad, our station manager, knows everything about any newsworthy stories in Denver. "I have to go. Interviewing a restaurant owner a few blocks away. Oh, Brad was looking for you, by the way."

Great.

I was hoping to go rest my eyes for ten minutes while eating lunch. Dragging my feet on the way upstairs to Brad's office, I hesitate at his door. What could he need? I rarely interact with him. He's more involved with the reporters than the meteorologists on staff.

Knocking twice, I wait until he tells me to come in. "Hi, Brad. Danica said you wanted to see me?"

"Yes. Close the door and have a seat, Becca." He motions for me to sit in front of his desk, shuffling some papers around. Are those photographs?

"Is everything okay?" I ask as I close the door.

"I'm not sure. You tell me."

As soon as I sit down, he flings a handful of eight by ten photos across the desk at me.

Jacob with the coffee outside my apartment.

By the pizza place, both of us dripping wet.

Walking hand-in-hand across downtown.

Me looking up at Jacob with a big smile.

"You care to tell me why you're gallivanting around town with our star forward, Becca?" Brad asks, a stern and imposing expression covering his face.

He's looking at me like my father would look at me. Disappointed. Embarrassed. Angry.

It's on the tip of my tongue to apologize. Admit my error in judgment. Tell him whatever I think will make this problem go away. Just like I had to growing up, even when most of the issues never had to do with me. They were almost always my brother setting me up.

I'd get chastised, demeaned, humiliated wherever we were. It didn't matter where. My brother would stand behind my parents, a victorious grin on his face, as he watched me slowly break down. It didn't happen all at once, this systematic breakage of my strength. It was so slow. Achingly slow. Like watching a car crash in slow motion. Years of emotional abuse.

Sitting here now, having Brad look at me with the same expression, it's as if I've been dumped in ice water.

And for some reason, that makes me incredibly pissed off.

"How is this any of your business?" I reply hotly, sitting up straight. My hands shake as I force myself to control the tremor in my voice. This isn't my father. I do not have to sit here and take it. I can stand up for myself.

Brad looks momentarily surprised when I speak. "I manage this station, Becca. And you are essentially a spokeswoman for the station. You have to be on your best behavior at all times. This is not what is in your contract."

"I'd like you to show me anywhere in my contract where it says I can't be friends with certain people."

Brad scoffs. "He's all over you. That isn't a 'friend.'"

I roll my eyes at his air quotes. "He was not all over me. He held my hand. That was it."

"You're honestly going to sit here and lie to me? You went back to your apartment with him."

"He walked me back there —" I stop. "What did you just say?"

Brad's nostrils flare. "He was there."

"How did you know he was there? Are you following me?" I ask incredulously. "And how do you know where I live?"

"One of the shots shows you walking into the building, so I assumed you lived there. I don't know where you live, Becca." Brad stands, placing both hands on his desk, and leans toward me. I recognize the power move, a move meant to be threatening and imposing to me. Instead of cowering or shrinking, I lean back against the chair, glaring up at Brad defiantly. Crossing my arms over my chest, I lift my chin.

"A photographer followed you. He recognized both of you. You're lucky he called me instead of selling the shots to the highest bidder."

"Was this coincidental, Brad? Or were you having me followed?" I ask slowly. His eyes narrow as he formulates an answer.

"Of course I'm not having you followed. Getting candid shots of people like Jax Mitchell is a big business. In any other instance, you'd just be a random woman. A puck bunny. But you've got a following here too, Becca. That makes this murky, and we don't need any more bad publicity at the station."

"It's not my fault some of your 'good ole boys,'" I say, mocking him with his own air quotes, "decided to make stupid choices this summer." Our evening news team and production staff went out one night and destroyed a restaurant. No provocation. No reasoning. Just straight destruction. Unfortunately for them, cameras were everywhere, and the restaurant went viral when the Denver Police released the footage. It was quite the spectacle.

Brad rounds his desk, coming to sit on the edge of the mahogany in front of me. Leaning forward, he places a hand on my shoulder. "Look, Becca. I only have your best interests at heart. Jax Mitchell is a player. He'll get what he wants from you, and then he'll drop you for the next piece of ass. Surely you don't want that."

When his thumb seems to jolt against my shoulder, causing it to flutter under the fabric of my sleeveless dress, I stiffen. My voice hisses out slowly as I utter, "Take your hand off of me."

Brad's eyes widen, and he swiftly lunges backward as his face pales. Standing, I move around the chair, putting it between the two of us. "Oh shit. I'm sorry. Really, Becca. I didn't mean anything by that —"

I interrupt him. "I don't care what you meant. Anything I do in my personal life is my business, not yours. If I want to date Jax Mitchell, or if I only want to fuck him, it's up to me. You keep your nose out of it."

Brad throws up his hand in a surrender gesture. "Okay. But the moment it becomes news, we'll be meeting again. And I can't guarantee I'll be this nice."

Turning, I storm out of the office, making a beeline for my cubicle downstairs, but pass it to head into my favorite women's bathroom on this floor. Yes, I have a favorite. I even have a preferred stall. Relieved to find the bathroom completely empty, I lock myself in my favorite stall and attempt to take a deep breath.

Focus, Becca.

Breathe, two, three, four. In through the nose.

Out through the mouth. Two, three, four.

In through the nose, and hold it.

You are in control.

How can you be so stupid?

No. My father isn't here.

I hate how his voice comes in crystal clear when I'm having a difficult time, right on the cusp of a breakdown. Hands shaking, I carefully withdraw my phone from my pocket. Whoever invented pockets, actual usable pockets, on dresses, deserves everything in the world.

My vision starts to blur with tears as I attempt to pull up a search engine. My therapist gave me a variety of different tricks for when I'm really feeling like my anxiety is taking over. The breathing exercises usually help immensely. Now I'm looking up kitten videos. Even though I have a dog, I've always secretly wanted a cat. For the longest time, my parents convinced me I was allergic to cats. I only found out recently that it was a lie. I'd love to get a Maine Coon cat, but I already feel bad about the amount of time I spend away from Thunder.

The kitten videos are calming my nerves a little, but I still shriek when my phone buzzes with a DM.

StickUM92: What's your favorite color?

NerdGirl1025: Turquoise. I've always wanted to go to one of those exotic places where the ocean water is so clear and turquoise that I could watch the fish for hours.

StickUM92: There's a place in the Maldives where you stay in bungalows above the water.

NerdGirl1025: I'd love that! It would be so nice to escape. I'd love to go right now.

StickUM92: Sounds like you're having a crappy day.

NerdGirl1025: You could say that.

StickUM92: Want to talk about it? I know we've maintained a rule of not sharing personal information, but I'm here if you want to vent.

NerdGirl1025: I just got reamed out by my boss for something incredibly dumb, and it was none of his business anyway, because it involved my personal life.

StickUM92: Are you a public figure?

StickUM92: Never mind. Don't answer that.

NerdGirl1025: In some ways, yes, I'm in the public eye. But mostly I'm not.

StickUM92: I love how you worded that, because it describes my life too.

NerdGirl1025: Oh? Has your boss ever told you who you can and can't be seen with?

StickUM92: Kind of, yeah. But more in a "don't make bad decisions" kind of way. Just reminding us that lots of people are dishonest, and trusting the wrong person can end up being an eighteen year sentence.

NerdGirl1025: Woah. That's blunt.

StickUM92: My boss is pretty blunt, but I appreciate it. He wants the best for me.

NerdGirl1025: Funnily enough, my boss used that exact phrase, wanting the best for me, and I'm not sure I believe him.

StickUM92: I'm sorry you're in a bind, darlin'. Sounds like your boss needs a reality check. My guess is he has the hots for you, and he's acting out because of jealousy. I bet you're a knockout, and he's grasping at straws to keep you in his claws.

NerdGirl1025: Don't you remember? I'm really a middle-aged man.

StickUM92: Fuck. I forgot that. Oh well. Maybe your boss swings that way.

NerdGirl1025: I don't think so? I guess I could be wrong.

NerdGirl1025: Thanks for this conversation. It's exactly what I needed.

StickUM92: I'm glad. Kismet, because I suddenly thought I needed to check in with you.

NerdGirl1025: Perfect timing.

StickUM92: I've felt that way about a couple of our conversations. Like the one about my mom and the olives. Had I not talked to you, I'd probably have spiraled into one hell of a depressive night with a bottle of Jack. Instead, you got me laughing about fake grapes. I don't know if I ever thanked you for that conversation, darlin'. But it was what I needed too.

NerdGirl1025: I'm glad.

StickUM92: Still think you're a gorgeous woman.

NerdGirl1025: How can you be so sure?

StickUM92: Sixth sense. It's a gift, honestly. All of my teammates make fun of me for instinctively knowing weird details about blind dates, catfishing, and other crap.

NerdGirl1025: Teammates?

StickUM92: Shit. Sorry. That was a personal detail. Forget I said anything.

NerdGirl1025: Extracurricular activities don't really count as a personal detail, do they?

StickUM92: It isn't extracurricular. It's my job.

NerdGirl1025: Your job.

StickUM92: Yeah. I'm gonna regret telling you this, I think. But I play hockey. Professionally.

NerdGirl1025: Oh.

StickUM92: I'm guessing that wasn't a good oh.

NerdGirl1025: I just haven't had a lot of good experiences with professional athletes. I've met a few, and they've all turned out to be assholes, StickUM.

NerdGirl1025: Not that I'm automatically assuming you're an asshole. Or that you'll turn into one.

NerdGirl1025: I shouldn't lump everyone into a general category based on one detail.

NerdGirl1025: But it's difficult, when all of my experiences are shouting at me that hockey is a red flag.

NerdGirl1025: I bet you have other red flags, though. You probably hate cats. Or sleep with socks on. And only have missionary sex in the dark.

NerdGirl1025: Oh my word. Can I delete a message in here?

StickUM92: Nope. And I already saw it. You're cute when you ramble.

NerdGirl1025: You're assuming I'm cute.

StickUM92: I know you're cute.

StickUm92: I like cats. All animals, really. I don't sleep with socks on. If you must know, I sleep in boxers.

StickUM92: And I'll fuck you anyway you want me to.

StickUM92: Shower.

StickUM92: Counter.

StickUM92: Wall.

StickUM92: Car sex isn't fun, but I can manage.

StickUM92: But NerdGirl?

NerdGirl1025: (blushing) Mmmhmm?

StickUM92: You promise me you'll do what I say when I finally get you wrapped around me?

NerdGirl1025: Oh my.

StickUM92: I think you will. You'll be my good girl, won't you?

NerdGirl1025: This conversation went off the rails so quickly.

StickUM92: No, darlin'. This is exactly where we were supposed to go. And for that reason, I think it's important for you to know my name, because at some point in the near future, I'm gonna make sure you scream it.

NerdGirl1025: I don't need to know your name. I highly doubt we'll ever meet, StickUM. You're in Texas. I doubt I'll ever get there.

StickUM92: I'm from Texas, but I don't live there.

StickUM92: I live in Colorado.

Warning bells go off in my head.

Details … details …

StickUM92: My name is Jax.

StickUM92: And I guarantee we'll be meeting soon, NerdGirl. Now how about you tell me your name?

I don't answer, because my phone slips from my fingers, dropping to the tile floor, and shatters the screen.

StickUM is Jax. My Jax. My Jacob.

I don't know why I'm surprised. My luck is abysmal.

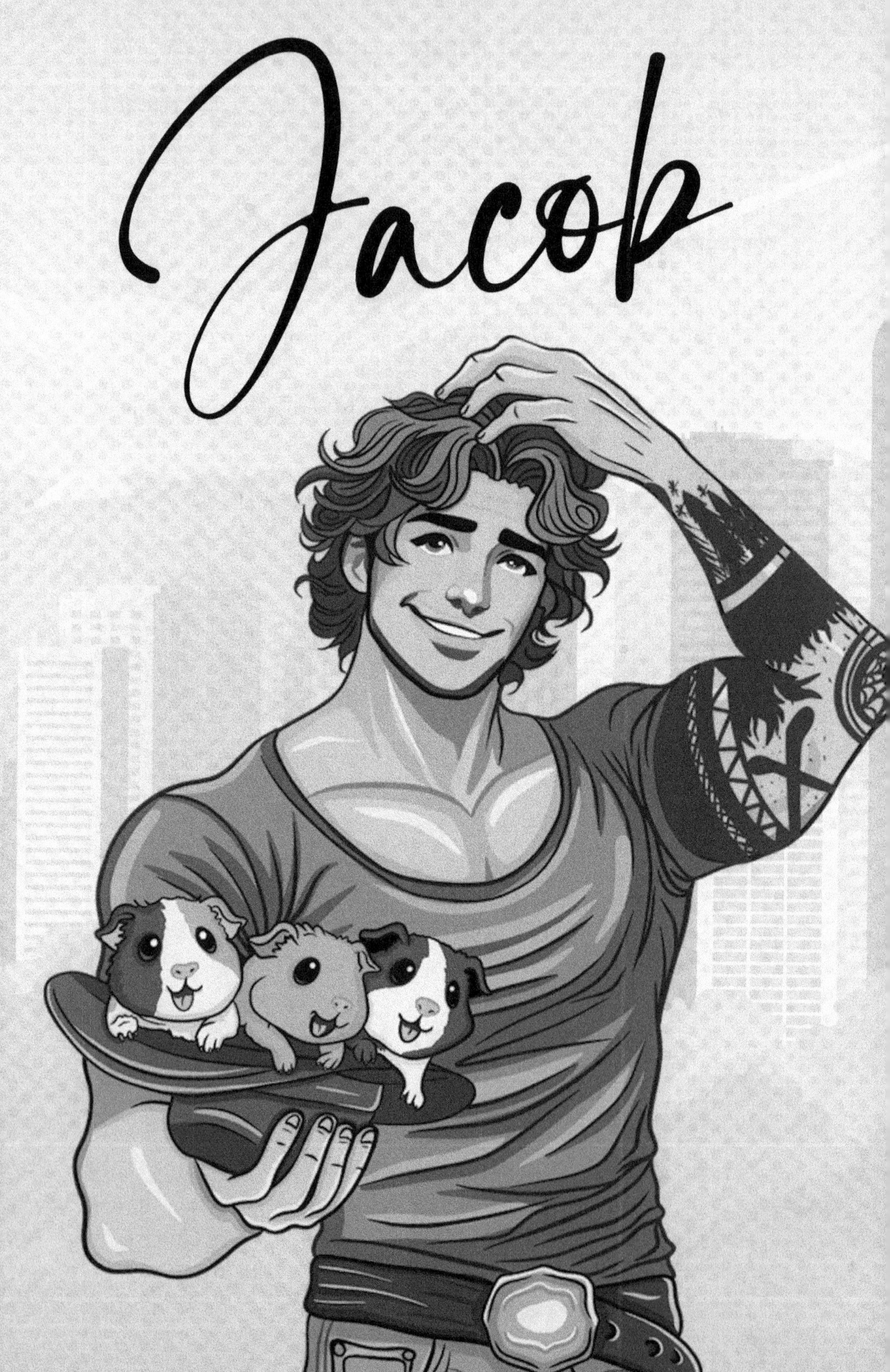
Jacob

CHAPTER 8

I waited for a while.

I could say it was only because I wanted to be a good friend to NerdGirl, but that wasn't the only reason.

It's Becca. It *has* to be.

That's why I started dropping personal details. I figured if it wasn't her, whoever NerdGirl is would ask some questions. Want to know where I play, what my last name is, and if I'd like to meet up. Knowing the little I know of Becca, I'm not surprised she clammed up.

If I could have willed my phone to ding with a new message from NerdGirl, I definitely would have done it. I hope it was coincidental timing. It's the middle of the day. She's clearly at work if she just got yelled at by her boss.

That little voice in the back of my head, however, is letting my self-consciousness come to the front. I told her my name and that I play hockey, and she goes radio silent.

I thought Becca was starting to like me.

Maybe not.

A week goes by with no messages from NerdGirl or Becca. From the moment I told NerdGirl my name and that I play hockey, I never heard from Becca again. I thought she'd at least acknowledge when I sent her the bouquet of hyacinths, considering her profile image on ChatBook is a picture of an incredibly similar floral arrangement. Hindsight, however, tells me I recognized her personality all along. Both Becca and NerdGirl are peaceful. Soft. Encouraging. Both make me want to be around them more. So why the radio silence? Am I that awful of a guy that Becca can't fathom interacting with me in person?

I texted her good morning a handful of times, but received no response. My self-confidence took a sizable beating, that's for sure.

Probably could also be because I talked about sex. I blame that mostly on the beautiful meteorologist who has taken up residence in my brain a good chunk of the day. Seeing how bashful Becca got when we talked about porn at dinner that night, I wanted to see if her online persona would also be shy.

I'm sure there's an element of the chase with Becca, because I've never had someone dislike me so quickly. But it's also just her. Dinner with Becca was a breath of fresh air. Puck bunnies want to talk about hockey. Money. Fame. I could immediately tell that Becca didn't care about any of that. We talked about pizza and bad dates, for fuck's sake.

I sent her flowers again, as well as a pizza from the restaurant I took her to. It's as if she never received anything. Hell, maybe she didn't.

Not wanting to bug Becca too much, I stop initiating texts. I don't want her to forget I exist, though, so I continue to send her flowers each week. I may not be texting Becca, but I always send her a note with the flowers asking if she'll go on another date with me. Fortunately, training camp is starting up, so I'll have lots of things to keep my mind off of both Becca *and* NerdGirl.

By the third week of September, I remember why I hate training camp. It keeps me really busy, which allows me not to think about the beautiful woman I've had on my mind since we last spoke four weeks ago. But I'm fucking exhausted.

I try to stay active during the off season, and I continue with four to five workouts per week. But it's nothing compared to what the coaching staff throws at us the closer we get to the regular season.

"Jesus, I'm getting old," Grant pants as we rest against the wall outside the cardio room. "Six miles is ridiculous. We don't go that long on the ice."

"It's called conditioning for a reason, dickhead," Gabe drawls as he strolls past us. Asshole looks like he didn't even break a sweat.

"How are you not exhausted?" I ask, taking deep breaths as my heart rate begins to slow down.

Gabe gives us a leering smile. "I get good cardio every day. Sometimes twice a day. My stamina is unbeatable."

"Jackass," Grant mutters.

"Green isn't your color, Nally," Gabe shouts as he continues down the hallway.

"The fuck does that mean?"

"It means he knows you're jealous that he's getting regular ass," I explain.

Grant shrugs. "Thanks for the explanation, oh Captain, my Captain. But don't you worry, Daws. I get it often enough. But I focus more on orgasms and less on stamina, so I can make that my focus from now on."

I shake my head with a chuckle. I'm sure Grant fucks more than enough. He almost has a chip on his shoulder that he's trying to erase by fucking it off. Even being a complete asshole to any woman he meets, they still line up ready to have their turn.

"Nally! Jax! On the ice in ten minutes!" Coach yells.

"Fuck," Grant groans. "I forgot he wanted us in full gear today."

A wave of nausea hits me. "I really think I might puke if he makes us do suicides."

"Don't even say that word out loud, man, or you'll give him ideas," Grant hisses. I've lost count on how many times suicides have made me puke.

They are miserable and every hockey player in the world hates them.

Quickly heading to the locker room, we put on our gear. It may look like we have a couple pads and two articles of clothing, but that's not the case. We've got shoulder pads and a chest protector. A jock strap and elbow pads. Hockey shorts and socks are put on separately, but the shin guards go on first. Depending on what our schedule is, we have different jerseys, also called sweaters. Protective gloves and a helmet finish the ensemble. It's a whole process, and every player has a routine for getting dressed. Some weirdos even go as far as putting their skates on *before* their pants. But don't get me started on what goalies have to wear.

Grant and I are the last on the ice, and Coach glares at us menacingly. I hear Grant swear under his breath, and I put up a silent prayer that we don't cause any more physical trauma to the entire team.

"You're one minute late," Gabe mutters.

"Alright, ladies," Coach says loudly. "We've got our first pre-season game tomorrow. Gonna do a full scrimmage today to prepare."

Multiple groans sound from my teammates, and Coach raises his eyebrows. "Oh? Is that a problem? I guess I could have you do a hundred suicides instead —"

"No!" Levi screams. "Scrimmage. We're all excited for a full scrimmage."

Coach mutters something quietly, then gestures for us to line up. Grant, Levi and I are the first line forwards, with me being the center. Coach warned me after our first pre-season game he will begin messing with the lines to see who I vibe with the best. I'm frustrated because I gel really well with Levi and Grant, but I know as Captain I need to be flexible, and aid where I'm needed.

The part I absolutely love about hockey is that I'm responsible for almost all of the face offs, and I love the anticipation of the puck dropping in front of me. I'm exceptionally quick getting the puck to my teammates.

I've always hated sports that take too long. You won't catch me golfing, and I definitely don't like baseball. Hockey is quick. We're on the ice for less than a minute each shift. The puck is constantly getting batted around, and I love the speed at which things change.

Thrilled at not having to do any suicides, I skate my ass off during the scrimmage. I know how to work hard. It sets a good example for the rookies, and also lets them know that I'm not going anywhere. We're still two players over roster, and my spot is secure. These guys must be nervous wrecks, this close to the start of the season, knowing two are going to be sent home.

After practice, I grab a quick shower, and once dressed, I get called into Coach's office. "You wanted to see me, Coach?"

"Yeah," he murmurs, typing something on his computer. When he finishes, he slams the laptop shut and turns to me. "You played harder today than most of last season. What's the deal?"

I shrug. "I don't know. Guess I was just happy for a scrimmage instead of suicides."

A tiny smirk appears. "I'm sure everyone thought that, but you were on another level. You know your spot is secure, right?"

"I know. Maybe it felt like a real game today, and I'm excited to be back to the daily grind and the busy schedule."

Coach studies me before sighing. "Who is she?"

"What?"

"The girl."

"What girl?"

"Jax, no one looks forward to the busy hockey schedule unless they're trying to get their mind off of a woman. Tell me who she is."

I shake my head. "It doesn't matter. She ghosted me, so it is what it is."

Coach chuckles. "That's the real issue. Someone didn't fall at your feet."

"No, it really isn't. I mean yeah, I didn't know how to handle that initially. And I fucked up with her more than once. But she was also the first woman I've met that I truly felt like I could be myself around. I wasn't Jax, the center for the Wolves. I was Jacob. And that was a nice change."

Coach nods, understanding dawning on his face. "I get it. Really. Maybe she hasn't ghosted you, or maybe she has. But I highly doubt she's the only woman out there who will want the real Jacob Mitchell. How the hell did you get the nickname Jax? That doesn't make any sense."

I let out a loud bark of laughter. "My first nickname was Mitchy, and I fought that hard. Even as an eight-year-old, I recognized how fucked up that sounded. I think a little sister of a teammate when I was around eleven couldn't pronounce Jacob or Jake, and somehow it came out Jax. The name stuck, and I was all too happy to go with that instead of Mitchy."

"I still want to know what Levi's nickname was. There's no way he went all the way through his career until now with no nickname," Coach says with a smile.

"Good luck with that," I joke. I know Levi's nickname, but I've been sworn to secrecy. I'd never do that to him.

Coach's eyes narrow. "You fucking know the nickname, don't you? Come on. Tell me, or I'll put you down to fourth line."

I stand up with a chuckle. "No, you won't."

"God dammit. I won't."

Whistling, I head out of his office, ready to get home.

A cacophony of squeaks and squeals hits my ears as I open the door to my apartment. "Alright, alright! I'll get you your treats."

Heading to the kitchen, I pull open my fridge to grab a smattering of fruits and vegetables for my girls. Today, it's blueberries, strawberries, watermelon, broccoli, and cauliflower. Their favorite is spinach, but I'm out of that. The squeals they let out when they hear the bag of spinach opening is pretty comical.

As soon as my foot hits the carpet in their room, my guinea pigs start squealing. All six of them.

Rose, Lily, Daffodil, Bluebell, Daisy, and Dahlia.

Yes, I have six guinea pigs. And I have a pet sitter that comes twice a day to make sure they have everything they need when I'm out of town.

My newest girl, Dahlia, hides in one of the huts. She's still unsure of me, as well as the chaos around her. I've set up one of my secondary bedrooms as their space. Multiple cages are connected by tubes. I even had someone 3D print special stairs that lead to tubes and slides halfway up the walls. As often as possible, I put them in their exercise balls and let them roam around the apartment.

I first became obsessed with guinea pigs in middle school. A kid at my school had one, and I immediately fell in love. I liked that they were bigger than hamsters, but could still be caged. For some reason, the thought of a dog or cat scared the hell out of me. Probably because I figured my mom would kill it and scar me for all of eternity.

So, when the NHL adult money started rolling in, I got myself some guinea pigs. Teammates bought cars or houses, and I bought myself a small rodent. Hardly anyone knows about the half dozen vermin with their own bedroom in my apartment, and I plan to keep it that way.

Rose, Lily, and Bluebell are my most outgoing pigs. They'll eat out of the palm of my hand, and Rose will even sit on my shoulder. I found out Lily likes to eat hair, so she doesn't get a chance to be close to my head. Daffodil and Daisy seem to have imprinted on each other, and will only cooperate if the other is involved. I found an extra-large exercise ball for them to use together.

After filling all of their food dishes with the fruits and veggies, I turn down the lights and quietly relax into the plush, cozy over-sized chair in the corner of the room. Watching my pigs inhale their treats is so peaceful to me. They don't have anxiety, or concerns about the future. They eat, sleep, play, and poop. That's it. Basic necessities of life.

I smile as my eyes drift closed. I wonder what Becca would say about my pig room. As NerdGirl, she would probably find it humorous, and expect me to regale her with humorous tales of their antics. I find myself thinking Becca would probably want to come see them. She'd be curious, asking a ton of questions, but be apprehensive about touching, or holding them.

The thought of having Becca in my apartment, in my space, brings a wave of peace across me, and I fall asleep thinking of her.

"Right there! Right there!" I scream as I charge toward the boards. It's a rare afternoon game in Indianapolis, two weeks into the season. We're tied late in the third period, but as I point toward Shears, he manages to snatch the puck away from the Hawks defensemen. He flips it to Billings, who passes it to me, and I'm in perfect position. Settling my weight on my back skate, I swing my stick, smashing the puck into the air. It soars right over the goalie's left shoulder, and the red goal light turns on. Red is my favorite color.

"Let's fucking go!" Billings shouts as the guys jump on me. Looking up at the clock, I see there's only thirty seconds remaining. All we need to do is keep the puck on this side of the ice, and we'll get our fourth win of the season. We lost our home opener, which was humiliating. None of us even went to our favorite bar after the game. Charlie's Pub has long been a staple for the Wolves players. With a back room that only some people are allowed to enter, we can relax and unwind after a game. But not after that first one. Nope, we all went home to sulk in private.

Coach switches out the defensemen, but leaves me, Shears, and Billings on the ice. We're typically not on the ice for this long, but I'm sure he's thinking we're his best shot at preventing a goal. I've learned that Shears has ridiculous skills with his hockey stick. Billings, in turn, is honestly half defenseman, and will run over anyone. I'm the quickest on the team.

"Goalie! Goalie! They pulled the goalie!" Gabe shouts from behind us. Shit. Now it's like a fucking power play, with the Hawks having four forwards to our three. We can't let our guards down for even a half second. Fortunately, the Hawks get their communication lines messed up, because one forward sits back, far enough that Shears swoops in to steal the puck. The crowd groans as he swiftly heads down to score in an empty net, right as the horn blows, signaling the end of the game. We win, with a final score of four to two.

"That's what I'm talking about!" Coach shouts as we pass him on the way to the visitors' locker room. There's a palpable energy as we cool off and unwind, especially after a win. Coach gives us a pep talk. He chooses the guy who essentially wins 'player of the game,' and that player gets a ridiculously large wolf medallion on a very heavy gold chain. Not surprisingly, Shears gets it this time, and gives us a few words.

"Nice game, boys. Let's keep it up," he says shortly. Nodding at everyone, he takes the obnoxious wolf necklace off and turns away from everyone. Shears may take the prize from Levi for quietest on the team. Levi has never been much for crowds, and he definitely hates when it's his turn to speak to the media. He just wants to play hockey, and not deal with any of the other bullshit.

Once everyone is showered and packed up, we make our way to the team bus. We're staying overnight at a hotel a few minutes from the arena before heading to Cleveland tomorrow for another game. I'm one of the first on the bus, and I pull up social media as I settle in to my seat.

I jump up as soon as I read the Denver news stories, including one about how chief meteorologist Becca Stephens is taking time off to be with her family due to the death of her father. "What the fuck?"

Opening up my texts, I immediately ask if she's okay.

ME

Are you okay? I just saw the news about your dad.

I'm definitely surprised when she immediately responds.

BECCA

No, I'm not okay. It's awful. My family is so horrid.

ME

What? How do you mean they're horrid?

BECCA

It doesn't matter. I'm only here because I'm expected to be, but they've made their opinions of me very clear. I hate it here. I wish I'd never come back.

ME

Where are you from again?

BECCA

Indiana. A small town outside Indianapolis.

ME

No shit? I just got done playing a game in Indianapolis.

ME

Send me your location.

BECCA

That's not necessary, Jacob. I'll be fine. I've survived them for over thirty years. A few more days won't kill me.

ME

Send me your location.

BECCA

Jacob.

ME

Becca.

BECCA

I don't have much extra time. I'm at my parent's now. There's a stupid dinner thing, and I still have to change.

ME

A dinner thing? When is the funeral?

BECCA

Tomorrow morning.

ME

Isn't the night before a funeral meant for something like a wake, or a viewing?

BECCA

Not in my family. It's all about presentation and appearances. My mother is hosting all of my father's bigwig investors and country club buddies. She actually doesn't care that he's dead. She can use it to build up her social standing.

ME

I'm sorry, Spitfire. That sounds hideous.

BECCA

She told me I have to stay silent. Even if someone addresses me, I'm only to nod, or shake my head.

ME

What the fuck? You're not a fucking child.

BECCA

To her I am. And my brother too. I'm an abomination. The black sheep. A waste of space. My dad died over a week ago, and they just called me two days ago. They weren't going to tell me, but people asked where I was. I'm only here because of that.

ME

Alright, Spitfire. You can send me your location right fucking now, or I'll find it myself. It'll just waste less time if you give it to me. I'll be damned if you're going to some stupid funeral party alone, like you're walking the plank. Nope. Not on my watch.

BECCA

A funeral party. I literally snorted, and my mother just told me I sound like the help. Women of good standing NEVER snort. We must not show emotion. We are robots. My mom looks like a robot with all the damn Botox she's got in her face. She won't show emotion because she CAN'T.

BECCA

I may have gotten into my father's bourbon.

ME

I have a feeling I'm going to like drunk Becca.

BECCA

I kinda like drunk Becca too.

ME

Send me your location, baby.

BECCA

Only if you promise that you'll be my pretend boyfriend for the night. Having a hot hockey player as a boyfriend will be good.

ME

You think I'm hot?

BECCA

You know you're hot, Jacob.

BECCA

Also yes.

ME

I'd be honored to be your pretend boyfriend. Does that mean I can kiss you?

BECCA

For pretend?

ME

Sure. We'll go with that.

ME

Looking forward to seeing you, Spitfire.

BECCA

Don't tell Jacob, but I'm looking forward to seeing you too.

ME

Don't tell Jacob?

BECCA

Yeah. My fake boyfriend keeps all my secrets.

ME

Alright. I won't tell him.

Becca

CHAPTER 9

I should have said no. Should have told Jacob I didn't need him. I'll be fine. I'm *always* fine. I knew from a very early age that I was despised by my family. I've never had a true explanation as to why, but they've treated me like shit for as long as I can remember. My therapist has some thoughts. I have the quietest personality of the four of us, but also the one who exudes the most peace. She thinks my mother hates me because I'm young and beautiful. I hold myself regally, whereas my older brother is only one inch taller than me, and has about one hundred pounds of extra weight on his frame. I don't ever remember my father treating me with anything resembling kindness, but my lack of interest in the family business sealed the deal there.

It's dumb, really. My brother has been groomed to take over from my dad since he was a teenager. What did it matter what I wanted to do with my life? Was I expected to take some kind of secretarial job, or another job with no responsibility? I know they wanted me under their thumb, where they'd pick out my husband, and then I'd be popping children out left and right. No thank you. I'm not sure if I even want kids. They're fun, but I like my independence.

So when my mother looks at me and loudly sighs, I roll my eyes. "What, Mother? How have I offended you this time?"

Margaret Atwood Stephens sits up straighter as my brother stalks into the room. Taking a good look at him, I notice how far his hairline has receded. Rodney Stephens, Junior glares at me as his nostrils flare, and I realize his nose is quite a bit bigger than when I last saw him.

"You watch your mouth, you little bitch," he snarls.

My eyes widen. "Excuse me?"

"You heard me. You are in our house. You will not speak to Mother that way."

"You still live here?" I screech. "You're thirty-six years old!"

I don't see the hand coming, and I don't register the pain until a few seconds after my head flings to the side. Rodney viciously grabs my chin, forcing me to look up at him. A metallic taste hits my tongue as I realize my lip is bleeding.

"I live here because I run this town. I will bury you, Rebecca. Just try me. You are only here to save face with our investors. After the funeral, we'll discuss how you'll be helping the future of this family." His eyes are full of hatred as he stares at me. I can see my mom out of the corner of my eye looking away, as if she can act like this isn't happening. Rodney squeezes my chin harshly, and I cry out in pain. "Such a waste of space. Do you understand? You're worthless. You mean nothing. They should have gotten rid of you when they had the chance, you spineless piece of shit."

Rodney slaps me again, harder this time, and I scream. "Stop it!"

He grabs my hair and yanks me out of the chair. "Get the fuck out of here. Make yourself presentable, Rebecca. You're such an embarrassment. People will arrive in an hour."

Grabbing my bag, I blindly lunge toward the front door. Tears block my vision, and I throw open the door with gusto. I'm unprepared to hit a wall when I step outside, but the familiar feeling is reminiscent of a handful of weeks ago when I ran into Jacob.

"Woah! What's the rush, darlin'?" Jacob drawls as he holds onto my shoulders. "You okay?"

"Do you have a car?" I whisper.

"I do."

"Can we leave? Just go anywhere. Please," I plead, my head bowed. I have a feeling if Jacob sees my face, he'll rush into the house and beat the hell out of my brother. As much as I'd love to see that, I know my brother well enough to know he'll press charges immediately. I can't be the reason why Jacob's career ends.

"Sure, Spitfire. You wanna help me get settled into my room? Apparently only the honeymoon suite at the Paradise Point Hotel was available, but the lady I spoke to promised to give me all the rose petals and a bottle of champagne, so I think I'm getting the better end of the deal." Jacob gently takes my elbow, leading me to a small sedan parked in the driveway.

"How did you get in here?" I wonder aloud. "The guards at this gated community barely let me in here, and I grew up in this house."

"Played the celebrity card and gave a couple autographs. I hate doing it, but it works," Jacob admits. He opens the passenger door for me, waiting until I'm safely inside before shutting the door and trotting around the car. "You alright if we head to the hotel?"

"Wait. Why are you staying here? Don't you have to go to Cleveland?" I ask suddenly, but Jacob shrugs.

"I explained the situation to my coach. I got a flight tomorrow at two that gets me into Cleveland by five. The game doesn't start until seven thirty. It isn't ideal, but I'm relieved he was so accommodating. I may have told him you're my girlfriend, but since you already asked me to be your fake boyfriend, I guess it wasn't a complete lie," he confesses sheepishly.

I let out an awkward giggle. "You don't have to stay. Your actual job is important."

"I know. But I also know you're hurting, and I'm not about to leave you alone around these vultures when you don't have anyone to back you up."

I feel a warmth in my belly. It's an odd sensation, but I'm not accustomed to having people ready to support me. "Thank you."

"Of course," he says quietly, reaching over and grabbing my hand. We're quiet for the few minutes it takes to cross town, with only the navigation directions breaking up the silence. As we pull up to the hotel, I realize I'm about to go into a hotel with a man who is pretty famous, and I possibly look like I've been beaten up. Dragging my hair over my shoulders, I push it to cover my cheeks. He doesn't even know I'm staying at the same hotel.

Jacob grabs a bag from the trunk, then waits for me to walk beside him. He again grabs my hand, and the feel of his hand against mine grounds me. He's the strength I need right now.

As he registers with the front desk associate, I keep my head turned and look at a wall of advertisements. Some are still the same from when I lived here over fifteen years ago. New ones include people I went to high school with selling various multi-level marketing schemes, or moms opening up at-home daycare slots. Why on earth would someone advertise a daycare at a hotel?

"You ready, baby?" Jacob calls out, and the butterflies erupt in my stomach. I don't know which one I like better: Spitfire or baby. Either of them said with Jacob's slow, southern drawl are like honey being poured over my skin. And boy, I sure would love it if he licked that honey right off.

Jacob takes my hand again as he leads me to the elevator. Heading up to the third floor, we walk silently to the end of the hallway. "It sure is quiet for a hotel that claims they only had the honeymoon suite available."

"I overheard my mother say that most of the hotels were completely booked because of the funeral tomorrow."

"Oh. I guess that makes sense. Your dad was a popular guy then."

I shrug. "No. He just schmoozed with a ton of people."

"How did he die?" Jacob asks quietly as we reach the door to the suite.

"I don't know," I tell him. "Anytime I've asked, I've been shut down. My guess is a heart attack. He never took good care of himself when I lived here, so I can only assume that continued."

Opening the door, Jacob gestures for me to walk into the suite, but I stop a few feet in, completely taken aback at the sight before me.

"Holy shit," Jacob breathes. "No wonder this was still available."

A circular bed with a heart shaped headboard sits in the middle of the room. Red rose petals cover a white bedspread, cascading over the edge of the bed and onto the floor. The petals lead to the corner of the room, where a large jacuzzi tub resides.

"Red rose petals were a bold choice," Jacob comments. "You'd think they'd go white or pink to match the walls."

"Uh-huh," I murmur, unable to formulate any other coherent thoughts. It's like a Pepto Bismol party in here. Every shade of pink imaginable. Pale pink carpet, which clashes horribly with the red rose petals. Textured wallpaper with what appear to be dark pink clouds with lightning bolts of white zinging through. I love the weather aspect of the wallpaper, but the colors are so bright it's giving me a headache. I'm about to comment that I want to put sunglasses on, when I hear Jacob loudly swear.

"What the fuck!" I automatically turn toward him, thinking he's found some other horrifying shade of bubblegum bullshit, but find his eyes wide as he stares at me. "What the fuck happened to your face?"

Shit. I completely forgot about Rodney. I try to duck my head, but Jacob is faster, carefully taking both of my cheeks in his hands.

"Who. Did. This. To. You?" he growls, but his touch is unexpectedly gentle. "Are you okay?"

I'm surprised at the tenderness in his voice. How his thumb gently swipes over my skin. "Tell me the truth, Spitfire. You don't have to put on a brave face around me. Just be you, and let me take care of you. Please."

A whirlwind of emotion overtakes me, and the dam breaks as I crumble. Jacob's arms encircle me, picking me up as I cry in earnest. He turns us, sitting on the bed before scooting toward the headboard. He leans back against the pillows, and I allow myself to rest my head on his chest. As I continue to cry, he patiently strokes up and down my spine. He doesn't rush me or push for me to stop crying. He just waits. And as the feel of his steady heartbeat against my cheek calms me, I finally speak.

"My brother hit me," I admit, my voice quivering. "Twice."

I feel Jacob tense under my head, but he doesn't respond, so I continue. "He's never hit me before. He's talked down to me. My therapist says he's the epitome of a narcissist who uses emotional abuse to belittle and break down women. With our father gone, he's now the head of the family company, and maybe that's made him feel a little too powerful. I really don't care that he hit me, you know? I don't want anything to do with him. I get to go back to Denver and continue living my life, and hopefully I'll never see him again. But my mom … she was right there. And she didn't say a word. Not even when he hit me the second time."

"I'm so sorry, baby. So fucking sorry," Jacob whispers as he places a gentle kiss on my forehead.

"I shouldn't have come," I whisper sorrowfully.

"Why did you? If you don't mind me asking."

I sigh. "Closure, I guess. I wasn't close with my dad by any means, but he wasn't as mean as my mom or brother. Slightly more apathetic, but he wasn't vicious as them. His insults didn't seem to hurt as much. I guess I wanted to say goodbye. But my brother … I wish I knew why he hated me. Why they all hate me."

"If you knew, do you think it would help?" Jacob asks.

I think about the question for a few moments. "Maybe it would give me some peace. I've wracked my brain for years trying to come up with their reasoning. I'd like to think I was a well-behaved kid. I didn't bring any big scandals to the family. I got good grades. I didn't party, stay out all night, or do anything that would explain their coldness and callousness."

"It wasn't you," Jacob says sternly, his hand pushing my chin up until our eyes meet. "I barely know you, Spitfire, and I can guarantee it has nothing to do with you. You're fucking perfect, and it's their loss. You hear me, darlin'? It is their loss. Say the words."

"It's their loss," I whisper, captivated by how his bright blue eyes glitter with a steadfast resolve I don't think I've ever seen before. He believes in me. It's been so long since I've had a man support me this way, and this man isn't even *my* man.

"Louder. I need to know you believe it yourself."

"I — it's their loss," I state, my voice clearly showing I'm not there yet, and Jacob chuckles.

"Nice try. Do it again."

I huff a breath, aggravated. I clear my throat and belt out, "It's their loss!"

A beautiful grin breaks across Jacob's face. "You're damn right it is. You're brilliant, talented, and beautiful. You're the light, not them."

"I'm the light?" I ask softly, and he gives me a one-shoulder shrug.

"Yeah. I guarantee they don't light up a room like you do, Spit-fire. You're a beacon, they're the storm. Of course they want you to snuff out your light."

No one has ever talked about me this way. Ever. Even Kevin, my boyfriend of one year while I lived in Cincinnati, and we'd actually talked about marriage. All my life, I've gotten so used to the constant repeating record of disappointment from the men in my life that hearing a man speak so positively about me is throwing me for a loop. Does he really mean all of this? Is Jacob Mitchell actually a good guy, and not the playboy hockey player that I assumed he'd be?

Looking deep into his eyes, I can't find one iota of falseness. Nothing hidden. He's looking at me so intently, so resolutely, that I'm taken aback.

Which is probably why I lose my head for a moment.

I push up and kiss him.

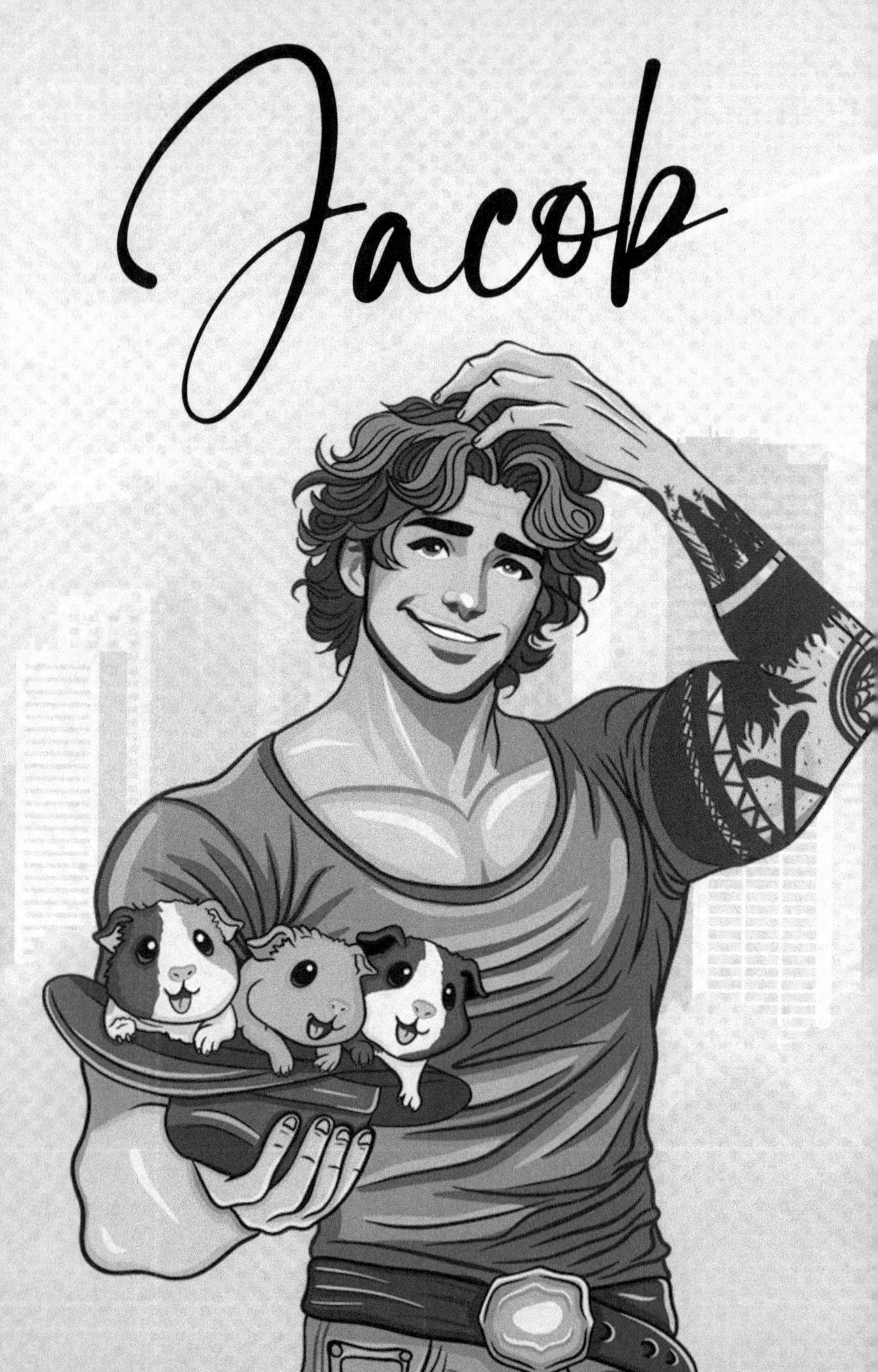
Jacob

CHAPTER 10

Holy fuck, Becca is kissing me.

Becca is kissing me.

It takes me a second to wrap my head around it, and I realize I'm not kissing her back. I fix that immediately, sliding my fingers gently into her hair and holding her head against mine, but being careful not to hurt her bruised face. Her lips are as soft as I'd imagined them to be, and when I feel her sigh softly against me, I groan. All of the blood in my body is quickly running to my dick, and I'm two seconds away from rolling on top of her and taking control of the situation. But I can't do that. I made the decision weeks ago that if anything were to happen with Becca, she'd be in control.

So, even though I'm fairly certain I can hear my cock cussing me out as he attempts to break through my boxer briefs and pants, I continue to let Becca run the show, moving my lips softly against hers.

But when her tongue tentatively slides out to skirt against mine, I clench her hair tightly in my fist and break off the kiss. I rest my head against the side of hers, taking a deep breath and attempting to calm my rapid heartbeat.

"Did I ..." she stammers breathlessly. "Did I do something wrong?"

"What?" I ask incredulously, whipping my head up to stare at her. "No. Fuck no. You did nothing wrong."

"Then why did you stop?" she asks quietly. I can see the uncertainty in her eyes. The emotion. The fear. I let out a long exhale as I rest my forehead against hers. There's a calming scent of lavender in the air, and I know it has to be a product she uses. Obviously this shitty ass hotel would have picked a pink flower to dump in this room, so I know the lovely lavender scent is coming from Becca.

"I don't want to push you too far," I confess.

Becca's eyes widen. "What? Why? How?"

A grin tugs at my lips. She's pretty fucking cute when she stammers like this. "I know it's been a really emotional day, and your head is all over the place. I don't want you to do something you'll regret later."

"You think I'll do ... you," she says with a tiny giggle, "and I might regret it?"

"Well, yeah," I answer. "Listen. I've been trying to get you to give me a chance for weeks, darlin'. I don't want this to happen because you're wanting to feel anything but sadness. I want you to want me for me."

Understanding dawns in her eyes. "Do you get that a lot? Women who want the celebrity of it all?"

"More often than I ever thought possible. At first, it was cool. Not gonna lie, I enjoyed it. But it gets old. I've been in the league for over a decade. I have no interest being a notch on a puck bunny's bedpost. And I've been lied to so many times. Fucking can't stand liars." People came out of the woodwork when I made the NHL. I became famous. But they weren't interested in me. Just the status it came with. And definitely my paycheck.

I feel Becca stiffen slightly against me, and I wonder what triggered her. Before I can ask, she sits up. "Are you StickUM92? I feel like you are, and I should have said something about it when you told me your name and that you play hockey, but I didn't know how to handle it. I couldn't process how the hot hockey guy and the online friend I had were the same person, you know? And then we had that really nice dinner, and you sent me flowers, and I got all up in my head. So, are you?"

"I am, in fact, StickUM92. Hello, NerdGirl1025."

Becca lets out a whoosh of breath as her shoulders slump. "You knew it was me? For how long?"

"I realized it the day I told you my name. Well, actually it was after our pizza date. You had told me your favorite flower was a hyacinth, and when I went to order you a bouquet, I thought of your ChatBook profile picture. The convo where I told you my name was me trying to sleuth out if it was really you or not."

"And then I just left you on 'read' for weeks," she breathes, her eyes filling with tears. "I'm so sorry, Jacob."

"I didn't think you'd ghost me for as long as you did, but now I can understand how surprising that must have been for you," I explain. "Looking back, I can hear your voice. I should have realized it earlier."

"I thought you lived in Texas," she blurts out, her neck reddening. "It never occurred to me I had befriended someone local."

"For a self-described nerd, we should probably work on your understanding of algorithms, Spitfire. They tend to lump people together by region," I tease.

Becca rolls her eyes as she lets out a light laugh. "I'm nerdy in *science*, not social media technology."

"Were you freaked out when you realized it was me?" I ask quietly.

Becca hesitates, looking down at her hands as she waits to answer. "I wasn't sure how to combine the two of you in my head. It was easier to shut the door, ignoring that it was something I had to deal with. Not that you gave me much time to think, though. The weekly flowers must have cost a fortune. I wanted to tell you to stop sending them, but secretly it was the highlight of my week."

"I'm glad," I whisper, reaching up to tuck an errant lock of hair behind her ear. "I'm the same man, darlin'. Just a Texan who loves hockey, cowboy hats, and pizza. And I'd really like to take you out on a proper date."

The corner of her mouth turns up in a soft smile. "I think I'd like that."

"So when we're back in Denver, you promise not to ghost me again?"

Becca laughs. "I promise."

I'm about to lean in to kiss her when Becca's phone blares with an awful ringtone. "What the fuck is that for?"

"The sound I have for my brother. Undoubtedly he's reminding me about the rules for the evening. I have to go get changed for their stupid dinner."

"Why? You look fine," I comment. She's wearing fitted black pants, a slate blue silk blouse, and black heels. I walked next to her, but I didn't realize she had heels on. I want to see where her height puts her now.

"It's expected to wear cocktail attire to this kind of dinner," Becca says snottily, flipping her hair over her shoulder to regard me with a dramatic roll of the eyes.

"But I'm okay like this?" I ask, standing to retrieve my suit jacket.

"They won't say anything to you. You could come in cutoff jean shorts and a bikini top, and they wouldn't care. You're a big deal. I'm a nobody," she says bitterly.

"Hey," I say, grabbing her hand and pulling her toward me. "You aren't a nobody. And I'm not a big deal. Yeah, I whip a puck around with a stick. So what? I'm not better than anyone just because I happen to play hockey well."

Becca gives me a hesitant smile as she nods. "Okay."

"Let's get you back to your parents' house," I say, placing my hand on the small of her back, ready to walk her down to my car. "Unless you want to skip the whole thing. We can head to the airport right now if you want, darlin'. I'm here for whatever you need."

"Oh, I'm not staying there. Not only because they'd never let me, but I don't want to. They'd probably go through my stuff and purposely antagonize me every minute of the day," she says with an exaggerated shudder. "I'm staying here, too. Right next door, actually."

"Seriously?" She nods. "Right next door? That's convenient."

"Convenient?" she asks with a breathy laugh. I'm seeing a little bit of sparkle come back to her eyes, and I let out a small exhale of relief. Becca is strong and resilient. Sure, she's got an expression sometimes that tells me she's dealt with some rough times. But a fully broken Becca is new to me, and I wanted to promise her I'd burn down the world for her to make her smile again.

I'm honestly wondering what I wouldn't do to make her smile.

"What time is dinner?" I ask, changing the topic. I feel like Becca is an injured bird, always a flight risk. If I tell her anything that I'm thinking — including how I'm probably going to have to get myself off tonight knowing she's asleep one wall away — I'll have her running for the hills again.

"Seven o'clock on the dot. We aren't allowed to be late. Punctuality is a strength," Becca says, standing tall with her chin high in the air. I feel my lips tug up with a smirk.

"Punctuality."

"Yes. The Stephens motto is four pillars: punctuality, oppression, discrimination, and psychological warfare," she says, deadpan.

I can't help the loud bark of laughter that bursts from my lips as Becca fights the urge to giggle. "Do we drink at dinner?"

"Oh, yes. There's no way any of us are making it through this monstrosity without more alcohol."

"I'll stay sober. I'll protect you, Spitfire."

She gives me a beautiful smile. "I know you will, Jacob. And thank you."

"For what?"

"For being here. For offering to go with me, or go to the airport. It's ... refreshing to have someone support me," she tells me shyly, her eyes trained on the floor by my feet.

"Hey," I say quietly, gently lifting her chin between my thumb and forefinger. Waiting until her eyes meet mine, I continue. "Whatever you need, Becca. I'm here for you."

Becca's hand trembles in mine as we walk up the brick walkway. She's changed into a modest pale pink dress, and has half her hair pulled back, allowing pearl earrings to appear. She applied a light layer of makeup — I assume to cover the bruises I am absolutely going to talk to her motherfucking brother about — and nervousness emanates from her body. She didn't speak on the short drive to her parents' home, instead choosing to wring her hands in her lap, and chew on her bottom lip.

"Pick an odd word," I blurt out. "A weather word."

"Cyclogenesis."

"What the hell is tha — you know what? Never mind. You can explain it later. Use cyclogenesis in conversation, or just say the word to me, Spitfire, and we'll leave immediately. I don't care who we piss off. You want outta there, at any point, and I'll get you out. Alright?" Reaching the door, I knock, then turn to Becca. "I got you, darlin'."

"Okay," she whispers. Someone answers the door stiffly, gesturing for us to walk into the home. Letting Becca lead the way, I follow her down a hallway and into a very large and stately dining room. Two obnoxiously large chandeliers hang over an ornate, dark wood table. I quickly count the chairs. Eighteen. Who the hell has a table for eighteen in their home? Insanity.

This entire room is horrid. The walls appear to be covered in fabric. Baroque style, featuring burnt orange, denim blue, and canary yellow. I have no doubt if I complemented Becca's mother on the walls, she'd undoubtedly boast about the cost of the materials. Even across the room, I can tell she's a woman who only responds to money.

"Would you like me to play your mother's game and flaunt my money? Or I can disregard her. Act like she's nothing better than the dog poop on my shoe. Or I can be a pompous asshole. Really, this can go a lot of ways, Spitfire. You tell me what you'd like me to do."

Becca's eyes whip to me, and panic is evident. "You don't want to be just you?"

My heart breaks wide open for this woman. So downtrodden, she thinks I don't want to be me with her. "No, baby. I'm definitely me. But I can flaunt my money. Talk about my NHL contract. Or I can treat your mother like trash, which honestly, is my first choice. I can also go to the good ole boys club over there," I tell her, pointing nonchalantly toward the group of men surrounding a small man who I assume is Becca's brother, "and begin talking about stocks, bonds, and any other ridiculous talking point I can come up with. They're all gonna know my name, and that I'm with you, by the end of the evening, though."

"My fake boyfriend, you mean," she whispers.

I gently take her chin between my thumb and forefinger. "How about you stop using the word fake? Let a man dream."

She gives me a soft smile as she nods, and I take the opportunity to kiss her temple. I have a feeling kissing Becca's lips would make her feel a twinge of embarrassment, and undoubtedly it would set off either her brother or mother. I don't want to bring any more drama and heartache to Becca tonight. My girl has had enough to last a lifetime.

My girl.

One way or another, I'm gonna make this girl mine.

After no more than thirty minutes of every person in the room ignoring me, barely speaking to Becca, and talking loudly about business acquisitions that really shouldn't be discussed at a wake — funeral dinner? What the hell is this supposed to be, anyway? — I'm ready to go the minute Becca says so.

These people are *horrid*.

I've been around my fair share of wealthy people. You don't own hockey teams unless you've got a tremendous amount of zeroes in your net worth. Our team regularly attends fundraisers and galas in the area, and Jamie always wants me to make an appearance at his events when I can. I've rubbed elbows with celebrities, politicians, and even foreign dignitaries. Yet none of them have ever gone out of their way to make me feel small.

Even worse is the fact that they're doing it to Becca, too. I can feel her getting smaller, pushing in against my side, as if I will somehow be able to hide her from the miserable looks we've gotten from every snake in this gaudy joint. Baroque tapestries, oversized dark furniture that looks as uncomfortable as it is, and paintings depicting unsmiling faces from centuries ago, tell me that even those people are unhappy here.

When some pretentious ass announces dinner is finally ready, I notice there are name plates at each seat. It's not lost on me that I've been placed as far away from Becca as possible. She's next to her brother, and across from her mother. Her brother is, of course, at the head of the table.

"They did that on purpose. They'll say it was due to not knowing about your attendance until earlier," she whispers, her voice trembling. I can hear how close she is to tears, and I'm two seconds away from pulling the garish tasseled tablecloth completely off the table to end this stupid dinner.

"I'm not having it, darlin'," I tell her, pulling her around the table. I grab my place holder, then swiftly walk to where hers is. I switch mine with hers so I'm next to her brother, then put hers next to me. Grabbing some random dude's name plate, I toss it across the table.

"I do believe my dear sister is sitting beside me," a nasally voice pipes up from behind us. "I don't think we've met. Rodney Stephens, Junior."

I turn, ready to meet someone eye-to-eye. Instead, I have to look down quite a bit at a man with a badly receding hairline, an incredibly large nose, and one hell of an overbite. It would appear Becca got all of the looks.

As Rodney attempts to squeeze between me and Becca to switch our name plates, I pull out Becca's chair for her. Once she's seated, I slam down in the chair next to Rodney. "We're good, Rod."

"You may call me Mister Stephens."

"Nah," I drawl, casually draping my arm on the back of Becca's chair. "Nice that you wanted to separate us, though. Good try."

Rodney's eyes narrow. "Presenting a unified family front at a meal to honor the life of our father has nothing to do with you. We didn't know about you until a couple hours ago."

"So?" I raise my eyebrows at him, sending a silent challenge.

Rodney glares as he slowly sits down. Becca's mother glides to her seat, her lips pursed so tightly I think she could cut glass if she wanted to. Honestly, I'm surprised she has the ability to move her face that much.

A line of servers walk in, each with one lidded plate. Once the plates are in front of us, the servers dramatically remove the domed lids to reveal … three pieces of romaine lettuce, and a dot of dressing? What the fuck is this?

Rodney carefully taps his fork against a glass of champagne, getting everyone's attention. Champagne. At a meal to 'honor' a dead man. I'll bet anything the champagne doesn't even go with anything at the meal. Rod's celebrating his father's death, and the look of superiority on his face only cements my hatred for him.

"Thank you all for coming. It is wonderful to have all of dad's esteemed friends here to celebrate his life," Rodney begins, his voice bordering on whining. How old is he? It's no wonder there doesn't appear to be a woman on his arm. No one could put up with that voice.

"Your father was a brilliant man," old fart number one calls out from my original seat.

"Here, here," old fart number two says loudly, pushing his almost empty glass of champagne into the air. Everyone follows suit, except for me and Becca. For the most part, I'm taking my cues from her. If she drinks, I will.

"Rebecca!" her mother hisses, her eyes bugging out of her head. When the woman next to Mrs. Stephens turns toward all of us, Becca's mother attempts a smile, and I jerk backward. This must be what a demon looks like as it tries to lure the unsuspecting into hell.

Becca giggles lightly next to me, and it breaks a little bit of the tension. I move my arm from around her shoulder, sliding my hand down her arm, and covering her hand with mine. She makes no move to eat the pieces of grass on her plate, nor do I.

So, Rebecca," the woman next to Mrs. Stephens says, "I hear you're moving back home."

"What?" Becca gasps. "No. No, I'm not moving back here."

The woman frowns. "I was told —"

"I don't know what you were told, Mrs. Betterson. I am not moving."

"How will you plan the wedding?" Mrs. Betterson asks.

"What wedding?" Becca asks.

Becca's mother jumps in. "Rebecca, may I speak with you outside?"

"No," I interject. "Anything you have to say can be said right here."

"You will not tell me how to deal with my daughter," Mrs. Stephens says stiffly. "You mean nothing. You are nothing. Probably just some trash Rebecca picked up to try and disappoint me."

Jesus. Is this the shit Becca had to deal with growing up? No wonder she got the hell out of here. "If you think you're going to make me feel bad about myself, ma'am, you've got another thing coming. I couldn't care less about your opinions of me."

"Oh, please," Rodney says with a stuffy laugh. "That's just because you don't know how much money we have."

I raise an eyebrow at him. "You also don't know how much money I have."

"Nothing, undoubtedly. That's why you sidled up to my unsuspecting sister," Rodney sneers. "You saw her on television and figured she's rich. Then a quick Google search of her family, and suddenly, you think you've hit the jackpot."

Mrs. Betterson glances warily between us. "This is hardly a topic for dinner. I don't understand why he's even here if she's marrying Benjamin Gaines' son."

"The fuck?" I blurt out.

"I'm not marrying him!" Becca shouts. She stands suddenly, knocking her chair over, dropping my hand in the process. She turns toward the end of the table, pointing toward old fart number two and a smarmy man grinning next to him. "I am not marrying you!"

"Rebecca, sit down!" Rodney booms. "You will marry who I tell you to."

"I will not!" she cries out. "Besides, I can't marry him. First of all, because I don't even know him, but also ..."

She trails off, looking down at me, and I know exactly what she's about to say before she says it.

"I'm already married. To Jacob."

Becca

CHAPTER 11

Am I married? No.

But it's the only thing I could think of saying, and I hope Jacob doesn't bolt.

"You're married? Without telling us?" Mother gasps, dramatically throwing her hand onto her chest in disbelief. "How could you?"

Oh, for a myriad of reasons, Mother.

"If you're married, why aren't you wearing an engagement ring or wedding band?" Rodney asks, his eyes narrowed as he stares at my hand. Before I can answer, Jacob stands up, sliding his right arm around my waist.

"We didn't think this was the right time to announce. We wanted this visit to be all about the life and legacy of your father," he says smoothly, and I breathe a sigh of relief. He's going along with my ruse. It really doesn't matter, because my brother is like a dog with a bone when he wants to humiliate me. He'll research marriage certificates, find out I'm not married, and then we'll be back at where we are now.

"Why was I being offered up to Benjamin Gates' son? For crying out loud. I don't even know his name!" I blurt out. I turn to Benjamin, then notice his son blatantly staring at my breasts. Gross.

He gives me a leery smile. "It's Richard. And we need an heir."

"And there aren't any other women you can force yourself on?"

"Your brother offered me a deal I couldn't refuse," Benjamin shrugs.

"What deal?" I say, my teeth clenched. I turn to my brother. "What deal?"

Rodney stands, attempting to look bigger. "Your presence is required at home. We've let you gallivant around the country for long enough. You can annul or divorce, and then you will marry Dick. We won't let this count against you."

"Count against her? You act like she's a child that needs to be grounded," Jacob says, his arm tightening around me. "There will be no annulment or divorce. Becca is mine."

Rodney laughs maliciously. "I will bury you in any way I choose. You have no idea who you're dealing with."

"Cyclogenesis," I mutter, humiliation burning up my spine, and I feel Jacob squeeze my waist reassuringly.

He leans forward slightly, forcing Rodney to peer up at him. "And you have no idea who you're dealing with. Might want to Google my name, asshole. I'm not the nobody you assume. Enjoy your dinner, folks. We'll see ourselves out."

Jacob grabs my hand and strides confidently to the door. I hear my mother shouting for me to stop, someone laughing hysterically, and another person stomping. I assume that last one is my brother, who, for a man in his late thirties, can throw an epic temper tantrum.

Quickly grabbing our coats from an attendant, we're silent as we walk to Jacob's rental car. I'm growing more and more anxious with each passing minute. The drive to the hotel is tense. So tense that I begin to hyperventilate. I don't know how to get out of this. Jacob probably hates me. He'll leave tonight, and I'll have to go to the funeral by myself. My brother will probably lock me in the basement and force a marriage to Richard Gaines by tomorrow evening. I'll never get back to Colorado, and who will take Thunder? My mother hates dogs. Richard Gaines probably hates dogs. I bet he has a hairless cat that he treats like a child. Richard has to be pushing fifty, but looks even older. Sagging skin on both him and his hairless cat undoubtedly, and I bet he'll want an heir the old fashioned way.

God, I'm such a fuck-up. I thought I could get through this week unscathed, and now I've brought someone else down into it. There's no way out of this. What am I supposed to do? How can I make sure Jacob doesn't hate me? Why did he even go along with all of this? I'm a mess in real life and online, but at least he now knows so he can sever all ties with me. I've managed to destroy a relationship with the real-life Jacob, and the online Jacob, in one fell swoop.

"Baby, I need you to breathe."

I hated my childhood. Hated it. Rodney was vicious. My mother horribly cruel. My father a constant force with his disapproving glare. Nothing I ever did was right. It took years of therapy for me to gain even one ounce of self-confidence after so much time dealing with psychological abuse. I don't know if I can recover from this one.

Every single person at that dinner looked down on Jacob as soon as I introduced him. When I gave his name to the butler, I wasn't surprised when it was misspelled on the name card on the table. Jake Marshall. But Jacob didn't even blink as he tossed the name card next to mine down the table.

He's such a good man, and I'm an absolute disaster.

"Spitfire. Come back to me, darlin'."

I feel something rub across my cheek, and my eyes suddenly focus. The passenger door is open, and Jacob is crouched next to me, holding my face in his hands. His eyes are full of compassion and empathy. He swipes a thumb across my skin again, and I realize he's wiping tears away. My breathing is choppy, and I take a deep inhale as I attempt to regulate my emotions.

"That's good. Slow and steady. I've got you," Jacob says quietly.

I look around, recognizing the back of the hotel parking lot. God, I didn't even realize we had arrived back here.

"I'm sorry," I say automatically, so tuned to apologize for any infraction.

"Nothing to apologize for. You have every right to be upset. What your family did back there …" he trails off. "I'm furious for you. Hell, it took every bit of my self-control not to throw your brother onto the table. And Grandpa better think twice before he comes after you for a wedding with Dick the Prick."

A snort bursts from my lips, and Jacob gives me a grin. "There's my girl. I've got you. I promise I won't let anything happen to you."

"I don't know what I'm supposed to do. I can't go to the funeral now. I can't face them," I whisper.

"Oh, we're definitely not going. In fact, we're getting the fuck out of this town right now. No time to waste, darlin'. Let's get inside and pack up." Jacob stands, extending a hand to me, and pulls me out of the car.

"What do you mean? Oh. You have to go to Cleveland."

"Tomorrow, yes. I'm hoping you'll go with me, but first, we have to go somewhere else."

"Where?" I ask.

"I'll explain once we get to the airport."

One hour later, we're changed, packed, and at the Indianapolis Airport. After turning in his rental car keys, Jacob turns to me. "I need you to breathe. Promise you won't freak out?"

My heart rate immediately increases. He's going to send me back to Denver. He'll probably block my number. I wouldn't blame him, but it'll still sting.

"Becca," he says with a laugh. "Don't spiral."

"It's hard. I don't like spontaneity," I admit.

He gives me a soft smile, pushing a lock of hair behind my ear. "I can tell. But I'm hoping you'll relax and let me take care of things. Do you trust me?"

I study him for a moment. He waits patiently, a small smile under his day-old scruff, and his blue eyes sparkling as they stay centered on me. And I realize that I do trust him. He's shown me nothing but steadfastness since we met. "I trust you, Jacob."

The small smile breaks into a wide grin. "Alright. That's good. That's real good, darlin'. Because the best thing I can think of to do, to ensure your safety and security, is for us to get married. Right now."

My mouth drops open as I stare at him incredulously. "I didn't mean that! It was the first thing that popped in my head. You don't have to do this, Jacob. Seriously. Your heart is in the right place, but I'll figure out something with my family."

He shakes his head. "I don't trust them. I can take care of you, Spitfire. I'll be a good fake husband, I promise. Hell, maybe even one day you'll consider me your real husband. But for now, I've got us booked on the last flight outta here. We've got a flight to Vegas with a layover in Dallas."

"Ho — how did you do this?" I stammer.

He shrugs. "I pack light. You took longer to pack, so I booked everything. We'll have a couple hours in Vegas before we have to fly back east. I can rebook you to Denver if you'd like, but I'd kinda like to have you in Cleveland with me, if that's okay."

He looks somewhat bashful as he waits for my response. "Why?"

Jacob looks down at our conjoined hands. "I want to introduce you to my teammates. Technically it'll be our honeymoon, and I figure together in Cleveland is still better than apart. And honestly, I'll feel better if you're with me. I don't know if your brother will lash out, and I can't protect you from a thousand miles away."

I can't help the sweet sigh that escapes my lips. I didn't expect such a thoughtful response. "A honeymoon in Cleveland? I sure am a lucky girl."

He lifts our hands to kiss the back of mine. "I'll take you anywhere you want to go during the All-Star break."

"Shit."

I look over to find Jacob clearly aggravated. "What?"

"The Clark County courthouse closed at midnight, and they don't open again until eight." After a slight delay on the tarmac in Indianapolis, we barely made our connecting flight in Dallas. Now we're heading to Vegas. "I'll have to change our return flights."

"Oh. And with the time difference flying back east, you may not make your game," I surmise.

"Maybe. Let me do some research." He types furiously on his iPad, and I take a moment to watch him. Smushed in this economy seat, he looks miserable, but I know if I asked him, he'd say he's fine. He commented earlier that he normally chooses first class just for leg room, but both flights tonight are completely full. I let out a yawn, and he looks at me out of the corner of his eye. "You can use my shoulder, darlin'. You've had a long day."

"No longer than you," I murmur, my eyes drifting closed.

"I'm used to it, and I didn't have the emotional trauma of my family this week. Rest your eyes, baby." I let my temple fall against him, and feel him rummaging around his lap before he covers me with his suit jacket. I feel his lips ghost over my forehead before the sounds of the jet engines lull me to sleep.

"Well, what do you want to do for six hours?" I ask Jacob as we leave the airport in an Uber. At just after two in the morning, I'm surprised at how bustling Las Vegas is.

"I was hoping to get a few hours of sleep," he confesses. "If I do make the game tomorrow, I need a little bit of shut-eye, or I'll be a menace on the ice."

"Oh, of course," I tell him. My power nap on the flight from Dallas has left me wide awake, but I'm fine reading a book in a hotel room.

"I got us a room at a hotel off the strip, but close to the court-house. I figure we need every extra minute we can get."

"You were busy," I comment.

"You were dead to the world," he says with a smile. "Besides, it kept me from focusing on the cute little snores you kept letting out."

"I do not snore!" I gasp.

"Yeah, you do. It was adorable," he laughs.

I cross my arms over my chest, popping my lower lip out in mild indignation. "Well, you won't think it's cute in twenty years when I'm sawing logs like a lumberjack and stealing all the blankets."

Jacob turns toward me, giving me a sweet smile. "From your mouth to God's ears, darlin'. Because that sounds fucking amazing."

"I — I didn't mean ..." I stammer, but he reaches up to place a finger over my lips.

"Let a man dream, Becca." His hand drifts across my cheek and into my hair. "I can make you happy."

"I thought you were just my fake boyfriend," I whisper.

His brow furrows as he stares at me. "Let me make you happy, baby."

"Okay," I finally say. I don't know what else to say. I can't believe this man is willing to marry me to ensure I'm not forced into a relationship with the son of some old geezer who is a friend of my family. I wouldn't have let that happen anyway. My brother might think he has pull when it comes to me, but he doesn't. I won't ever go anywhere near him again.

But the way Jacob looks at me makes me wish for this to be real. To have a happily ever after. Maybe I can believe in this. Just for a little while.

Upon entering our hotel room, I stop when I notice the single king-size bed.

"It's all they had available. I promise I'll behave," Jacob says, winking at me. "I really need some sleep. Let me use the bathroom to brush my teeth, and then you can do whatever you need. I'll be asleep before you come out."

"You fall asleep that easily?" I ask.

"Yeah. It's a gift."

"I'm jealous," I say as he rummages in his bag, pulling out a toothbrush and toothpaste. "It takes me hours sometimes."

"Oh yeah? At home I have a sound machine that gives out the most perfect amount of rain noises. Maybe that will help you."

"You'll have to give me the name. I'll try anything."

Jacob stops abruptly on his way to the bathroom, before turning to look at me. "Why would I give you the name?"

"So I can buy one?" I say sarcastically. I mean, duh.

"Darlin', I don't think we discussed what happens after today," Jacob says slowly. "I naturally assumed you'd have thought about it."

I shake my head. "I figured it was dumb to think too far ahead. I've only wrapped my head around today and tomorrow."

"Okay," he drawls, walking leisurely toward me. "You know how I said I wanted you with me in Cleveland, because I wasn't sure what your brother might do?"

I nod.

"I'm gonna feel that way in Denver, too."

"Okay?" I ask, confused.

Jacob's lips tug with a smile. "I want you to move in with me."

My eyes open comically wide. "What? Why? You don't have to do this. It's too much. You didn't sign up for this. God, no. People will know you married me to help me out. What am I supposed to do with my apartment? Or my dog? My things?"

Jacob's lips overtake mine in a searing kiss, his lips pulling against mine with perfect suction. One hand snakes around my waist and onto my ass, cupping it and pulling me into his body. I gasp, giving Jacob the perfect opportunity to slide his tongue against mine. The gasp quickly turns to a moan as I drag my hands up his chest and into his hair. I feel a groan emanate from his body when I scratch my nails against his scalp, and his arms tighten around me. He breaks off the kiss to rest his forehead against mine.

"I love dogs," he says, his breaths quick.

"What?"

"You said you have a dog. I love dogs. Boy or girl?"

"Boy."

"What's his name?"

"His name is Thunder."

A puff of air hits my lips as he chuckles. "Perfect name for a meteorologist's dog. He can come too, darlin'. He's okay now, right? He's not just stuck in your place alone?"

"No, he's not alone. I've got someone watching him." I take a deep breath, uttering one single confession. "This is a lot, and I don't know how to process everything."

Jacob lifts his head to look in my eyes. "One day at a time, Becca. We'll get it all figured out. Let's worry about getting married today."

After Jacob is done in the bathroom, I spend a lot of time trying to calm my nerves. How am I supposed to wrap my head around all of this? I started the day just trying to get through dinner with my family and the funeral tomorrow. Now I'm not even going to the damn funeral, my brother is trying to marry me off, and a man I hardly know is willing to marry me as a what, a favor? Insanity.

When I creep out of the bathroom, tiptoeing over to the bed, I hear Jacob's deep breathing. I don't know how long I stand there, watching him sleep. It's so steady, and I feel myself relaxing as I climb into bed. Before I even get myself comfortable, Jacob rolls over, throws an arm around me, and drags me into the middle of the bed. I'm about to say something when I feel him bury his head in my hair.

I fall asleep before I say a word.

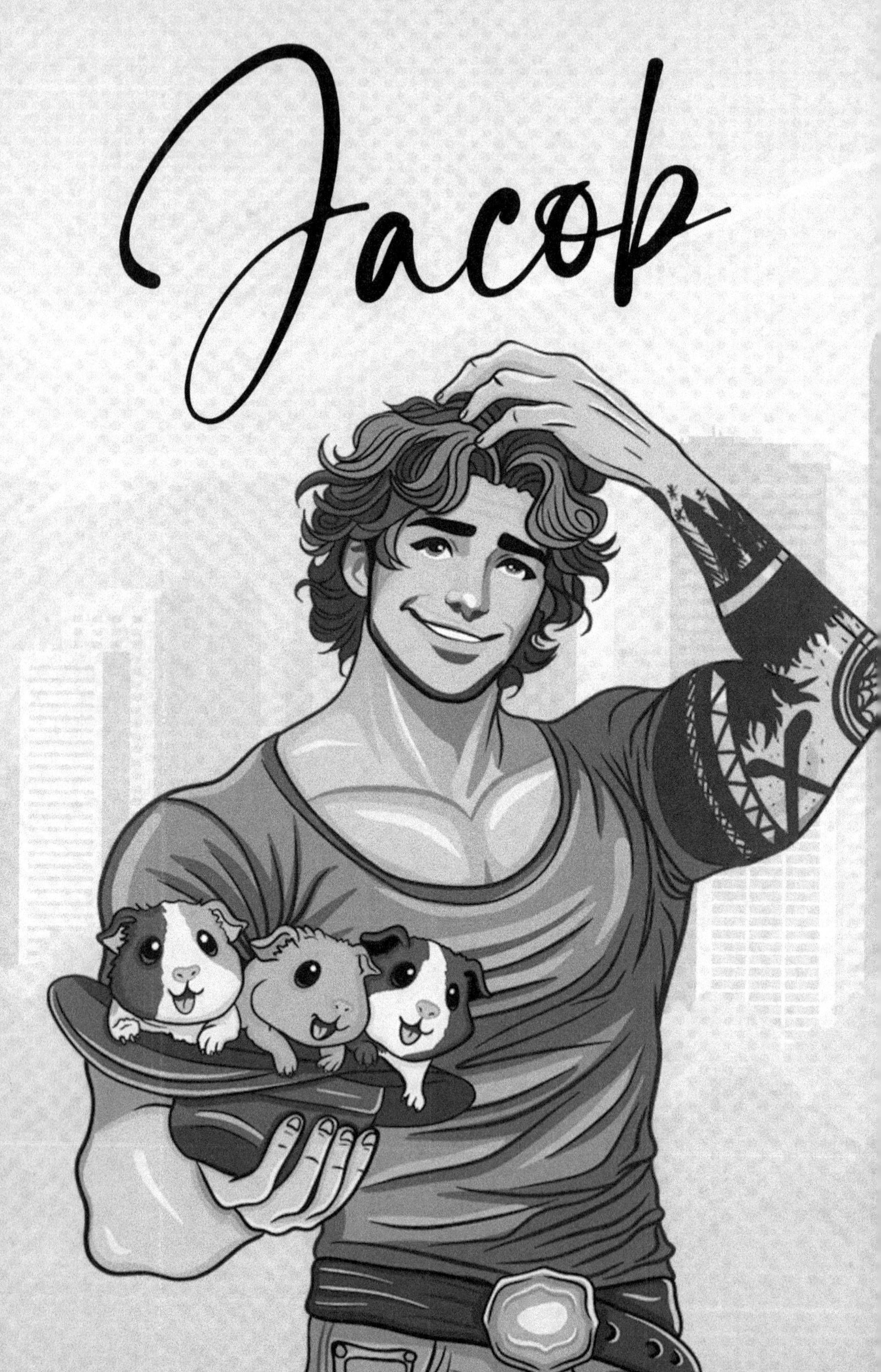

Jacob

CHAPTER 12

I wasn't asleep.

I tried to fall asleep, but I couldn't. I knew Becca was stalling in the bathroom, and I honestly thought she might try to sleep in the bathtub. So when she finally emerged, I kept myself completely still as I waited to see what she would do.

She watched me sleep.

It was so hard to keep my breathing even. As soon as she was under the covers, my body moved on its own accord, rolling toward her and yanking her into the middle of the bed. Becca fit perfectly into my arms, an exquisite little spoon to my big one.

And after her telling me sometimes it took her hours to fall asleep, Becca fell asleep before I did.

It was still a surprise to find her cuddled against me in the morning, with me on my back and her head on my shoulder. I manage to sneak a peek at my watch, seeing it's just after seven, and I know I need to get up. But feeling Becca against me is like the first hit of a drug, and I can't seem to force my body to move. And then I realize she's cupping my morning wood.

It takes me a minute or two to realize the sensation I'm feeling, and I bite my tongue to keep from groaning out loud. Her hand isn't moving, but the pressure — and knowing it's *her fucking hand* — is enough to get the endorphins going.

Okay. I have a bunch of options here.

I can gently lift her hand by her wrist, relocating it to anywhere less erogenous.

Or, I carefully slide out from under her and bolt to the bathroom.

I could lay here and visualize every coach I've ever had completely naked, hoping my hard on deflates.

There's always thrashing around like I'm having a bad dream, thus dislodging Becca's hand, then roll over to hide my erection.

What I should do is daydream about her touching me for real, then come in my boxer briefs.

Wait. That was very clearly a thought from my engorged and miserable cock, who hasn't had any real action in quite some time. Since well before I even met Becca, but there wasn't a chance since we met. My mind — and my dick — have been focused on her since that day.

Alright. The best option here is probably to escape to the bathroom. Inching my left foot closer to the edge of the bed, I slowly begin moving my right leg. Becca threatened to steal all the blankets, and she did do that, because all I have between her and my skin is one thin sheet and my boxers. Which is probably why the movement of my legs wakes her up. I figure she'll freeze, feel mortification, remove her hand and run to the bathroom.

Instead, she lifts her head, looks at her hand, and fucking squeezes my length. Who is this vixen?

"Oh," she whispers, as her pinkie finger hits the barbell frenum piercing on the underside of my cock. She curiously traces the metal for a moment before giggling to herself and climbing out of bed. Once the bathroom door closes, I let out the deep exhale I didn't know I was holding.

Holy shit.

This morning has not evolved how I thought it would.

An hour later, after getting our marriage license at the county courthouse, we arrive at Vegas Weddings, only because it's a block away from the courthouse. As we look at all the options, I'm suddenly apprehensive. I don't really know Becca that well. Will she be okay with this ceremony? Should I offer up anything different?

Fortunately, both of us have clothing that is appropriate for a wedding, but as I see a couple waltz out of the venue wearing a bikini and an adult Stitch onesie, I guess we can wear whatever. Becca could be dressed in a paper bag, and I'd still find her beautiful. I'd still want to marry her, regardless of the circumstances.

It just so happened that I packed my favorite purple plaid tie, and it perfectly matches Becca's purple dress. Kismet? Serendipity? Meant to be? I sure as fuck hope so.

"Oh my God, they have one with an Elvis impersonator!" she shrieks, then slaps a hand over her mouth. "I'm sorry. That was really loud. I've just always had a thing about Elvis. It would be cool to be married by him."

"Seriously?" I ask, a smile spreading on my face. This woman keeps surprising me.

She gives me a coy look. "I like his music. And I find his life story to be incredibly fascinating."

"So you're really okay being married by an Elvis impersonator?"

Becca nods. "I think it's a cool idea, and a great memory to share."

As we're waiting for the chapel to open up, Becca gasps. "What?"

"We don't have rings!"

"Shit. We'll stop at a jewelry store on the way to the airport."

"Don't we need them for the ceremony?" she asks.

"Uh, sir?" A voice calls out. "We sell rings here."

"Great," I reply, standing to go see what rings are available. Becca follows behind me, and we pick out simple silver bands.

The ceremony is a trip. Why do all Elvis impersonators pick the period of his life where everything is bedazzled and he wears those awful looking oversized sunglasses? Why don't they feature him when he first began his career. Or when he was in the military. How about the time right before he died when he was overweight and miserable? Nope. We all get Elvis with the bell bottoms from the late sixties.

"Repeat after me," Elvis says to me. "I take you, Becca Stephens."

Looking deep into Becca's eyes, I feel my world tilt. This isn't just to help her out. It's not me just being a good guy. I believe wholeheartedly that this is my forever. "I take you, Becca Stephens."

"To be my wife, for better or worse."

Becca inhales sharply as I continue. "To be my wife, for better or worse."

"For richer or poorer, in sickness and in health."

"For richer or poorer, in sickness and in health." A sheen of tears covers Becca's eyes.

"To love and to cherish, until death do us part."

I squeeze her hand as I slide the silver band onto her ring finger. "To love and to cherish, until death do us part."

Becca repeats the vows to me, and the reverence I hear in her voice is like a balm to my soul. I think she knows this is more. I have no doubt she'll fight me, assuming I want something different for my future. No, darlin'. All I want is you.

"By the power vested in me by the great state of Nevada, I now pronounce you husband and wife. Lay one on her, man."

Grinning, I pull Becca into my arms and kiss the hell out of my wife.

Quickly heading back to the hotel to get our suitcases, I Google jewelry stores. I'll be damned if my wife is going to wear a simple wedding band. Frankly, I want her to wear the biggest fucking rock I can find that lets everyone out there know that she's spoken for. I know it sounds medieval of me, but there's something about Becca that makes me feral.

"Why are we stopping?" Becca asks a little while later. Her eyes zero in on the jewelry store sign. "Jacob, no. This ring is fine. I don't need anything else."

"*You* may not need it, but *I* do."

"You need a different wedding band?"

"No, I need you to get another ring," I tell her, before turning to the taxi driver. "Keep the meter running. I'll pay for it."

"I know you will. You've got the money," the driver answers with a chuckle. "I watch hockey, and I know how much your last contract is worth."

Shaking my head in amusement, I help Becca out of the cab and quickly walk into the store. "Where are your engagement rings?"

A speechless employee points in the direction of a case of diamonds. I pull Becca toward the case as I peruse the options. "No, those aren't big enough. Nope. She doesn't like gold. Marquis is a weird shape. Oh, this cushion cut is nice. Can she try it on?"

"How did you know I don't like gold?" Becca whispers, her eyes wide.

"You never wear gold. I've seen you in different silver necklaces, some silver earrings, but never gold. And before you ask how I know all of this, I'll admit I may have done a little Internet stalking of your social media posts. How many carats is this?"

"It's a little over two carats, sir," the woman says. I study Becca's reaction to the ring, and watch as her eyes keep darting to another ring. The stunning ring has a sign next to it saying it's a custom design by some famous jeweler I've never heard of before.

"Let's try a different one, baby," I say quietly, as I carefully take the ring off.

"Okay," she replies, her eyes still on the other ring.

"I think this one is a good one," the woman says, also aware of what Becca is looking at. "The center diamond is just at two and a half carats, but the band holds another carat in pavé diamonds. I think it'll work perfectly with your wedding band."

I take the ring out of her hands and slowly slide it onto Becca's finger. Her hand trembles ever so slightly as she stares at the ring. "It's so beautiful."

"Yes, she is," I murmur, my eyes on Becca's face.

"It's a lovely choice," the salesperson says. "Will you be purchasing today? I can get the ring shined up for you."

"Yes, we're definitely taking the ring," I respond. Becca reluctantly removes the ring and places it on the glass display case. Once the salesperson leaves, Becca finally looks at me.

"Did you even look at the price?" she asks.

"No," I laugh. I don't care if it was a hundred thousand dollars. That ring is meant to be Becca's.

"It's probably thousands of dollars!" she hisses.

"And? I've got the money, Spitfire. I couldn't give you the wedding of your dreams. Let me give you this."

"You're already doing too much," she whispers, her head dropping.

"Hey," I tell her, grabbing her chin between my thumb and forefinger. Pulling her chin up, I wait until I can see her gorgeous eyes. "I don't regret one moment of the last couple of days. Well, I take that back. I regret not punching your brother."

Becca giggles. "I'm glad you didn't. He's a litigious jerk, and I'd hate to see you dragged in the media because you were protecting me."

"I'd happily deal with a PR nightmare every fucking day if it meant shutting your brother up," I say with a grin, then lean forward and quickly kiss her lips. "Let me take care of you, darlin'."

Becca excuses herself to use the bathroom before we leave, and the salesperson brings out the ring immediately after. "Will you be financing the purchase?"

I chuckle again as I pull out my Black Card. "No."

"It really is amazing how the ring fit her perfectly," she comments. "Like it was made for her."

"Completely agree. It was definitely made for her."

Once the sale is finalized, I wait for Becca to finish before we head back out to the waiting taxi.

"Oh, wow. It's over a hundred dollars for the fare already," Becca comments.

I couldn't care less. "We were in there a while."

"We didn't have to stop for this."

Yes, we did. "I'm happy we did. This ring is perfect for you."

Becca sighs as I open the box, pull out the ring, and slide it back onto her finger. "It really is perfect. How much was it?"

"Enough."

She slaps my arm. "Don't play that game with me. It had to have been at least a couple thousand dollars. How much?"

"Sure, we'll go with that," I respond with a devilish smile. Eight thousand is the same as a couple thousand, right? "It doesn't matter how much it was, Spitfire. The only thing that matters to me is seeing how happy this ring makes you."

Becca's head falls to the seat behind her as she gives me a sweet smile. "You really are a good guy, aren't you?"

"I'd like to think so," I say, then lean toward her so I can whisper in her ear. "But not all the time."

I don't miss the shiver that wracks her body.

Looking up at the board with all the flights leaving the Las Vegas airport, I feel Becca's hand slip into mine. "How much trouble are you going to be in?"

"I don't know."

Our nonstop flight to Cleveland is delayed, meaning I won't make the game on time. It was already going to be dicey, with our arrival time only an hour before puck drop, but I'd hoped to at least get there and be moral support if Coach decided to keep me on the bench.

"Can we find somewhere to go so you can call your coach?" Becca asks.

"Yeah, there's a lounge past security. I'll call from there." Even though I have TSA Pre-Check, I've chosen to wait with Becca in the standard security line. I'm apprehensive about leaving her alone for even a few minutes right now. It's probably unlikely that her brother sent someone after us, and I doubt he tracks her location. But if something happens to her because I'm impatient and waited in a shorter line, I'll never forgive myself.

Once through security, I grab Becca's hand and lead her into the private lounge I only know about because Levi pointed it out on a weekend trip a couple of years ago. Grabbing a loveseat, I take out my phone.

Here goes nothing.

"Jax," Coach Davenport says. "You got an ETA?"

"I'd just like to start off by saying that I feel I've been an exemplary employee, and I've never been late to anything," I blurt out.

Coach sighs. "What the hell happened?"

"Our flight is delayed."

"Our?"

"Oh, uh, yeah. Some stuff went down, and Becca's coming with me."

"Alright. So the delay means you wouldn't get here before the game? It's five hours from Indy to Cleveland, man. Rent a car."

"So," I clear my throat, "I'm not exactly in Indianapolis anymore."

Silence.

"Coach? You still there?" I ask.

"What did you do."

"That didn't sound like a question," I joke.

"It wasn't. Just explain what happened, please."

"Long story short, Becca's brother tried to demand she marry some dipshit who's dad was friends with their dad, so I said she was already married to me. Since we weren't exactly married yet, we took a red eye to Vegas and got married this morning."

Another loud sigh. "So your delayed flight is actually in Vegas."

"Yes."

"Jesus Christ," Coach mutters. "I'd really love a week where all of you behave and I have zero public relations disasters to deal with."

"Sorry," I murmur.

"Alright. You are correct about always being on time, and while this PR will be a nightmare to cover, you're definitely one of the better behaved on the team. I'll put you as a healthy scratch for a private personal matter, and I'll have the PR team reach out to you to work on a strategy for a statement if needed."

I let out a relieved exhale, smiling at Becca. She's been attentively watching me, waiting on a reaction. I see the moment she relaxes, and she lays her head on my shoulder.

"Thanks, Coach. Should I still come to Cleveland?" I ask.

"Yes. You can still fly home with the team tomorrow morning. I'll have your wife added to the manifest so she can fly with us."

"Wow," I breathe, slightly stunned at how my heart jumps in my chest.

"What?" Coach and Becca ask simultaneously.

I look over at Becca. "He called you my wife."

"Do I really need to explain the concept of marriage to you?" Coach asks dryly.

"I just didn't realize how much I'd like the sound of it," I confess.

A sweet smile breaks on Becca's face. "And you're my husband."

"Fucking hell," I swear. "That's even better."

"For fuck's sake," Coach mutters. "I'm hanging up."

As he hangs up, I vaguely remember hearing a few shutter clicks, but I can't peel my eyes away from Becca to see what the sound is.

Click! Click, click, click!

And that's how Becca and I are unknowingly photographed together for the first time, staring adoringly at each other in the Las Vegas airport.

Becca

CHAPTER 13

"This is surreal," I comment as I look around the first class cabin. We've reached our cruising altitude, and I've yet to stop taking in every detail. How Jacob managed to procure two first-class tickets only yesterday is beyond me.

"Marriage?" Jacob asks.

"No, this," I say, gesturing around us. "Why is there this much space?"

"It's not that much, actually. International flights have insane business and first class cabins. The seats fold flat to make beds."

My mouth drops open. "Isn't that ridiculously expensive, though? I mean, I knew those kinds of seats existed, but I guess I figured only Hollywood celebrities and millionaires could afford them."

Jacob looks at me, cocking an eyebrow. "You can't tell me you haven't Googled my net worth yet, Spitfire. I may not fall under the former category, but I definitely fall into the latter one."

I feel heat rush to my cheeks. "I have Googled you, yes. Does it make sense if I say that you seem normal, and that I don't really see you as a millionaire?"

He chuckles lightly. "I don't go around splurging on things. I know guys who live in houses worth millions, and have so many cars they need their own parking garages. I know this career isn't going to last forever. I'd rather make sure I can live comfortably for my entire life instead of lavishly for a few years."

"How many cars do you have?" I blurt out.

"Two. Plus a motorcycle, but I rarely ride that anymore. People started recognizing me, and I couldn't take the chance of someone trying to jump on at a stop light."

"People would do that?"

He nods. "Happened twice, and that's twice too many. Plus it's cold in Denver. I'm a wimp with the wind."

I giggle. "The wind is something else. I love to hike, and on sunny winter days, I can still get out there. But if it's windy, it freezes me to the bone."

"I like to hike, too. Does your dog go with you?" Jacob asks.

"He does, although our hikes take twice as long because he has to greet everyone."

"That sounds about right for a golden retriever," Jacob comments.

"I don't remember telling you he's a golden," I say warily, making Jacob give me a sheepish smile.

"I may have done a little Googling on my own," he says quietly. He reaches over and gently picks up my left hand, sliding it into his palm. His fingers rub carefully against my wedding band and engagement ring, making butterflies erupt in my stomach. "I felt a connection from the first moment you ran into me, Becca. Once I recognized who you were, I needed to know more. I saw a pic of you and a golden, but didn't know if it was a current photo until you mentioned having a dog."

"I'm glad you aren't anti-dog, because we're a package deal," I joke lightly. "I guess I should have asked if you have any pets. Thunder is pro-animal, so I doubt you'll have something he doesn't want to befriend."

Jacob lets out a nervous laugh. "I do have pets, actually."

"Pets?" I inquire. "Plural?"

"Yeah."

I wait for more information, but Jacob stays tight-lipped. "Are you going to tell me about them, or do I need to start a guessing game?"

"I highly doubt you'd be able to guess," he chuckles.

"Alright," I say giddily, swiping my hands together in excitement. "I love games. I bet people associate you with big dogs, so I'm guessing three long-haired dachshunds."

He lets out a loud bark of laughter. "Not even close. Well, the size isn't too far off, but definitely not dachshunds."

"But it's three?"

"No." He smiles innocently at me, not giving me any kind of clue as to the correct number.

"You really don't seem like a cat person," I murmur, and he shrugs. "Hmm. Interesting. Maybe it's something incredibly off-the-wall like a Savannah cat."

"Honestly I don't know what that is, so I can confidently say I don't own a Savannah cat."

"A reporter for my station did a report on exotic animals that can be legally owned in Colorado. Did you know you can own a wallaby?"

"What the fuck is a wallaby?" he asks.

"They look like small kangaroos. Which, on the topic of kangaroos, the red kangaroo is also legal in Colorado."

"That must not be the size I'm thinking of, then," he says.

"Oh, I bet it is. They get to be about a hundred pounds as an adult."

"God," he says, laughing, "I can see it now, walking down Colfax with my giant kangaroo."

"I guess it's safe to say you are not currently tending to any Australian wildlife in your home. If I ask you some yes or no questions, will you answer?" I ask.

"Shoot your shot, Spitfire. But I'm only allowing five questions."

Tapping my finger to my lip, I watch as Jacob's eyes drift to zero in on my mouth. He subconsciously licks his lower lip, drawing my own attention. When his eyes focus on mine, I find his pupils dilated and full of restrained lust. He reaches toward me, grabbing the lip I didn't know I was biting, and pulling it from between my teeth. He drags a finger along my lips, and my panties are immediately soaked.

Goodness. I think the temperature jumped twenty degrees in here.

"Ask your questions, Becca," he commands quietly.

"Oh. Sorry." I shake my head to remove the NSFW images currently carousing through my mind. "Do you have three or less animals?"

He smiles. "No."

"Do your pets bark or meow?" I have a gut feeling that he's harboring some unique animals.

"No."

"Do you have more than five pets?"

Jacob's grin gets bigger. "Yes."

"Are your pets the size of your hand or smaller?" I ask.

He holds up a hand, noting its size. "That doesn't really help you out much, baby, but yes, they're the size of my hand or smaller. One last question."

The size of his fingers — focus, Becca. Jeez. "Do your pets have tails?"

His eyes widen dramatically. "No."

I smile triumphantly. "Guinea pigs."

"How the hell did you do that?" he asks incredulously.

"I read a lot as a kid. My parents never let me have any of the science kits that I wanted, but they didn't put a limit on books I could read. We only lived a half mile from the local library, so I'd walk there almost every day in the summer. I'd borrow full encyclopedias, and I loved reading about animals."

"What would you have guessed if I said they did have tails?"
"Rats."

"Why a rat?" he laughs.

"Well, you don't seem like a guy that would keep gerbils or

mice. Rats are actually quite intelligent, and I imagine you'd teach them to do tricks."

He nods. "Now I kinda want to get some rats."

"No," I say sternly. "I don't do rats."

"You'll learn about them, but you won't interact with them?"

"Alright, smart-ass. What are you scared of?" I ask.

"Not too much. I'm not a huge fan of spiders, I guess."

"What if I said I loved tarantulas, and I wanted to bring my five different species of tarantula into your apartment?"

He shudders. "Point taken. No rats, and no tarantulas."

I smile sweetly at him. "Now tell me about your guinea pigs."

"I will, but you have to promise me you won't tell anyone. They aren't exactly a secret, but I don't go out and publicize that I have six of them."

"Six? Why six?" I ask, intrigued.

"I like even numbers. Originally I had five, because that's how many the kid at the farm suckered me into buying when I went a year or so ago with a buddy's family," he says sheepishly. He then tells me all about his harem of flower-named guinea pigs, their favorite foods, and the setup he has in his apartment. "But, like I said, I've got this thing with even numbers. Grabbed the sixth one a month or two later."

I figure now isn't a good time to tell him that Thunder will probably try to eat at least one of them.

Two and a half hours later, Jacob shakes my knee. "We're about to land, Spitfire. Didn't want the landing to jar you."

Lifting my head, I realize I fell asleep on Jacob's shoulder. I frantically wipe at the drool spot on his shirt, then wipe my mouth. Lovely. I look through my lashes to find Jacob struggling to withhold a smile, but I'm thankful he doesn't tease me about my drooling. As the wheels touch down on the runway, I ask, "Where are we again?"

"Cleveland," he says dryly. "A city famous for having a river filled with so much debris and oil that it actually caught fire."

"Seriously?"

"Yep. I remember a teammate in college talking about it. Michigan and Ohio have a hate-hate relationship, and since I went to the University of Michigan for college, I learned all about the ridiculous Ohio facts I could throw around when needed."

"The river catching on fire changed how we view pollution and the city's industrial landscape. There's a lot more to Cleveland than just one detail about a fire," the man sitting across from us states loudly.

Jacob leans forward to stare at the guy. "Let's just ignore the fact that you were so blatantly eavesdropping on my conversation with my wife, and chat about that one detail, shall we?"

I find myself reaching to rest my hand on Jacob's. Not only to support him, but he just called me his wife — in public — and my body is reacting pretty quickly to it. I need to touch him.

"How many times did the Cuyahoga River catch fire?" Jacob asks sternly.

The man's face pales. "Uh, I'm not sure, but so many changes have been made to benefit the environment and the city since then, so does it really matter?"

"The answer is thirteen. It's caught fire thirteen times."

"Over the last century."

"That doesn't make it any better, my guy," Jacob chuckles. "It's great that your city has made improvements. Doesn't change the past, though."

"True. Would you like me to comment on all of your faults, hockey boy?" the man asks aggressively.

"Sure," Jacob answers nonchalantly. "Go ahead."

"What?"

"You're welcome to it. Yeah, this is a sport, but it's also my job. I don't do it perfectly, but I'm paid a hell of a lot of money to be the best. Two years ago I had a shitty season. Too many penalties, well below my average for both shots on goal and points. So if you'd like to discuss that, have at it."

The man stares aghast at Jacob. "I really didn't expect you to be so open to taking criticism."

Jacob shrugs. "You're talking about my job. You start to come after me as a person? How I treat people? Then we'll have a problem."

The man nods gruffly before reaching for his belongings. Jacob catches my eyes and gives me a soft smile. "You okay, Spitfire?"

"You really don't care if someone gets mad about your hockey stats?"

"No. I know I have value. I wouldn't be playing where I am, or be the captain, if I didn't. I devote my life to hockey, and I'm damn good at it. Yeah, I have off games. Or, like I mentioned, an off year. But I'm proud of what I've accomplished in my career so far. Most of the people who come at me spouting off nonsense are fans from rival teams, and they're just trying to get in my head. I've learned to just ignore the chirping."

"When you had an off year, did you lose your focus? Or your confidence?" I ask. The ding letting us know we can remove our seatbelts interrupts our conversation, but as soon as we've gathered our things and exited onto the jetway, Jacob continues.

"I did briefly. I wondered if I should think about retirement. A buddy of mine recently retired from the Wolves, and he was at the top of his game. The difference was this: he didn't find it fun anymore. He didn't look forward to practice. He hated leaving his girl. He wanted to put down roots, not spend half the year galli-vanting around North America. I still love hockey. I get off on the smell of the ice every fucking time I step onto it. I feed off the roar of the crowd, whether they're rooting for or against me. It's in my soul."

"What's the normal age of retirement?" I wonder aloud.

"There's no set number. Many guys get forced out due to injury or poor performance. I know I'm nearing the end of my career. I have two more years on my contract, and I'm not gonna take anything else. I want to retire here. I've spent the majority of my career with the Wolves, and I hope to end it here, too."

I find myself letting out a loud exhale of relief, and Jacob looks at me with amusement. "Worried about me moving, darlin'?"

I attempt a nonplussed look, but fail miserably. "I don't like spontaneity. I'm very Type-A. I know things are … new with us, but you suddenly telling me you're moving wouldn't sit well with me."

Jacob grabs my hand, pulling me off to the side, near an empty gate. "Why?"

I shrug. "I'd like to be prepared for it. That's all. If the end is coming, I don't want the bottom to drop out unexpectedly. I'll need to prepare. Put my game face on."

Jacob's eyes search mine, flitting between them as he squeezes my hand. "You wouldn't want to go with me?"

"What?" I ask, stupefied. What the hell does that mean?

"Let's just say I got traded next week. Nothing I could control. It can happen, Becca, but I'm fairly confident it won't happen to me. But if it happened, that's it? We're done?"

"I'm not even sure what we are, Jacob," I answer with an irritated tone. "A faux spouse does not a husband make."

He steps closer to me, so close our noses almost touch, and pushes one hand into my hair. Holding my head, he latches into my waves to tilt me back, waiting until my eyes meet his. "Let's get something straight here, Spitfire. Nothing about this is fake to me. Nothing. You are my wife. Not a pretend one. Or a momentary one. You are it. You can deny all you want, but this is happening. We've got the marriage license and these rings to prove it. In case that wasn't specific enough for you, let me say it this way. If I get traded, I want you with me. End of story."

Jacob leans down to press a harsh kiss against my lips before turning to march toward baggage claim. Stunned into silence, I follow.

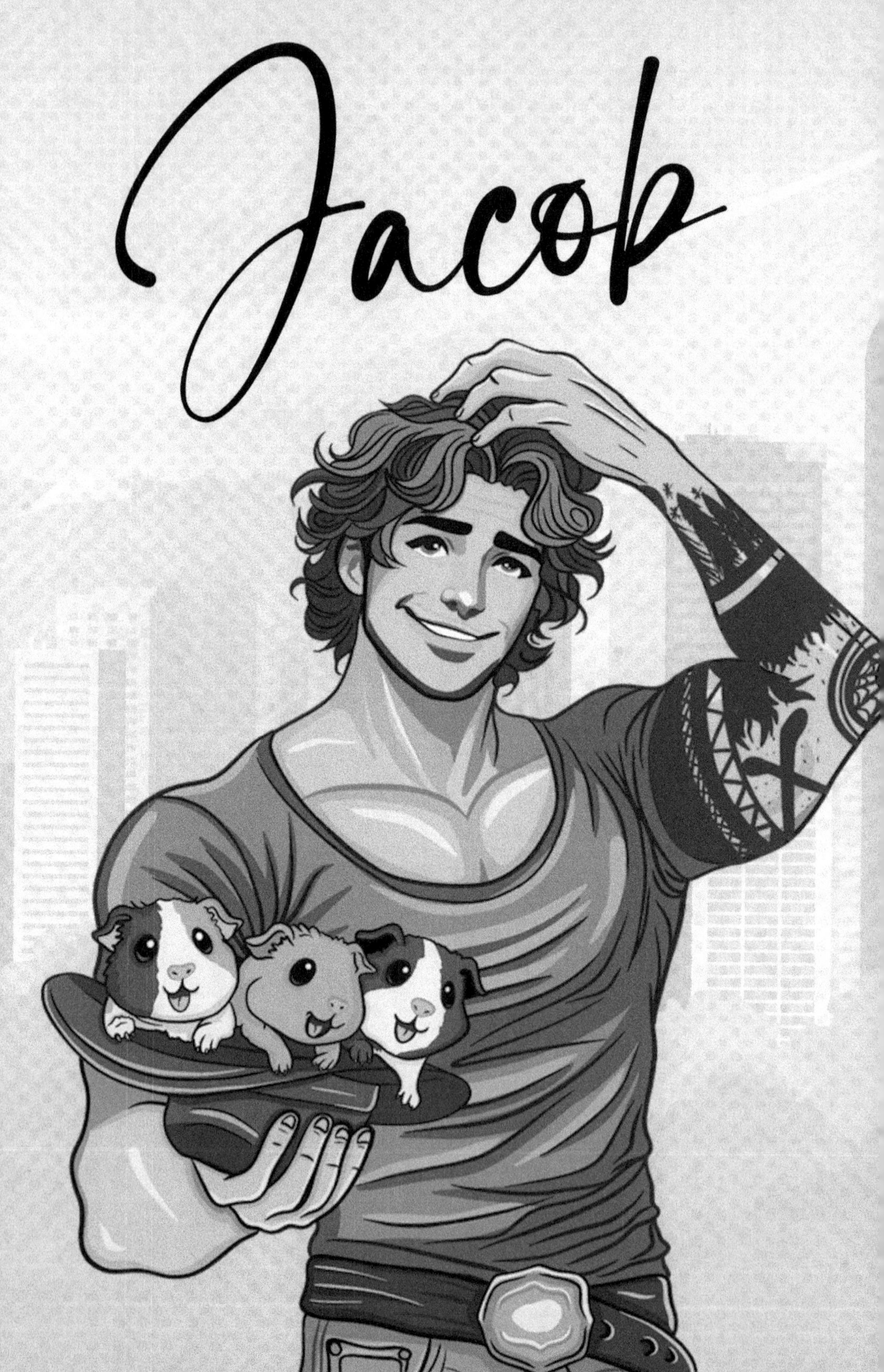
Jacob

CHAPTER 14

This woman gets me all twisted up. I probably freaked her the fuck out. Honestly, it's better than what I could have said. I could have told her what I was really thinking. Feeling. Wanting.

Yeah, you're my wife. But I'm pretty sure I'm falling in love with you, and I have been since I first felt your lips on mine, and I can't fucking wait to get you into my bed so I can show you properly how much I need you.

If she's freaked by me telling her our impromptu marriage isn't fake to me, she'll probably hyperventilate if I tell her I'm in love with her. I'm just gonna lock those thoughts up in the Jax vault for now.

"Do we need to rent a car?" Becca asks quietly as we wait for our baggage.

"No, the team sent a car service," I murmur, pulling my beanie further down onto my head. I sure am glad I didn't wear my favorite cowboy hat on this trip, because I'd really stand out then. A couple of people have noticed me. I'd rather word not get out that I'm at the airport, instead of with the team, and the game has already started. Honestly, I'm surprised the douche from the plane didn't comment on it, since he obviously knew I was a hockey player. I'm in a suit, knowing we'd most likely head straight from the airport to the arena, but I know I'm recognizable. Because of the circumstances, Becca is wearing a dress, and she explained that her family always expected it. I'm not complaining, as she looks absolutely captivating. My wife is a knockout.

I feel Becca's hand tentatively sliding into mine. "Do you want to go outside? I can get the bags."

"No, I'm fine."

"Jacob," she says softly, waiting until she gets my eyes. "I know you're uncomfortable. You helped me so much this week. Let me return the favor."

"I don't want to leave you alone," I finally grit out, bending so I can rest my forehead against hers. "Someone might harass you. Your brother —"

"Is not here," she interrupts. "Go find the car. I see my bag, and I'm sure yours is right behind it. I'll be fine."

I warily let go of her hand and trudge outside, immediately finding the car service Coach told me to look for. Honestly, he's been incredibly accommodating this week. It probably also helps that I haven't so much as missed a game, or practice, in his entire tenure as head coach, and he knows it won't be repeated. I honor my obligations.

"See? I told you it would be fine. Look at me, I'm being a grown up," Becca says, huffing as she drags our suitcases behind her. "What the hell is in this thing? It weighs a ton."

"I'm an over-packer," I tell her with a grin. I like shoes, and I know I travel with too many. I make a mental note to message the pet sitter who checks in on my girls while I'm on away trips, to see if she wants to make some extra cash. I've spread out in my walk-in closet, and I'll need to make room for Becca. I'm sure she's going to fight me on moving in, but this is one area where I will not make concessions. I don't trust her brother ... and I want to be close to her.

After throwing the bags in the trunk, I open the back door with a flourish. Gesturing to her to get in first, I say, "after you, my lady."

Once settled, Becca turns to me. "Are we going to the game, or a hotel?"

"Game. I'd rather not piss off Coach."

"Is it bad that you weren't here earlier?"

"Yes and no. He knew we'd be late, and it's unusual for me to be off schedule in any way. But I also don't like to deviate from things, especially on a game day."

"I'm nervous," she admits.

"Why?"

She gives me a shy smile. "They're your family."

I love that she recognizes how important my hockey family is to me. Levi already told me he got a good first impression after our failed double date, and he's rarely wrong about people. But Becca doesn't know that yet. "They're going to love you."

"Are there any other wives or girlfriends there? Do any others travel with the team?"

"Sometimes. It's more likely when they're from that city. I don't think anyone from the team is from Cleveland, though. Had I traveled from Indianapolis, I'd know more. I'm nosy when I'm bored," I tell her.

Becca giggles lightly. "I don't find that hard to believe at all."

I do the old move of stretching my arms up, then sliding one around her shoulders. "Just wait until I start sending you tons of memes and videos."

"Oh, you're *that* guy?" she laughs.

"Only for my wife."

I don't miss the subtle shiver that dances down her spine. Yes, wife. I like calling you that as well.

Becca has an absolute death grip on my hand as we walk through the halls of the Cleveland arena. She's been completely silent since we pulled into downtown, and I haven't forced her to talk. I'm a pretty patient guy, and something tells me I need to let Becca work through things in her own time.

"Why are there pictures of basketball guys on the wall?" she whispers, making me chuckle quietly. "Are we in the right place?"

"They share the facility with the professional basketball team, just like we do in Denver," I explain. When she doesn't respond, I say, "I'm guessing you didn't know that either."

"It didn't occur to me, but now I feel like a dummy, because I've been to both kinds of games, and I never realized they were at the same place," she admits, her cheeks turning pink.

"You're not a dummy. I think at least half the population assumes every sports team has their own space, but in reality, most hockey and basketball teams share the same arena."

"I should know more about Denver, I guess," she says somewhat sullenly.

"Why?" I ask as we're led past the locker rooms. A dull roar begins to increase the closer we get to the ice, and even out of uniform, I can feel my blood begin to pump. If Coach let me dress, I'd get on the ice right now.

Becca shrugs. "I'm an introvert, and I don't do the nightlife scene. My idea of a fun night is reading on the couch. I love my job, but I think I live in my own bubble while there. I should know more about what my co-workers report on, for crying out loud."

"Well, I don't think you should feel forced to learn about things you have no interest in just because you think it's expected of you. If you don't like sports, why would you know about the teams, or where they play?" A Wolves employee sees me, and I tip my chin to him. "Let me go talk to this guy and see where we need to go. Stay right here."

"Wait, uh, Jacob?" Becca says, tugging me back to her as I begin to walk away. "Is my makeup okay?"

"Yeah, why?" I ask.

She looks embarrassed as she explains very quietly, "I don't want people to see where my brother hit me."

Fuck. No wonder she's apprehensive about meeting the team. I reach up, cupping her cheek softly. "You look absolutely breathtaking, darlin'."

Becca leans into my touch, her eyes softening almost imperceptibly. "Really?"

"Really."

"You wouldn't lie about that, right?"

I step closer to her, letting my hand slide down to bracket her neck. "I will never lie to you, Becca. I promise."

"Okay," she replies, giving me a cute smile. Satisfied, I walk away.

"Sup, Jax." Tim, a physical therapist who often travels with the team, greets me. "Coach said you'd be getting here at some point."

"Yeah, our flight was delayed."

"That the new missus?" Tim gestures toward Becca.

"That's her."

"You're all everyone talked about during warm ups. Team seems pretty stoked to be welcoming a new WAG."

I roll my eyes. "I haven't even explained the WAG mentality to her. Not too many are worthy of meeting."

"I know. Dunner's girlfriend had the audacity to ask me to get her a drink at the last event. She couldn't grasp the concept of me being an employee and *not* hired help." Gavin Dunn's girlfriend, Avery, became social media famous a few years ago, and nabbing a hockey boyfriend made her think even more highly of herself. After one interaction with her, I knew immediately she wasn't someone I wanted to be around. Fortunately, I think her boyfriend is a piece of trash too.

"She's the first person I'll be warning my wife to steer clear of," I tell Tim. God, I fucking *love* calling Becca my wife. "I'm not sure where we should go. Does Coach want me on the bench? Back here? In the stands? What period are we in?"

"Just about to finish the first period," Tim replies.

"Seriously? That's a long-ass first period."

"Way too many penalties, and a lengthy delay because of an injury to a defenseman for Cleveland."

"Oh, shit," I say. I never want to hear about injuries, no matter what team the player is on. Most injuries are simple things like bloody noses or minor cuts. We get stitched up, and we're back on the ice. Rarely, there are injuries that involve a lot more care.

"Yeah. He got slammed into the boards pretty hard. Completely knocked out. Took a while to get him secured and off the ice. At the same time there was a fight, and all those penalties took time to sort out as well. Honestly, it was a mess."

A buzzer sounds, alerting us to the end of the period. Knowing how my team exits the ice, I nod at Tim before going back to Becca's side. My teammates are likely to bum-rush her in their haste to get back to the locker room, and I don't want her to get frightened or hurt.

Levi is the first through the doorway, and he immediately throws both arms around us. "Mr. and Mrs. Mitchell!"

"Oh, wow, that smell," Becca blurts out, making both Levi and me laugh. He pounds me lightly on the back as he continues toward the locker room. Each of my teammates walks past with a nod to me, and most acknowledge Becca as well. Gabe Dawson stops to introduce himself, telling Becca he can't wait for her to meet his wife, Cassie. Becca will love Cassie, as well as their daughter, Mackenzie.

"Jaxy boy! Thanks for bringing me a present," Grant says loudly, whipping off his gloves as he takes Becca's hand in his. "Hello, beautiful."

"Uh, hi?" Becca says, confusion laced in her tone. As Grant brings her hand to his lips, my immediate frown turns to an amused smile when Becca yanks her hand away from Grant. "I don't think so."

"What?" Grant asks innocently. "I figured you'd want to upgrade from Mitchell here."

Becca burrows into my side. "No, thank you."

Grant cocks his head to the side, glancing at me as I proudly slide my arm around Becca. "Huh. Found yourself a keeper, I think."

"Nally, move it along!" Coach Davenport barks from behind him. Grant winks at me as he strides past us. "Jax. Fashionably late."

"I do like to make an entrance," I joke, making Coach crack a smile. "Coach Davenport, allow me to introduce you to my wife, Becca Stephens. Uh, Mitchell. Becca Mitchell? Becca Stephens-Mitchell. Shit. We haven't discussed the name thing yet."

Becca giggles as Coach extends a hand. "Hello, Becca. My wife is a huge fan."

"Really?" Becca asks incredulously.

"She's a quintessential nerd, as she puts it. She loves the long-term forecasts you put out every year. Tells me all about La Niña, the polar vortex, and all of that stuff. Every conversation we have includes weather in some form," Coach says with a smile.

"Awe, I love that. Tell her I'd love to meet her. Would she like a tour of the studio, do you think?"

"She'd fucking love that. Her name is Elsie. I'll tell her to email you." Coach looks at me. "If I had known you'd be here with two full periods to play, I wouldn't have left you off the official roster for tonight, Jax. The NHL is pretty damn specific about repercussions for giving what they refer to as false statements, so I can't let you dress and play."

"I didn't expect to play. I'm happy to be here and support the team in any way I can."

"Go watch from the box. I'm sure your wife will have questions about the game," Coach says with a smirk. He shakes Becca's hand again. "Welcome to the team, Becca. You're part of the family now."

As he strides away, Becca turns to me wide-eyed. "I think I blacked out. Did they all greet me?"

"Pretty much." Well, except for Gavin Dunn. Fucking asshat.

"Except that one gremlin-looking guy," Becca snorts, then gasps. "Oh my God, that was so mean. Is he your friend? Please tell me he's not your friend."

I throw back my head in raucous laughter. "He is absolutely not my friend. Also his girlfriend is heinous, so be advised when you meet her."

She frowns, a look of distaste crossing her face. "Do I have to meet her? My poker face is pretty nonexistent. She'll immediately know how I feel."

"You'll meet her at some point. It's bound to happen. We have team events where the wives and girlfriends attend. She likes to size up the newbies, acting like she's the queen bee of the group. She'll probably make it her mission to seek you out and put you in your place."

"I'm so out of my element," Becca mutters. Grabbing her hand, I pull her to walk beside me as we head toward the elevators.

"I'll introduce you to people I know you'll like. The gremlin-looking guy, as you called him, is Gavin Dunn. His hockey nickname is Dunner, and his girlfriend is Avery. Once Avery realizes you aren't going to cower, she'll leave you alone."

"But I am a cowerer. And I'm one hundred percent okay with cowering. You know what I don't like? Confrontations. She can very much be the queen bee, and I'll stay hiding in the corner where I'm very comfortable."

Arriving at the elevator, I push the button, before looking down at Becca. She chews on her lower lip nervously, and I resist the urge to pull her lip from between her teeth with my mouth. Instead, I gently grab her chin between my thumb and forefinger, tilting her head up to look at me. "I am totally a fan of confrontations. You cool if I do the confronting? Then I'll join you in your comfy corner."

Becca gives me a relieved smile. "You're gonna fight for me?"

"Darlin', there isn't much I wouldn't do for you."

Becca

CHAPTER 15

I'M QUIET AS WE TAKE AN ELEVATOR UP. JACOB CHATS AMICABLY WITH an arena employee, but I tune them out.

Is he being for real?

There isn't much he wouldn't do for me?

Double-negative aside, that might be the most romantic thing anyone has ever said to me. I didn't think he could top his whole 'nothing about this is fake to me' line from the airport, but he proved me wrong.

Everything I've experienced about Jacob Mitchell so far has created a war in my mind with what I thought I knew about the entire male species, and I'm having one hell of a time coming to terms with that. He's been nothing but thoughtful and kind, patient and compassionate. My heart is ready to leap in, feet first, but my brain is putting on the brakes. He can't be real. His flaws will show up, and they'll be awful. He's bound to let me down.

Should I trust in this?

I'm really in over my head. I should tell Jacob I don't feel well, and go back to the hotel. Or maybe even the airport. There has to be a red-eye back to Denver, right? As I'm about to speak up, Jacob opens a door.

"You ready for Hockey 101?" Jacob asks as he guides me into what he described as a 'box,' but is actually a room with padded chairs and a partition separating the room from the stands. A handful of men in suits stand around the space, talking loudly, but Jacob walks to the edge and motions for me to sit down.

"Now you're a teacher?" I ask wryly, and he gives me a big grin.

"Best you're gonna get tonight. Do you know what that thing is called on the ice?" he asks, pointing down at an odd machine driving along the ice.

"Not a clue."

"It's called a Zamboni. It shaves off the top layer of ice, then puts down a heated layer of water that freezes onto the leftover ice. It gives us a smooth surface to skate on for each new period."

"Why's it called a Zamboni?" I ask.

"For the dude who invented it."

"Makes sense," I murmur. "What's the other word for jersey?"

"They're called jerseys or sweaters."

"Who is the most popular guy on your team?" I wonder aloud.

"Levi. He's an enigmatic mystery, which means he's a chick magnet," Jacob laughs. "Gabe Dawson is right up there too. He's a top scorer, and he gets the female vote because of how he became a dad."

"How?"

Jacob leans toward me. "A sad story, honestly. He found out about his daughter because the hospital where she was born called to tell him that the baby's mom died in childbirth. Gabe had no idea about the baby."

I gasp. "Oh, I can't imagine. How horrifying. He wasn't in a relationship with the mom, then."

"A one-night stand. It was during the season, and Gabe was completely unprepared. The team helped him with everything, and Nally's sister started nannying for him."

"How old is the baby now?"

"I think about one and a half."

"And Nally's sister still nannies for him?"

"Yes and no," he chuckles.

"I don't see how that question is funny," I say with a frown.

"It is when you hear the whole story. Just know they're together now. As a couple. So yes, she technically still takes care of Mackenzie, but it's mostly because Kenz calls her Mama."

"If I had a nickel for every time I read a single dad and nanny story," I say with a laugh.

Jacob's brows raise. "Single dad and nanny?"

"Yeah. In romance books."

"The spicy kind?" he inquires.

Crud. "They usually are, yes."

A wicked smile crosses his face as he leans in, his lips ghosting over my ear. "Promise to share your favorite books with me, wife?"

My stomach leaps as pure lust pools in my core. "I didn't take you as a reader of women's fiction and romance, husband."

He groans against my skin, letting his forehead rest on my temple. "I enjoy learning, Becca. And if reading a romance book helps me to learn what you like, then I'll happily buy a Kindle and take it with me everywhere."

"What I like?" I ask breathlessly as he places a hand on my thigh, and my eyes flutter shut as I bite my lip to refrain from moaning out loud.

Jacob absentmindedly draws across my leg, and I'm thrilled the dress I'm wearing is thick enough to hide the goosebumps he leaves in his wake. The fabric *should* be thick enough to hide goosebumps, but my eyes are closed, and I can't seem to force them to open enough to look. "You're a tough nut to crack, darlin'. If I read enough of the same books, I'll learn what you veer toward. If you want it sweet, or if you like it rough. If you like a man to take control, or if you want to make the decisions. Hell, I might even be able to determine what area of your body is the most sensitive, and what gets you off the quickest. Because here's the thing, Spitfire. I want to learn every fucking thing about you, your body, and what you need, and I plan on giving it all to you."

"Holy cow," I pant. "I wasn't ready for that."

He gives me a pained smile as he nods, sitting back and discreetly adjusting himself. "Yeah, I know. I came on too strong."

"No, I liked that part," I admit quietly, aware that anyone could be listening. "I guess I had you firmly in the golden retriever category, so hearing you speak differently is outside of the character I've built you up to be in my mind. Which is dumb, really. You're a real person, so why do I have a caricature of who I think you are roaming around in my brain? I sometimes feel the need to test-run how conversations might go, from any angle I can think of. And I think I've made you out to be —"

"A golden retriever." Jacob's dry remark makes me giggle. "I'm sure most men have been called dogs before, but I've never been called a specific breed. This is new."

"It's a romance book thing," I blurt out. His gaze meets mine. "A golden retriever book boyfriend is one who has a glass half full mentality. Finds joy in everything, and has friends everywhere. Has a great sense of humor, and people love to be around him. I smile when I'm around you. I'd bet other people think you bring joy to their lives, too."

He looks down, a subtle smile showing in the corner of his mouth. "I bring joy to your life?"

Now it's my turn to feel bashful. "You do."

Jacob turns his head slightly, peeking at me from under his thick lashes. "But you liked the part where I told you all the things I want to learn about you and your body?"

Oh my. Did the temperature just jump fifteen degrees in here? Maybe I need a ride on that Zamboni to cool off.

No, I need to ride Jacob.

Good God. I'm a little too keyed up to deal with this man, and my vagina is about to take over all decisions if I don't get a handle on things.

"Where's the bathroom?" I blurt out. Quickly standing, I attempt to scoot past Jacob, and instead, fall into his lap. Onto it. Well, him. All of him. That one quick squeeze I snuck in while he was asleep really didn't give me an estimate on his full length, and my eyes widen as I realize he's likely to puncture something if — or when — we have sex. "I need the bathroom. Right now."

Jacob lets out a rather pained chuckle as he grabs my waist, pushing me to stand, before rising to his feet. "I'll go with you. I don't know this level of the arena, and I don't want us to get separated."

That makes sense, I guess. I reluctantly trudge out of the box with Jacob in tow, hoping I can settle my whirling mind and raging hormones in the few short minutes I'll be able to use in a public restroom before Jacob inevitably gets nervous. I assume his golden retriever tendencies could also show up in the form of barging into delicate situations because he needs to check on me. Thunder certainly does that to me fairly often.

"Oh. It looks like the only option here is a unisex bathroom," Jacob comments as we stop in front of a door with every bathroom picture on it. Crud. Now I don't even get three minutes to rein in my chaotic thoughts.

"We have one of these in our building," I explain as nonchalantly as I can, pushing open the door. As I expected, there are four separate stalls with floor-to-ceiling partitions enclosing the space. A shared wall of sinks sits opposite the stalls. A television hangs from the ceiling corner, showcasing the game, with the volume turned low.

As I walk toward a stall, Jacob grabs my hand, yanking me back to him. Two quick steps and my back is against the wall, with Jacob pressed against me as he locks the main door. "You want to tell me what that was back there?"

"What?" I ask, struggling to keep my breathing even. I feel surrounded by him. Every atom of my body buzzing with adrenaline and chemistry, just aching to feel him.

"Why you tried to get away from me as fast as possible," he murmurs, ducking his head to drag his nose along the length of my neck. I can't withhold the deep moan that escapes my mouth.

"I feel overwhelmed," I whisper.

"How?"

"Because it's been a while for me, and you're saying all these things that get my motor running. But you're … you, and I'm struggling to gauge if how much I want you is normal."

"Fuck," he whispers against my skin. "Tell me that again."

"Which part?" I ask with an airy giggle.

"The part where you tell me you want me. It does something to me, hearing you say that. Because darlin', you have no fucking idea how much I want you," he rasps, before kissing the spot where my shoulder meets my neck. My knees buckle, but Jacob's arms clamp around me, holding me upright. "Tell me you want me, Spitfire."

There are so many things that I want to tell him. I want to whisper all the things I need him to do to me. How I know he'll own me like no one ever has before, and that I want to memorize every inch of his body. I'd love to tell him that I do want him to take control. To take me to the edge again and again before he finally sends me over. I'd explain how anxious I am about my body. And that I have more confidence because of him, but I still have a ways to go. How he'll need to tread carefully.

But I can't say all of that. Instead, I slide my hand up his chest, over his shoulder, and into his thick curly hair. Grabbing a fistful, I pull until his head lifts and our eyes meet. Gorgeous blue eyes are glassy and hooded as Jacob waits for my words. "Tell me, darlin'. Say it. Please."

"I want you," I blurt out, and Jacob crashes his lips against mine.

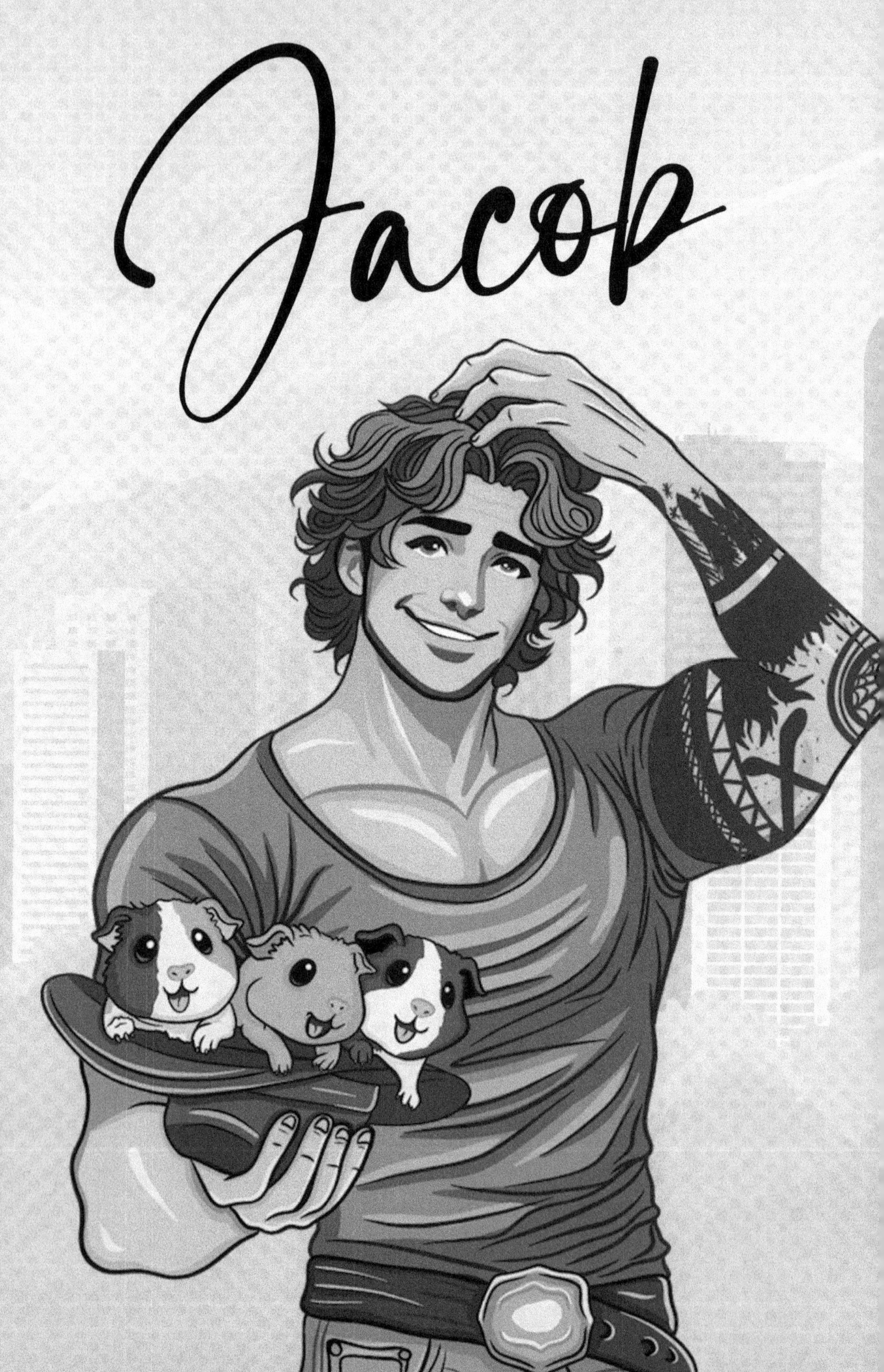

Jacob

CHAPTER 16

She thinks she doesn't give anything away. That she's got her shutters up tight, letting no one see the real Becca and what she thinks.

But I do. I see so much in her beautiful eyes. The pain. The wariness. The expectations that I'll let her down, because every man in her life has so far. I'm all too ready to show her how different I am from the assholes she's dealt with, including her shit-for-brains brother.

When I asked her to tell me she wanted me, I saw it in her eyes. She wanted to tell me all kinds of things. But she doesn't trust me fully yet. I'm a somewhat patient man. While I'd love to fast forward the process of Becca learning to trust me, I know I just have to bide my time. I know, deep in my soul, that Becca is my end-game. She's worth the wait.

While I can't force her to fall in love with me more quickly, I can show her that she'll love how I fuck. Considering this is the first time Becca has blatantly expressed her attraction to me, I'm not giving up this opportunity.

I grab Becca's leg and yank it up and around my hip. She immediately grinds down on me as my tongue circles hers. She gasps into my mouth, and I feel her fingernails dig into my scalp. It's a pleasure that borders on pain, and I fucking love it.

She called me a golden retriever. I can see how that would be correlated. I am generally pretty happy. I can find light and joy in most things. I'm the life of any party. Becca is about to find out, though, that golden retriever does not equal vanilla and boring.

Ending the kiss to drag my tongue down her neck, I nibble on her collarbone before lifting my head to put my lips beside her ear. "The first time I fuck you will not be in a bathroom at an arena in Cleveland. The first time I feel you come on my cock will not be here. Our first time will be when I can take my time to unravel you. Spread you out. Make you mine."

"Wow," she pants, and I smile against her skin. "Jax!"

"No," I correct her, pushing back. Eyes closed and mouth open, Becca looks like a goddamn wet dream. "Open your eyes and look at me."

Her eyes open, the gaze is glassy and unfocused.

"I'm Jacob to you."

"What? Why?" she asks breathlessly. "Everyone calls you Jax."

"That's why. You're not everyone. You're my wife. You're the only one who gets to call me Jacob." I barely blink as I tell her this. I can't remember anyone ever calling me Jacob. In school, I was Jake or Jax. My parents never even called me Jacob. But from the moment Becca referred to me as such, I knew I never wanted her to call me anything else.

Well, except husband. That was fucking hot.

"Okay," Becca replies, her voice apprehensive.

"I love that you call me Jacob, darlin'. It's like you see me differently than everyone else. You don't see me as a hockey star, or a dollar sign. You see me as … me."

Her eyes soften. "Hockey isn't what you are, Jacob. It's a job. You're so much more than that."

Not knowing how to respond, and feeling like I might shout out a love proclamation that scares the hell out of her, I lean forward to kiss her again. Becca sighs as she melts in my arms.

"We should get back," she murmurs between kisses. I nod, but I don't stop. I'm not kissing her as a precursor to anything right now. I like the feeling of Becca in my arms. Against my body. On my lips. She feels right. Like comfort, home, and happiness.

"In a minute," I whisper against her.

Becca giggles, and I love how the feeling vibrates my lips. "Jacob."

I shake my head, making her laugh again.

"Husband."

"Fuck," I groan. "That will not make me leave this room any faster."

I hear the muffled noise of the horn signaling a Cleveland goal at the same time as someone tries to enter the bathroom. Becca gasps, shoving me away as she drops her leg from around my waist. "Get that —" she hisses, pointing at my crotch, "— under control."

Head held high, she unlocks the door, opens it, and steps outside.

"Why was it lo — oh." A surprised man stares at us as I grab Becca's hand. "Hey, aren't you …"

"Nope," I reply.

"But you really do look like him," he stammers.

"Not him," I answer, swiftly walking away with a snickering Becca in tow.

"You don't know who he thought you were," she laughs. "Maybe he thought you were Jack Harlow. Or Justin Timberlake. Or that dude from *Shameless*. Maybe Jesse Eisenberg!"

I stop walking, turning to stare at her incredulously. "Are you seriously just naming men with curly hair?"

She gives me an adorable grin. "I would have picked out athletes with curly hair, but I really don't pay attention to sports."

I dramatically place a hand over my heart. "You wound me, darlin'. I may have to request a divorce now."

Becca rolls her eyes. "I didn't say I hate sports. Just that I don't pay attention to them."

"Gonna have to change that. Maybe not all sports. Just pay attention to hockey."

"Okay," she says with a breathy giggle. Her green eyes sparkle, and I'm relieved to see some joy in her expression. I hope with every passing hour, and the further we get away from her toxic family, Becca will feel confident and happy again.

A couple of hours later, I pull a very nervous Becca onto the team bus. She's gripping my hand so tightly the blood is pooling in my fingers, but I don't shake off the connection. I like that she's depending on me, and that she trusts me enough to take care of her.

"Uh-oh, Jax brought his ball-and-chain with him this time!" One of the rookies shouts, a huge grin on his face, but before I can react, Levi pops the guy on the back of his head.

"Dude, that's fucked up," Levi snaps. "You better watch how you talk, Rookie."

"Does that mean we can bring bunnies?" asks another rookie.

Oh, hell no. "She's not a bunny, she's my wife. Say another nasty thing about her, asshole, and I guarantee you'll be eating your breakfast through a straw."

"Jacob," Becca whispers. "It's okay."

Turning to her, I stare down into her gorgeous green eyes, which look like pools of water in a mountain reservoir. "No, it's not okay. I won't stand by and let them talk about you this way."

"Alright, alright," Coach says from behind us. "Gentlemen, this is Jax's wife. No, we don't normally allow anyone on the bus that isn't part of the team, but this is a unique circumstance. Don't think you can just turn up and get anyone on board. Now I'm fucking tired, so let's get this show on the road."

I motion for Becca to scoot into an available row, then sit beside her, extending my left arm along the back of her seat. It's a power move, designed to inform everyone that Becca is mine, and no one better fuck with her.

"Still can't believe you got married," Grant grumbles from the row behind us. Turning my head slightly, I cock an eyebrow at him, and he shrugs. "Who the hell am I supposed to drag out with me now?"

"Dude, I rarely went out with you before I got married. It'll be the exact same thing," I point out. I can count on one hand how many times I've been Grant's wingman in the last year, and half of those instances had us home before midnight because even he got bored.

"But now I can't call you," he grumbles, and Becca turns around to stare at him.

"I have no problem with you guys continuing to hang out. Honestly. I have an early bedtime anyway," she says.

"An early bedtime?" Grant says with a chuckle, but I don't miss the bitterness that oozes along with his words. "Do your mommy and daddy come tuck you in, too?"

"I'm the chief meteorologist for channel twelve in Denver. I get up around three in the morning, because our broadcasts start at five."

Grant stares at her, dumbfounded. "You're a weather girl?"

Becca sighs. "No, I'm a meteorologist. I have a couple degrees to prove it."

"What's the difference?" he asks.

"I'm trained to read weather models, make forecasts, and provide information to the public to keep them safe. A person who is not a certified meteorologist is usually just reporting a forecast someone else has made," she explains.

"Who makes the forecasts I get on my weather apps? Because those suckers are never correct," Levi pipes up from behind Grant.

"Weather apps just compile information from the different weather models. It's all computerized, so there's no human connection. Weather models don't have the ability to factor in other variables, such as how mountains can impact the weather. The Palmer Divide, between Denver and Colorado Springs? It'll create vastly different weather between the two locations. Meteorologists understand how to take topography and factor it into a forecast."

The bus is eerily quiet as we begin the short drive to the downtown hotel, while everyone listens to Becca as she animatedly describes different weather scenarios we experience in Denver. I watch, completely captivated, as she glows with happiness. It's clear Becca is doing what she loves, and it shows. I'm incredibly proud of my wife.

Wife.

That word does something to me, and as if she knows, her soft hand tentatively finds mine. As her hand closes around mine, her fingers graze the fabric of my trousers, and her words falter as she realizes what she's feeling.

I assume she'll move her hand away, or squeeze my hand tightly to avoid touching my cock. I grunt quietly when Becca doubles down, dragging two fingernails along my length. She does it again, and I swallow a moan.

How fucking far is this hotel?

I cannot come in my pants. I cannot come like a fucking teenage boy just because I got a brief touch from Becca.

"Are you okay?" she whispers, a twitch in the corner of her mouth telling me she's fighting a smile.

"What do you think?" I reply quietly. Her fingers move again, dragging from the tip all the way to the base of my cock, and I squeeze my eyes closed as I capture her hand in mine. As the bus slows down, I visualize every ball sack I can think of, trying to will my damn dick to calm the hell down.

Shit. It's not working.

Saggy old man balls.

Saggy and hairy old man balls.

Okay, that's working. Fuck, the bus has stopped, and it's so obvious I'm rocking a full chub right now.

Becca's brother's balls.

The old dude's balls who wants to marry off his son to Becca.

Alright, we're getting somewhere.

"Jacob," Becca whispers.

"Hmm?"

"Everyone is waiting for you to get up," she says. I snort as I carefully stand. Getting it up isn't the problem. Getting it down is. I rip my beanie off my head, choosing to hold it in my hand in front of my groin, as I exit the bus. Coach tells me to head to the desk to get a room key. Once we grab our luggage that the team so nicely brought over from the arena, I get a room key from the concierge before heading up to the eighteenth floor.

"Let's hope we don't get the honeymoon suite this time," I tell Becca with a grin.

"I don't know," she muses. "It might be nice to compare and contrast the two. It couldn't be as bad as the one in my hometown, right?"

"Only one way to find out," I tell her as we arrive at the room, furthest from the elevators. I wave the key card in front of the sensor, but as I grab hold of the door handle, I realize I'm forgetting an integral part of our wedding night. I push the door open, then shove our two rolling suitcases through the door. "Hold on, Spitfire. Gotta carry you over the threshold."

"What? Oh!" Becca shrieks as I pick her up gently, kicking the door open with the tip of my nice cowboy boots that I wear on many game days. Her hands immediately wrap around my neck, and I can't help but think about how nice it feels to have her in my arms. As I go to set her down on her feet, Becca doesn't let go, instead slowly sliding down the length of my body. I find myself tracing her hairline, tucking pieces behind both ears. She softly sighs, leaning in to my touch.

"I don't think I've ever wanted someone as much as I want you, darlin'," I confess, my voice husky as I drag a finger down the curve of her neck. Placing my thumb against her pulse point, I find it's beating wildly, and I wonder if mine is beating quicker than hers. I'm like a tightly coiled rope, desperately needing to be unraveled. Fuck, do I want to be unraveled by Becca.

"I've never had a man be so forthcoming with his desire for me," she whispers, her pupils darkening with lust. "If I'm being honest, it both excites and terrifies me."

"Terrifies you how?" I ask. "You know I'd never hurt you, don't you?"

She nods as her hands find purchase inside my suit coat, gripping my shirt tightly. "I'm terrified about what you make me feel. I'm afraid you're going to break my heart."

"Oh, darlin'," I say quietly, leaning forward to rest my forehead against hers. "I think I'm much more likely to end up with a broken heart."

I want to say so much more. How I feel like I've been waiting for her. That she's meant to be mine, and I'll proudly tell anyone that I'm hers. How just feeling her hand in mine brings me a peace I never knew existed, and that she already holds my heart in her hands.

But Becca isn't ready for me to profess my love and adoration for her. Instead, I'll patiently wait until she's as obsessed with me as I am with her.

Becca

CHAPTER 17

His beautiful blue eyes seem to be staring deep into my soul, and I'm suddenly apprehensive about what he might find. I know he's doing me a big favor by marrying me, and undoubtedly we'll go our separate ways at some point. But with every conversation, every intense look, I'm growing more connected to Jacob. And that scares the hell out of me.

"Jacob, please," I murmur, not sure what I need him to do. My entire body feels lit up, an energy buzzing along my skin as his eyes rake down and up my body.

"What do you need, darlin?" he rasps, dragging a fingertip between my breasts. "I need your words. Tell me what you want, and I'll give it to you."

"How do you know it'll be something you can give me?" I ask breathlessly.

"Because," he says with a lopsided smile that makes my heart skip a beat, "I'd do just about anything to ensure you get what you need."

Oh *my*.

"Kiss me," I whisper, unable to take one more second without feeling his lips against mine.

Jacob grins wickedly. "With pleasure."

He takes my mouth in a delicious kiss full of promise and lust. I can faintly taste the mint he popped at the end of the third period. He groans quietly, and the sound reverberates throughout my entire body. His tongue traces the seam of my lips, begging for entry. As soon as I feel the velvety softness rub against mine, my knees buckle, but Jacob catches me, slowly lowering me onto the bed.

"I promise I'll take my time with you later, okay, Spitfire? I swear I have every intention of memorizing your body, but if I don't bury myself inside you here shortly, I think I might die," Jacob says hoarsely. I have a momentary flash of disappointment, hoping he'd at least get me off first. I've never come from just intercourse, and I usually just tell the guy I came. I'm not the most experienced woman out there, but most men don't know what a real female orgasm feels like, and they take my word for it.

"What's that look for?" Jacob asks.

"What look? There's no look," I respond, a slight tremor evident in my voice. Jacob cocks his head to the side as he studies me.

"I literally just told you I want you to tell me what you need. I can't read your mind."

"It's nothing," I stammer, waving a hand nonchalantly. "I've just never been able to come from intercourse."

Jacob's mouth drops open. "Never? Never ever?"

I shake my head. "I can come other ways. Lots of women don't have orgasms when only penetration is used."

"Huh," he muses. "Can honestly say I've never noticed it."

I can't help the giggle that bursts from my lips. "Of course not. Most men don't know what a real female orgasm is."

"I never said that. No woman has ever told me she can't get off that way, but I guaran-damn-tee you that every woman I've ever slept with has left feeling incredibly satisfied."

"They could be lying to you, you know," I point out.

Jacob shrugs. "Darlin', there are a lot of things I'll admit I'm not good at. I suck at driving in snow, and I'm shit at organizing a grocery list. But pleasuring a woman? Knowing when she's coming so hard she blacks out? Yeah, I'm fucking amazing at that."

"She — she blacks out?" I whisper. "Is that normal?"

He shrugs again. "Not sure. Might just be normal for me, because it happens fairly regularly. I've got a good tongue."

Jesus. "You do have a good tongue."

He gives me a wicked grin. "When I said I needed to bury myself inside you, did you automatically assume I'd take care of myself, and not make sure you got yours too?"

I nod slowly.

"Hmm," he hums. "Seems my wife needs to learn a little more about how giving her husband is."

Jacob kisses me hard on the lips, then slowly slides down my body until he's kneeling next to the bed. I sit back on my elbows so I can watch him, and I notice a subtle pink flush on his neck. Is he as turned on as I am? As my breathing picks up, I watch as he leans forward to rest his chin against the juncture between my legs. I'm wearing a dress, as we went straight from the wedding chapel in Las Vegas to the game in Cleveland, and now I'm so happy I did.

Easy access.

I should push him away. It's been an incredibly long day where I haven't showered. But I just … can't. I can't stop the train that is Jacob, and I'm hoping he takes me straight to Orgasm Town.

I giggle under my breath as his hands slide underneath the dress, grabbing onto the sides of my panties. He pulls them down slowly, his eyes never leaving mine. It should be vulgar when he pulls them off my feet, leaving my heels on, and brings the fabric to his nose. Inhaling deeply, he lets out a guttural moan. "Jesus, Spitfire. You smell divine."

Finding my voice, I say clearly, "How about you find out if I taste better?"

A crooked grin grows on Jacob's handsome face as he chuckles. "That's my girl."

His girl. I almost comment on how much I like the sound of that, but Jacob takes the opportunity to bury his face between my legs, and I forget how to breathe, much less talk. His tongue hits my clit perfectly, circling it over and over again, and I feel my body tense up in preparation for an orgasm. It's been so long — too long — since I've been eaten out, and I didn't know how much I missed it.

Jacob drags his tongue to my entrance, lapping up the evidence of how turned on I am, before bringing it to my clit. Circling it rapidly, he pushes one finger inside me, immediately finding my G-spot. "Eyes open, darlin'. I want your eyes on me as you come."

He pushes another thick finger inside, and I clench tightly. When he sucks my clit between his lips and nibbles gently, I detonate. Eyes rolling back into my head, I arch my back as the wave of endorphins crashes over my body. It seems to go on for minutes as my body vibrates with shudders. I suddenly realize I'm panting, as I was so caught up in the orgasm that I forgot to breathe. I'm not sure the last time I had that intense of an orgasm. Maybe never.

"Wow," I mutter, and I feel Jacob chuckle against my pussy as he slowly laps at my release. Eyes unfocused, I can't seem to make eye contact with him. "There appear to be two of you."

He snorts, and the rush of air hits my skin like dynamite. I push away from him, closing my legs. The move pushes against my clit, sending a new rush of pleasure to my core. I could probably come again just by shifting my legs around a few times, that's how turned on I am.

When I finally open my eyes to focus, I find Jacob standing above me, his legs open in a perfect masculine stance. Belt open but still hanging through the loops of his pants, Jacob palms his rigid length as he stares at me wolfishly.

"What's that?" I ask, pointing to an odd indentation on his left shoulder.

He looks down at it before smirking. "The heel of your shoe."

I gasp. "Oh my God! Seriously? Why didn't you take them off?"

"Because," he says huskily, as he crawls over top of me, "I've had dreams about fucking you with your heels on. I'm all too happy to live my fantasy."

"They're normal heels, Jacob. They aren't even that sexy," I tell him. They aren't anything special, but I know they make my calves and butt look pretty spectacular.

"Anything you wear, Spitfire, I'm bound to find sexy," he says before kissing me deeply. The taste of myself on his tongue is an aphrodisiac, and I wrap my legs around his waist. "Get this dress off. I need you naked."

"Take it off me then," I reply sassily.

He cocks a brow at me. "You should set up some parameters for me, darlin'. If the only objective is to get the clothing off, I will rip each piece from your body. If you'd like to save the clothes, you gotta tell me beforehand."

Holy shit. "I'd, uh, like to keep this dress."

"It is a nice dress." Jacob looks me up and down. "Any dresses at home you'd be okay with me ripping off you?"

"I'm sure I can find something," I answer. He pulls me up to standing, motioning for me to turn around. He finds the zipper quickly, following its path with his tongue along my spine.

"Fucking hell, Spitfire. You've been without a bra all damn day?" he spits out.

"Well, I don't like strapless bras, and the top of this dress doesn't really account for wearing a bra anyway. My boobs are so small I don't need bras most of the time." As president of the itty bitty titty committee, I stare down at my A-cups with disdain. The only way my boobs get bigger is if I eat a hell of a lot more, and then the rest of my body gets bigger too. My dress drops to the floor, and I wait to see his next move.

"I only need a mouthful, baby," Jacob whispers as his arms slide around my waist and up to my chest, cupping my breasts reverently. "These are perfect. *You* are perfect."

I whimper as he plucks my nipples between his fingers. Tiny but super sensitive, and Jacob seems to hone in on that fact immediately. I feel his lips press against my pulse point, and I'm so close to coming. So close, in fact, it's almost embarrassing. I think it's been a slow foreplay with Jacob for weeks. Ever since he walked me home after dinner, holding my hand, I couldn't stop myself from imagining all the things he might do to me. I reach around to grab the backs of his thighs, and I feel the tension rippling through his muscle and sinew.

Turning around, I throw my arms around Jacob's shoulders, pulling his face down to mine. I need his mouth on me. He reaches down to grab my ass, lifting me, and I automatically wrap my legs around his hips. I feel his length hit me perfectly, and my body trembles with need and anticipation.

Jacob lowers me slowly, then stands to his full height. Grabbing on to one of my calves, he brings it to his mouth and applies the lightest of kisses, feathering his way down to my heels. "Don't you dare kick these off, darlin'. I want to feel them digging into my back."

I giggle breathlessly as he lets go of my leg, beginning to slowly unbutton his shirt. His gaze never leaves mine as I watch inch after bronzed inch appear before me. I knew he had tattoos on his left arm, but he has a smattering of tattoos across his chest as well. And oh, dear God, his abs. They look carved out of stone, and I subconsciously reach out to touch them.

Jacob grunts as my fingers find purchase, his eyes closing in bliss. His body trembles underneath my touch, and I'm emboldened by this. I've never had a man react so blatantly to me before, and it's intoxicating. I grab hold of his waistband, pulling him toward me, then unbutton his pants. "Eyes open, husband."

He groans, but dutifully opens his eyes. Pupils blown wide with lust, his gaze is intense. "Call me that again, wife."

"Husband," I whisper, loving the power one word has. He groans again, falling on top of me and crashing his lips against mine. This kiss is passion personified. It's unlike anything I've ever experienced. His tongue circles mine furiously as one hand latches into my hair, and the other pulls my leg up and around his waist. If

I died right this moment, I'd die happy, knowing I had the perfect kiss.

The orgasm a few moments ago didn't hurt either.

Jacob breaks off the kiss, panting. "Do you trust me?"

"Yes?" I answer, a questioning tone obvious.

"I'm clean."

"Okay?" Is he suggesting I need to shower? He just went down on me and didn't complain, so clearly I'm not understanding.

Jacob chuckles. "I'm telling you I've been tested recently, and I don't have any STD's."

I feel the burn of embarrassment coat my cheeks and neck. "Oh."

He presses his lips against mine for a moment. "Are you clean?"

"Yes," I whisper.

He exhales slowly, the heat of his breath searing across my skin. "I have a condom. I'll use it if you want me to, but there's nothing I want more than to feel you, darlin'. I want to feel every bit of your pussy clenching around me."

Holy hell. My voice squeaks out as I answer. "I'm on the pill."

He lets out a harsh exhale. "Fuck. I'm not going to last long, Spitfire."

Jacob stands, only to yank his pants and boxer briefs down, then grabs me underneath my arms and tosses me toward the top of the bed. Crawling after me, he fits himself perfectly between my legs, and as he bends to suck a nipple into his mouth, I feel the head of his cock at my entrance. I gasp when the cold barbell hits my skin. "Will that thing hurt?"

"My dick or the piercing?" he asks as he nibbles on my nipple, making me moan.

"Uh, both, I guess," I say with a laugh.

He raises his head to look at me. "Baby, you were made to take me."

Jacob inches forward, breaching my entrance, and I let out a guttural moan. It's been quite some time since I've had sex. I'd begun to accrue quite the supply of bedroom helpers to get me off when needed. I couldn't justify a one-night stand, or a friends-with-benefits situation, and I don't trust many men. Being in the public eye makes me extra cautious. Maybe I've just refused to settle, because I can already tell, as Jacob slowly fills me, that he's going to be a hard act to follow.

"See?" he groans as he bottoms out, circling his hips to rub against my clit. "Fuck, darlin'. You feel spectacular."

Pulling out almost to the tip, he slides in quickly, and I feel the frenum piercing stroke along nerve endings I didn't know I had. Jacob begins thrusting, those powerful thighs I grabbed moments ago being the star of the show. Grabbing one hand, he intertwines our fingers together and holds it next to my head, then slides a hand between our slick bodies. Finding my clit, he rubs steadily, and I feel another orgasm building.

Jacob's movements become unsteady, his eyes glazed over and unfocused. "Get there, baby," he grunts. "I need you to make me come."

"I like you calling me baby," I pant. He doesn't answer as he continues to stroke my clit, and my legs tense up as the exquisite wave crests over me. Arching my back, white spots dot my vision as I come harder than I've ever come before, clenching around Jacob so tightly he can barely move. He lets out a loud moan as he comes, and I feel his release coat my inner walls. We're panting in unison as he collapses on top of me, falling to the side so the bed bears the brunt of his weight, but he pulls me with him so we stay connected.

I've always been the kind of woman who found a lot of aspects of sex to be fairly gross. Intimacy in general has been somewhat difficult for me my entire life. It undoubtedly stems from my relationship with my father and brother, but sexual intimacy has been a challenge as well. I never wanted to feel a man's release leaking out of me. I didn't like a man's sweaty body against mine. Once we were done, I wanted to get dressed or shower, and go about my day.

But with Jacob, I'm reveling in this connection. I want to keep him buried inside me. I want him to cover me in his cum. I move my head slightly to stare up at him, my eyes wide as I take in his profile. He has a contented smile on his face, a sheen of perspiration across his skin, and I don't think I've ever seen a more beautiful man.

I'm falling for this man.

I am in big trouble.

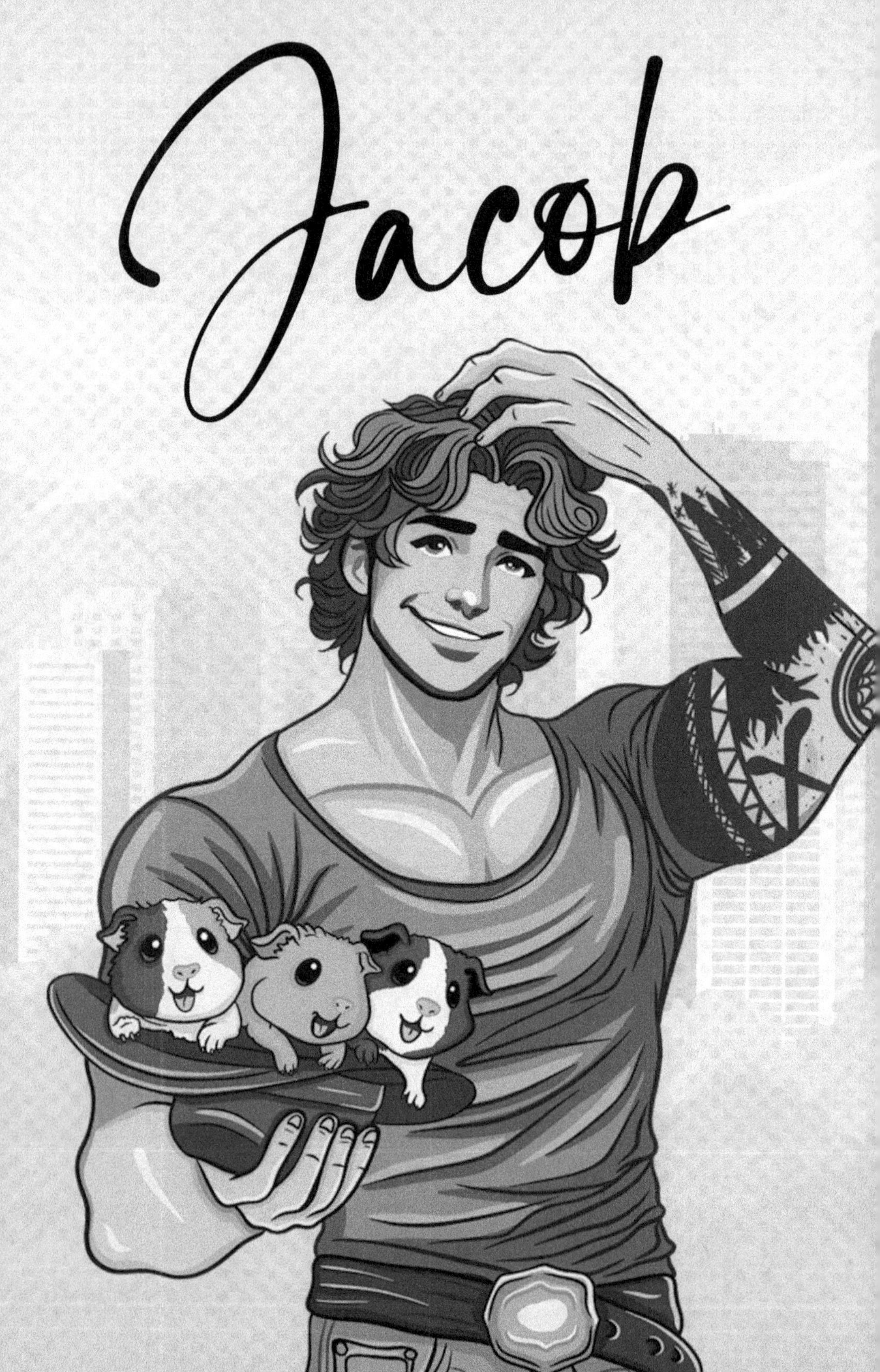
Jacob

CHAPTER 18

Sweet Jesus, I could live inside Becca's pussy and be incredibly happy.

The way she responded to me, and all the sounds she made, were fucking phenomenal. I'm not even sure she knew how responsive she was. Little moans, gasps, high-pitched sighs that had me two seconds from blowing my load.

Did I visualize my team all lined up in tube socks and jockstraps in an attempt to last longer? Yes. Yes, I did.

Becca sighs against me as she snuggles into my side, nuzzling my neck in contentment. Shit. I need to get a washcloth for her, and get her under the blankets. It's been an incredibly trying few days for her, and I know she's exhausted.

"No," she whimpers as I slide out from inside her, but I see the wince as my piercing drags along the nerves. "I like that thing."

"My dick or the piercing?" I ask with a chuckle.

She smiles softly. "Both."

Climbing off the bed, I head to the bathroom to retrieve a washcloth. Wetting it with warm water, I return to Becca to find her slowly scooting up to slide under the blankets. I grab her ankle to stop her before tenderly wiping between her thighs. She watches with eyes as wide as saucers. "Something wrong?"

"You just cleaned me," she whispers.

"I did."

"Is that normal?" she inquires.

My brow furrows in confusion. "I'm gonna need a little more information, darlin'. If you're asking if I take care of my woman after sex, then yes, it's normal. If you're wondering if I can last longer, then yeah. If you're wanting to know when we can do that again, I have every intention of waking you up at some point tonight."

Becca's ears tinge pink as her cheeks flush. "I meant the first part."

I fight the urge to smile. I'm loving how bashful she is right now. Tossing the washcloth onto the bathroom floor, I turn off the light and climb into bed beside my wife.

My wife.

Fuck, I love that.

Not giving Becca a chance to argue, I put my arm around her and pull her into my side. Burying my face in her hair, I speak. "There are a few things you'll learn about me, Spitfire, and some of them might piss you off because of how independent I know you are. Whenever you're with me, you won't open a door. Anywhere. I'll always make sure you're comfortable, no matter where we are. Better expect that I won't let you pay from now on. I'm open in the bedroom. You want to try something? Just talk to me. Rest assured, though, because you'll come first, and you'll come often. And yes, I'll be cleaning you up every time."

"Wow," she breathes. "Part of you is a gentleman, and part of you is a rake."

I let out a bark of laughter. "I don't know about that."

I feel her tense and hear her intake of breath as she debates on saying something, so I squeeze my arm around her tighter. "It's okay, darlin'. Just say what you want to say."

"Well, it's just —" she stammers. "You say you're open in the bedroom. What exactly does that mean? Open to trying positions, or bringing in some toys? Or open as in you'd want to bring other people in —"

I interrupt her immediately. "There will be no other people. I don't fucking share, Becca."

She lets out a loud exhale. "Oh thank God. I don't want anyone else in there. I don't like sharing either, you know."

"Good," I tell her, smiling against the top of her head.

I fall asleep with Becca tightly in my arms, and get the best sleep I've had in months.

Six hours later, we're boarding the team plane back to Denver. Coach must have warned the team, because every one of my team-mates stands to greet Becca warmly. As soon as I have Becca safely into the back of the plane, Levi motions for me to come to where he's sitting with Gabe and Grant.

"Care to explain why you didn't even have a girlfriend, and the woman who is now your wife wasn't even replying to your texts a week ago?" he asks pointedly.

"Long story. Becca has a shitty family, and I gladly helped her out by marrying her."

"Is this just a temporary thing?" Gabe asks.

I shrug. "She might think it is. But I'm gonna make her fall in love with me."

Grant snorts. "Pretty sure that's not how love works, oh Captain, my Captain."

"Can you quit it with the *Dead Poets' Society* reference, Nally? I had to Google that shit, and now my suggestions are weird." I cast a quick glance back at Becca, who is trying to seem nonchalant, surrounded by hockey players, but failing miserably. "I'm telling y'all, she's it for me. I knew she was different from the first moment I saw her."

I vaguely hear the door closing, but don't fully register it until I notice everyone around us stand up and start removing their clothes. "Fuck!"

Turning, I lunge back toward Becca, frantically waving my arms. Eyes bugging out of her head, and her mouth open in shock, I reach her and cover her eyes. "Jax!"

"God dammit, woman, I told you to call me Jacob," I mutter, forcing her head into my chest.

She laughs openly against me. "What is going on? Is this normal? Aren't there any females that travel with the team? They didn't do this for my benefit did they?"

I watch my teammates, suddenly furious that she saw them all in varying stages of undress. I'm by no means self-conscious. I know I'm in shape. Kinda have to be in this line of work. But I'm in my mid-thirties. I know some of the younger guys are packing more abs than me. "How much did you see?"

"Just everyone standing up, a couple shirts coming off, and then you flying back here to protect my virginal eyes," she cackles. "What was that?"

"You'd have done the same thing if a group of women suddenly started undressing in front of me."

"Are they done yet?" she asks, her voice muffled. "I feel like they all think I'm giving you a blow job right now."

Shit. She's right, and as soon as I let go of her head, she pops up, her hair in disarray. Fortunately, no one is looking at us. They're all comfortable and in their seats. "Sorry about that. Guess I got a little self-conscious there for a sec."

She gives me a sweet smile. "I don't see why you'd be. You're pretty impressive, Jacob Mitchell. Now tell me why they all did that."

"We always do it. No one wants to fly for hours in an uncomfortable suit."

"Do all teams undress on the plane?" she asks. "What about other sports?"

"No clue. Guess I'll have to ask my friend Jamie if the NFL teams do this as well. The NHL is a stickler for game day travel outfits, though. Other sports let guys dress however they want."

"Do you want to get undressed?" she asks shyly. Her hand finds my tie, tugging on it. "You do look handsome all dressed up, but I understand it must be cumbersome for a three or four hour flight."

"I'm fine. You better stop looking at me like that, though, or I'll have us joining the mile high club here before long."

Becca blinks rapidly. "You most certainly will not. Have you seen those bathrooms? They're disgusting, and there isn't enough room for anything good to happen."

I fake stretching before laying my arm around her shoulders. "I don't know how much you know about hockey players, but we're actually pretty flexible."

She cocks a brow at me. "Is that so?"

I nod, leaning toward Becca and pecking her lips quickly. "If you want to find out how bendy I am, just say the word."

Usually on trips, I'm in my own little world. I might read, take a nap, or zone out while listening to some music. None of that happens with Becca next to me. When we weren't talking, I found myself just watching her. I truly don't think she knows how beautiful she is. Physically, yes. But her soul is what speaks to me. Her breathtaking soul makes me want to do anything to make her happy.

We talked about where we both like to hike, and how she thinks her dog will react to me. I've yet to broach the subject of my guinea pig room to her in full. Most people think I'm embellishing details.

That it's probably just a big cage or two. Nope, it's a whole ass room.

We discussed what we both like to eat, and I found that our daily diets are pretty in tune with one another. At first, when Becca started talking about clean eating, I worried she thought she was fat. That isn't the case. She's very conscientious of what she puts in her body, especially colorants and chemicals. When I told her I love to cook when I can, she excitedly began making plans for all the healthy meals we can prepare together each week.

I asked if she'd be okay with moving in with me, and she agreed. I have the space. My apartment is probably too big for just me and the pigs. Besides, I like knowing she'll be in a safer apartment building when I'm on away trips.

Becca falls asleep as we're beginning our approach into Denver, and I'm surprised when her phone vibrates with an incoming call. Being a nosy husband, I look at the screen, only to growl when I see it's her brother. Leaning away from Becca, I answer the call.

"What the fuck do you want, asshole?" I hiss.

"Oh. It's the *husband*," Rodney sneers. "Interesting that it seems you only got married last night, when my dear sister insinuated you were already legally wed."

"Really doesn't matter now, does it? She's my wife, and you can go fuck yourself."

"My, my. Hockey players sure do have vulgar mouths," he says cheerfully. "It doesn't matter. Your marriage will end, one way or another, and I'll get my way."

"The fuck you will," I snarl. "Let me make something perfectly clear, Ronald."

"It's Rodney."

"I literally don't fucking care." I cast a quick glance down at Becca, wondering if she's faking sleep, as I continue. "You so much as glance at my wife, and I'll make you pay. You've very much underestimated me. I will stop at nothing to protect her. Understood?"

Rodney laughs heartily. "You won't do a damn thing. It would end your precious hockey career."

"You think I care about that? I've got the girl of my dreams and millions in my bank accounts. Test me, Randolph. Just fucking test me. Lose this fucking number."

I end the call, then go into Becca's contacts and find Rodney's info. First, I forward his contact to my phone, and then I block him from Becca's. Good riddance.

"He won't stop until I do what he wants," Becca says clearly, jarring me. Her head pops up, and a sheen of tears threatens to spill down her cheeks. "He won't stop. He'll drag you through the media. He'll get you fired. He'll go after your money. It won't end until he gets his way."

Turning, I gently grasp her chin with my thumb and forefinger. "Sounds like your brother and I share a couple of traits. Tenacity being one of them, but also stubbornness. I'll be damned if I let that little jackass try to bully me into giving you up. You're mine, darlin'. And I protect what's mine."

She gives me a shaky smile, but it doesn't reach her eyes. "No one has ever called me theirs before. Does that mean you're mine as well?"

"Fuck yes, it does," I whisper as I kiss her deeply. No one has ever called me theirs either, and fuck if that doesn't make me realize something monumental.

I'm in love with this woman. I know it. She brings a peace to me that I never thought possible. I felt a pull toward her from the moment she ran into me, and it didn't lessen, even when we didn't talk.

I told the guys I would make Becca fall in love with me, so now I have to figure out exactly how to do it.

Becca

CHAPTER 19

"You said he's friendly, right?" Jacob murmurs as he follows me into my apartment building elevator.

I laugh. "Thunder has never met a stranger. He'll probably lead you to where I keep the knives."

Jacob's brows shoot up to his hairline. "Why the knives?"

"I would have said he'd lead you to where I keep my jewelry, but I don't have anything worth any money. Knives are probably the nicest thing in my apartment. Well, a couple pairs of shoes were fairly costly."

Jacob slides an arm around my waist, squeezing me into his side. "I happen to think heels are an excellent use of money, darlin'."

I feel a blush cover my neck as I shyly look down at the floor. I love how Jacob flirts with me, but I'm still pretty awkward, and I'm not sure I even know if I'm flirting back or not.

"Let's hope Thunder doesn't bring any criminals to the knives. Speaking of the kitchen, I just want to confirm that you weren't exaggerating about liking to cook. If so, that really makes me happy," Jacob says with a hint of a smile.

I nod. "I'm really happy that you like to cook too."

"I use a meal service for a lot of healthy meals, but when I have down time, I really enjoy cooking. It's pretty calming. I'm not the best chef out there, but I can handle some easy things."

"I've taken cooking classes to help me learn," I confess. "My parents wouldn't let me in the kitchen very much growing up. We had a chef, and my mother worried if I learned to cook, or had too much free time in the kitchen, I'd get fat."

"I fucking hate that woman," Jacob mutters under his breath. Reaching my floor, he follows me down the hall. I hear Thunder's woof as we approach. "Who watched Thunder while we were gone?"

"My neighbor's daughter, Ainsley. She's saving for college, and was all too thrilled to make a couple hundred to feed Thunder and walk him a few times a day. Usually I have Thunder at a doggie daycare facility, but they didn't have room for him on such short notice."

Perfectly timed, we pass Ainsley, and she tells me she just walked Thunder, and played with him for thirty minutes. As we approach my apartment, I'm hopeful it means Thunder will be calmer.

Unlocking the door, a flurry of yellow fur dances next to me, whining, but then stops completely. Thunder looks up at Jacob for a moment before barking, then leaps into Jacob's arms. "Woah! Hey, buddy. Guess we're friends now."

Thunder licks the entire length of Jacob's face, making him chuckle. "I told you he doesn't know a stranger."

"I hope he's okay with the pigs," Jacob comments as he carefully puts Thunder down. "They've never had a dog in the apartment, but I rarely let them just wander around. Probably best to keep him out of their room, though."

"I thought you were embellishing about them having an entire room" I say.

"Yeah, I wasn't kidding about that. They have an entire room," Jacob answers, ambling around my apartment. I know his apartment has probably double, or triple, the amount of square feet, but I love my space. Soft purple lace curtains cover the large windows, and little trinkets, from all the places I've lived, cover a coffee table and bookshelf. A few of my favorite romance books lay haphazardly on the bookshelf. I prefer to read on my Kindle, but every now and again, I'm so struck by a book that I need to have it on my shelf as a constant reminder of how much I love it.

"This space is so … you," Jacob says quietly.

My hackles go up. "What does that mean?"

His head pops up, and his eyes widen. "Oh, not in a bad way, Spitfire. I can see how much you love living here. It represents you, and your path to get here. I can imagine you cuddling on the couch with Thunder, undoubtedly under that thick blanket you have across the back, and watching a movie. I can see you happily cooking in this kitchen."

"Oh," I whisper.

Jacob approaches me slowly, lowering his voice. "I gotta be honest with you, darlin'. I'm afraid once you get to my apartment, and you see how … bland it is, you won't want to be there. It's nothing like this. But I really want you to be with me."

Looking into his blue eyes, I can see the sincerity in them. "I like that you're honest about what you're thinking. You don't hide things."

He cocks his head to the side, studying me. "I have no reason to hide things from you. I believe communication is the most important part of a relationship. I hope that you'll trust me enough to tell me what you're thinking, too."

"Okay," I answer, nodding as a smile breaks across my face. "But maybe we could bring some of my things to your apartment? That way there's more color."

"Darlin'," Jacob says as he pulls me into his arms, "I don't care what you bring. Hell, bring it all if you want. I just want *you*."

Butterflies erupt in my stomach as he places his lips on mine, and I sigh softly into his mouth. One hand comes up to tangle in my hair as I circle my arms around his waist. I'm against the nearest wall before I even realize Jacob walked us there, and he lifts me to wrap my legs around his waist. He nips at my lips as I settle my core against him, feeling his rigid length hit me perfectly. Emboldened, I decide to tell him what I'm thinking.

"I've never been with a man who's pierced before. Well, before you," I blurt out against his lips.

"What?" Jacob asks, the word harsh as his breath hits my face.

"Well, I haven't. My experience is pretty limited. So I researched it. Yours. I mean your piercing. I learned way too much about penile piercings, to be honest, and somehow that led to me learning about female piercings, and holy moly, there are a lot of options down there. But for yours, it suggested I'd enjoy it best if you were behind me? So I'd like to do that. Sex. The behind kind. Wait! Not the *behind* kind. Not that sex. I'm so not ready for that. Oh my word. Can I just be put out of my misery right now?"

"Fucking hell, Spitfire, you are an absolute treasure," Jacob blurts out before throwing his head back in laughter. My face burns in complete humiliation. I attempt to loosen my legs from around him so I can go hide in the bathroom, but his arms clamp down on my thighs, his hands on my ass. "No. You're not running away. I don't know anything about piercings, other than my own, but if that's something you're interested in, I can learn. What we had last night was phenomenal, darlin', and I'm not rushing you into anything else, even the behind kind. But you are right, you'll feel it best if I'm behind you. The piercing will hit your G-spot that way. And I want you to always trust me to hear your thoughts. You don't have to act around me, Becca. I don't expect the perfect version your family expected. Just you, baby. I just want you."

Not knowing how to respond, I pull him toward me for a kiss. He kisses me softly, slowly, and so tenderly that I feel tears pool behind my eyelids. It's an odd juxtaposition to go from talking about G-spots and piercings, to feeling like he's getting ready to make love to me. The hand that was wrapped up in my hair slides around to cup my cheek, and I'm immediately a puddle of goo.

"Where's your bedroom, darlin'?" he asks against my mouth. I point down the short hallway on the other side of the kitchen, and

Jacob takes off, his legs making long strides across the short distance. He stops at the doorway, looking down at Thunder, who faithfully trotted behind us. "Sorry, buddy. Adults only this time, but I promise we'll make it up to you."

Shutting the door, Jacob doesn't look around. His eyes are solely focused on me, and I can't look away. His gaze is intense, and now that I know what he can do in the bedroom, I'm all too excited to experience it again. He kneels, placing me on the edge of the bed, and begins removing my shoes and socks. I quickly begin unbuttoning his shirt, then spread my hands across his pecs. He really is beautiful.

"Arms up," he whispers huskily, and I oblige. He removes my shirt, then pulls my bra straps off my shoulders. I reach around to unhook it, letting it fall into my lap. "You are so fucking spectacular, Becca. I don't think I'll ever get over feeling like this. I can't believe you're mine."

Goosebumps erupt as his fingers leisurely stroll along my skin, and I whimper softly. "Please, Jacob."

"Please, what? What do you need, baby?" he asks, leaning in to place a light kiss on my collarbone.

"I need you. I need you to make love to me."

He lets out a muffled curse as he rests his forehead against mine. "I hope this doesn't scare you. I really hope you don't freak out. But I can't not tell you. I'm falling for you, Becca. And hearing you say you need me to make love to you? It's like my dreams just came true. I'm not letting you go. Whenever this drama is done with your family, I'm not letting you go."

I'm falling for him. I know it. But I can't say the words. Every man in my life has failed me, for one reason or another, and I'm petrified Jacob will do the same. Instead, I pull him to me again, kissing him deeply. He helps me remove my pants, then slips out of his. Climbing onto the bed above me, only our underwear separate us, but now it's not so much about sex. It's about the connection we're both feeling, whether I'm able to verbalize it or not.

We make out like teenagers for an ungodly amount of time. I

find myself paying attention to his body, and reactions, to see how I can make him unravel. Jacob likes it when I suck on his tongue, and when I drag my fingernails up his spine. He really loves when I scratch his scalp, and the guttural groan he lets out whenever I nibble on his lower lip tells me he's a big fan of that move. Without stopping a deep kiss, we each slide our underwear off so we're fully skin to skin.

When Jacob suddenly sits up, I let out a sputtering, "What's wrong? Did I do something wrong?"

"No, not at all. Just want to try something." He grabs my arm, pulling me up, then motions for me to climb in his lap as he sits on the edge of the bed. Once I do, I realize how intimate the position is. He's all I see. Feel. Hear.

I wonder if our heartbeats are in sync, and if he can hear mine pounding.

Jacob shifts slightly, and I feel him notched at my entrance. Pushing in slowly, his eyes never leave mine. I forget to breathe as he fills me, feeling so overwhelmed with pleasure and lust. It feels so right, and that scares the hell out of me.

I shimmy my hips a little, then gasp when I feel his piercing hit a deep spot inside me. Jacob grabs hold of my waist, picking me up before slamming me down again. Over and over he moves me along his shaft, and my orgasm builds. Then everything stops again.

"You wanted me to hit it from behind, so stand up," Jacob grunts, his face covered with a sheen of perspiration. I stand, then look down at his lap.

"Wow," I breathe.

"What?"

"I've never seen one like this before."

"You saw mine last night, darlin'. It's the same dick." While his voice is deadpan, a hint of a smile twitches on Jacob's face, and his eyes sparkle with amusement.

"But I didn't see it covered in me," I blurt out, and the amusement fades from his eyes.

"Turn around and back up," he demands, his voice a full octave lower. As I do what he says, unsure what is about to happen, I wonder if when he said, "hit it", did he mean spanking? I really don't think that's my kink, but I don't know how to explain that. "Put your legs up on each side of me. Like before, but backwards."

Oh.

I carefully position my legs as Jacob's arms encircle me, pushing my back against his front. His breath is hot against my ear. "This also means I have better access to your tits and your clit. How many times you think you can come before I do?"

"Is that a rhetorical question?" I wonder aloud.

"No, I'd like you to take a gander at a guess."

"Two."

Jacob laughs. "I'm thinking at least four."

"Jacob, I don't think I've come four times when I'm masturbating, much less with someone else —" I lose my train of thought when he pushes inside me, and that piercing slides right across my G-spot. My head drops back to rest on his shoulder as I'm completely overcome by the wave of pleasure that hits me. When he slides in again, he simultaneously pinches my clit and one nipple, and I immediately come.

"That's one," he grunts. He continues to manipulate my body, and I am a quivering, sweaty mess. Orgasms two and three are of the same caliber, and I'm close to passing out. The intensity of the barbell sliding along my G-spot is unlike anything I could ever imagine.

"Jacob, no more," I murmur, unsure if my voice is loud enough to be heard. Honestly, I may have only said that in my head.

"You've got one more in you. You're coming with me this time," he responds, his voice strained as his thrusts pick up in speed. He grabs my neck to turn my head, kissing me harshly as his other hand finds my clit again. I scream into his mouth as I come, then completely black out.

"Earth to Becca. Come on, darlin'. I need to see those pretty eyes."

Eyelids slowly opening, I peer up at a serious Jacob. "What happened?"

He lets out a relieved breath. "You passed out. Scared the hell out of me, Spitfire."

"I thought you said you knew when a woman was about to pass out," I murmur.

"It's different because it's you," he responds quietly.

I stretch my arms above my head, and notice my body hums with pleasure. "I'm not even a little bit sorry."

"I'm not surprised. Told you I could get four out of you. We'll have to work up to six, but I think we can do it. I'm more than willing to practice," he says, a cheeky glint in his eye.

"What a gentleman," I tease. A muffled bark sounds from the other side of my bedroom door, and I gasp. "How long have we been in here? I should walk Thunder."

"How about I walk him while you pack up some things for the two of you?" Jacob offers.

"Oh, I assumed you'd want me to move in sometime later. Not today," I say nervously.

"We're both off today, so it makes the most sense to get you over there and somewhat settled. I have to leave for another away trip in a couple days, and I want you in my building before then."

"Why?"

"Security is tight there, and I have a parking garage that'll be safer for you. There's even a dog run and park for Thunder on one of the roofs."

"Seriously? On a roof? I'd be a nervous wreck on a high rise roof with a dog," I confess. Thunder is my baby. I'd be inconsolable if something happened to him.

"No, it's on the third floor, I think. It's above the building pool and gym. Thunder will like it. Some of my teammates that live in the building have dogs, and they all say it's nice and convenient. Really great for winter storms too."

I'm quiet as we both get off the bed and dress. Too many questions stream through my head. If and when this ends, how does it play out? Should I keep my apartment as a precaution? How will Thunder handle moving? Am I really in danger in my building, or is Jacob just being a little overdramatic about my brother?

"Darlin'," Jacob says softly, sliding an arm around my waist. "I want you with me. You're my wife. I want to wake up every morning next to you, and cook dinner with you whenever I can. I can't wait to see your makeup cluttering the bathroom counter, and have your shoes next to mine at the door. Please."

God, he's so sweet.

I'm not sure what I did to deserve a man like Jacob, but I don't want to give him back.

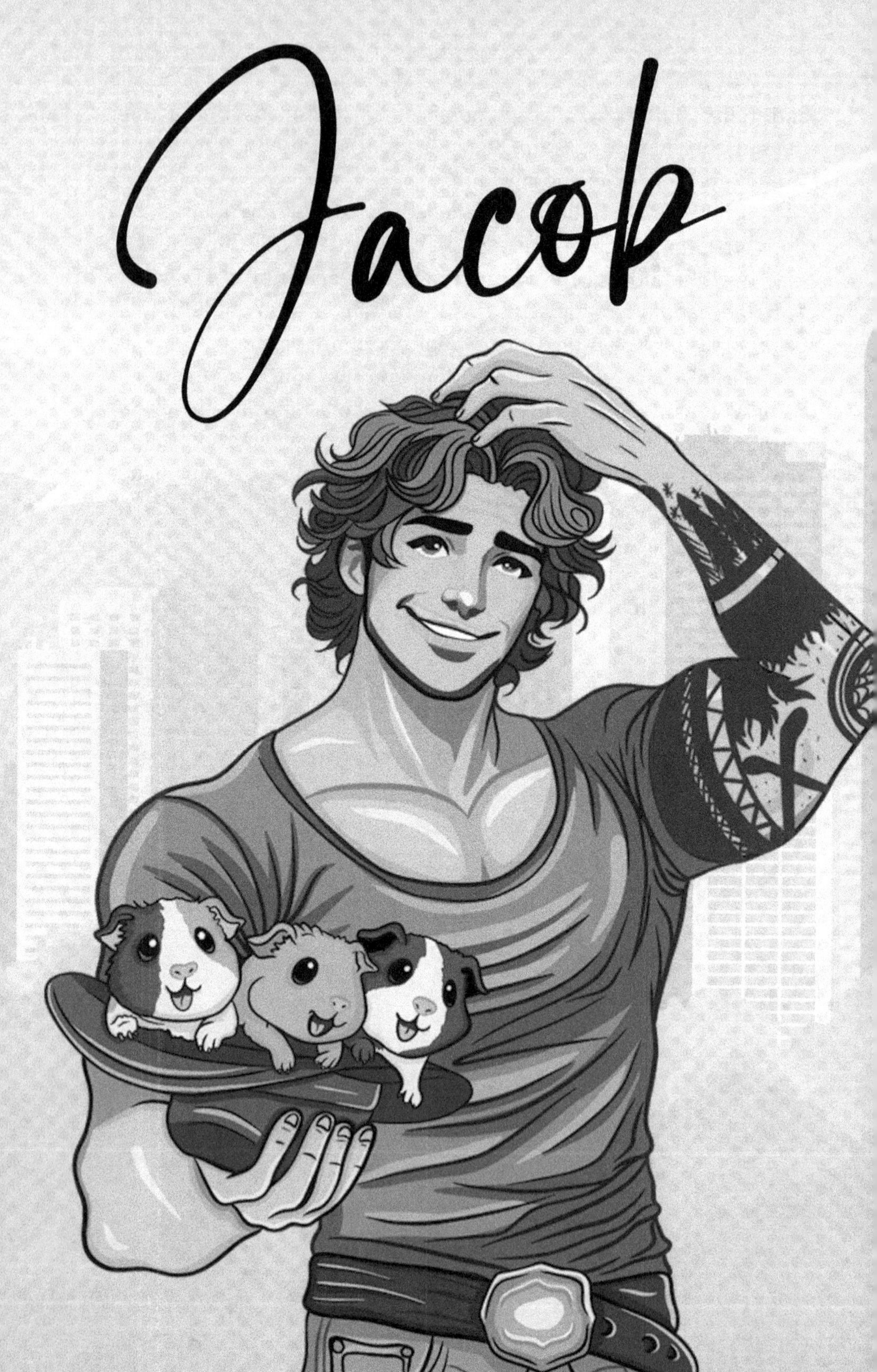

Jacob

CHAPTER 20

As Thunder and I make our way down to the street, I realize this is the first time I've ever walked a dog.

When we get outside the building, Thunder looks up at me in confusion. "I don't know what I'm supposed to do here, dude. Lead the way."

Evidently, that worked, because Thunder launches to the west, dragging me with him. The walk takes much longer than I anticipated, due to stopping at every pole along the way so Thunder can sniff and then mark his territory. Didn't the neighbor say she had just walked him? Where is he storing all of this fluid?

"You can't have any more pee in there," I murmur as he squats, but then I realize what he's actually doing. "Shit. I'm supposed to clean this up, aren't I?"

"You better clean it up, young man! This is a nice block," a woman shouts.

I wave at her. "I got it."

I don't got it.

I should have asked more questions. I volunteered to walk Thunder to give Becca a bit of time to herself. I could tell she was overwhelmed. Clearly, I handle spontaneity better than her, because I've always rolled with the punches of life. But her world has really been thrown a curveball with the death of her father. Then she's suddenly married to me. She has a trial-by-fire into the hockey WAG lifestyle, and now I'm asking her to move in with me.

So she gets a few minutes without me breathing down her neck.

"The bags are on the leash!" Jesus, old lady. I would have figured it out.

"Yeah, okay. I'm good."

"No, you're not," she cackles.

Yeah, I'm grossed out that I'm going to be picking up dog poop with only the thinnest pieces of plastic known to man separating it from touching my skin.

Once I get the bag pulled out of the odd contraption Becca has attached to the leash, I decide to double — no, triple — bag it as a precaution. Sue me, this is my first time. I'm a dog shit virgin.

Thunder gives me one hell of a side-eye as I grimace while cleaning up his mess. "Did you eat a whale, my guy? Why is there this much?"

He sighs, completely over me. Trust me, I get it.

Carefully tying a knot in the bag, I look around for a trash can to dump Thunder's droppings. Spotting one across the street, we jog over to get rid of the nastiness. Thunder continues west, away from Becca's apartment, and as I'm about to pull him to turn around, my phone dings with a text. Hoping it's Becca, I'm only slightly disappointed when it's my group text with the guys.

I've managed to master the art of texting while walking, and while adding in a leashed dog is a new challenge, I open the group text to see what shenanigans my teammates are up to.

LEVI

I think we should break this text into the marrieds and the non-marrieds.

NALLY

I agree.

DAWS

Why?

NALLY

Because all you guys do is talk about your wives and babies and shit like that.

DAWS

It was literally just me married until yesterday. Well, technically Santzy was in the group chat for a bit, until someone pissed him off and he left.

ME

YOU pissed him off, Daws. You did that. I tried to add him back in, but he wouldn't let me.

DAWS

Me? No. It couldn't be.

NALLY

Oh it was totally you. You reminded him that you hit on his wife before he was with her.

LEVI

In Gabe's defense, he teased Luca about that more than once, but that last time Luca decided enough was enough.

ME

It weirds me out that you refuse to call anyone by their nicknames, Levi. I really should share YOUR nickname.

LEVI

I will end you.

NALLY

Still can't believe Jax knows it but no one else does.

DAWS

It has to be something good.

LEVI

ANYWAY. How is married life treating you, Jacob?

ME

No. You don't get to call me Jacob. Only my wife gets to call me that.

NALLY

Ooooooo, his WIFE! Look at him being all possessive and married.

DAWS

Just wait, Nally. You'll find out when you meet your person. It's different. Any of you piss off Cassie, I'll end you, too.

NALLY

Dude. That's my sister you're talking about. I piss her off daily.

DAWS

Yeah, she won't let me murder you. Something about sibling love and that your parents would be upset. I don't know, man. Not sure what she's thinking.

NALLY

Nice. I feel the love. Hey, Cass said you guys were getting Chinese tonight from that restaurant we all love. You got enough for me?

DAWS

I swear to God, Nally, if you show up here for food AGAIN I will not be held responsible for my actions.

LEVI

Can you two take the lovers quarrel into a
private text exchange? The rest of us don't
need to see this.

ME

Speak for yourself. It's like a soap opera.
Don't take away my fun, Levi. My show
is on.

DAWS

You'd really think it was a soap opera if you
knew what Nally told his sister last week.

NALLY

GOD DAMMIT IS NOTHING SACRED
BETWEEN A BROTHER AND SISTER??

DAWS

Not when I know exactly how to get secrets
out of my woman.

NALLY

Ew.

LEVI

I stand by my original statement for
separate group texts.

DAWS

Nope. I enjoy terrorizing everyone in here
way too much. In fact …

(DAWS ADDED LUCA SANTO TO THE GROUP.)
SANTZY

NO.

ME

Come on, Santzy. Betcha don't even know I
got married this week.

SANTZY

The fuck? Seriously?

DAWS

This is why you have to stay in the group text, asshole. You miss very important information.

SANTZY

We define "important" differently, Daws. You shared a picture of a dirty diaper a while ago.

DAWS

I had to ask someone if it was normal!

SANTZY

None of us had kids at that time.

LEVI

That was an overshare.

ME

I found it fascinating. Crazy how a little baby can drop that much shit.

SANTZY

No more diaper pictures. No pics of weird moles or growths anywhere. If you wouldn't ask your parents a question, don't ask it in here. Those are my stipulations for staying in the group text.

DAWS

Party pooper.

DAWS

What about pictures of Mackenzie covered in food, finger paint, or any kind of goo?

SANTZY

I'll allow it.

DAWS

(sends picture)

"What's got you smiling over there?" My head pops up as I hear Becca's sweet voice. "You were gone so long I was getting worried."

"Sorry. Thunder had to mark every surface he could find, and then I got caught up in a group text with some of the guys on the team. Did you get everything that you want to bring to my place packed up ? Wait. Our place."

Becca giggles. "You've really gone all in on this."

"I have. I'm the kind of person that embraces life. Once I'm settled on something, I'm all in. Why half-ass your way through life?"

"I guess, it's just …" she trails off.

"What?"

Becca sighs. "It's hard for me to go all in with things. I keep thinking of every worst-case scenario. It seems like we're moving at warp speed, and that scares me."

I pull her into my arms, and she burrows her face into my neck. "I can understand that. I want you to trust me, that I'll never consciously try to hurt you. Take it to heart when I say that I'm playing the long game here. This isn't just a blip on the radar. But if it freaks you out to think about the future, how about we just take it day by day?"

She nods against me, her hand drifting down to pet Thunder's head. "Will it offend you if I keep my apartment for the time being?"

A little, but I'm not telling her that. I'm trying to be patient. "If that's what you need to give you some peace, then keep your apartment. But you're sleeping in my bed."

She laughs again, and the sound is the most beautiful melody. "Okay."

"Wow." Becca's eyes are enormous as she looks around my apartment. I don't have the biggest place on the team, but it's more than enough space for me and the pigs. Even adding Becca and Thunder to the mix won't be a problem. Hell, they could both have their own rooms — which absolutely will not happen, because I meant what I said about Becca sleeping with me — and we'd still have extra space.

"Woah," she says, as she looks at a prominent wall featuring bookshelves and most of my cowboy hats. Once a Texan, always a Texan. "Do you wear those often?"

"Not as much anymore," I admit. "It's more that I like to collect them. Each hat has a memory attached to it. They all matter to me."

Becca glances at me with a smile. "I like that. You're sentimental. That's cute."

"I'm not cute," I huff, crossing my arms over my chest in mock anger. The move makes my muscles pop, and Becca's eyes immediately drop. My lips twitch as I try to contain the responding grin. "Cowboy hats are manly. Sophisticated. They're making a statement."

"Okay, Mr. Cowboy," she laughs. "Settle down. I like the hats."

"Good." I'd already planned to take the hats down. Now that Becca is here, I want a more stylish space that showcases both of us. A wall of cowboy hats ain't it.

"This view is phenomenal!" she gushes, stepping up to the floor-to-ceiling windows looking out to the northwest. "I can totally visualize drinking my morning coffee on your balcony. I bet watching sunsets is amazing, too."

"They are pretty spectacular," I answer simply. I want to correct her again. It's not my balcony, it's *our* balcony. *Our* apartment. *Our* bedroom.

Patience, Jax.

"You want the dollar tour?" I ask, and she nods gleefully. I look warily at Thunder, who has parked himself outside the pigs' door, his nose smashed against the slim opening. "He can't open doors, can he?"

"I don't think so. I've never seen him try," Becca answers as Thunder scratches at the door. She looks at me with a laugh. "Probably best to put a lock on it, though. Just in case."

"I can ask the building superintendent if they have doorknobs with locks. It never occurred to me until right now that none of my secondary bedrooms have doors that lock," I muse.

I make a mental note to ask the building staff about a locking mechanism. I'll be the first to admit I'm not the handiest guy out there. I don't know my way around cars, and my tool set was a gift from someone years ago. I'm not even sure I've opened it. My expertise is focused on a hockey rink, and a farm. I may not be able to fix a broken dishwasher, but I can hold down a calf that needs to get an ear tag. That has to count for something, right?

I show Becca the kitchen and spare bedrooms, then the small office I rarely use. Her eyes light up at the space, and she shyly asks if she can use it for creating long range weather forecasts. She explains that she does a quarterly video where she goes into detail about how each weather model works, as well as explaining different weather terms like the jet stream and El Niño, which is a climate pattern when ocean temperatures are unusually warm around Christmas. She tells me that she makes dozens of visits to local elementary schools every year, helping kids learn some terminology, and not to be afraid of some of the scarier weather phenomena.

Becca's eyes sparkle as she launches into a monologue about women in STEM fields, and how less than ten percent of chief meteorologists in the country are female. She's determined to spotlight the field, and I love the fire and tenacity I can hear in her voice.

My girl is one smart cookie.

"I've sort of taken over this closet, but I'll make room for your things. In all honesty, I didn't expect to be coming home from a road trip with a wife, or I'd have had half the closet ready for you. I mean, I asked the gal who checks on my pigs to move some of my clothes, but she wasn't available." I'm somewhat chagrined as I tell Becca this, as if either of us could have predicted our whirlwind marriage.

"What?" Becca says sarcastically, rolling her eyes. "I bet you ask women to marry you before every away game."

"Only the chief meteorologists," I quip, and Becca beams. "The en suite bathroom is through this door."

Becca gasps when she sees an enormous soaking tub and steam shower in the large gray bathroom. "I'd have moved in here just for that tub."

"Feeling the love here, Spitfire," I remark dryly. She shoots me a glance and lightly slaps my arm.

"I haven't had a soaking tub since I left home. Baths are my favorite kind of self-care. I could never justify the expense to get an apartment with one though."

"This one is all yours. I use it occasionally, but only if my legs are really sore and tight." The thought of sharing a bath with Becca, though, makes me rethink my stance on baths.

"I can't wait to get some bath bombs, bubble bath, and Epsom salts!" she exclaims gleefully, clapping her hands together with a giant smile covering her face.

"Glad that makes you happy, baby," I say quietly. Clearing my throat, I motion for her to walk out of the bathroom. "You ready to meet my girls?"

"Your girls?" she asks quizzically.

"Yup."

"Should I be concerned? Nervous?"

"Concerned? No. You're the top girl. Nervous? Also no. As long as you bring them fresh produce, they'll love you."

Stopping in the kitchen, I notice that the pet sitter brought some more vegetables, and grab the last portion of spinach. As soon as I crinkle the bag, all six guinea pigs start squealing. Becca lets out her own surprised squeal, then giggles at herself. "Noisy bunch."

"If you think they're noisy now, you may be unprepared for the sound when we're in the room. I had contractors come out to add insulation around that room because the neighbor upstairs complained. I had no idea the sound carried that much."

Thunder waits patiently at the guinea pig door, and he jumps up hopefully as we approach. "Sorry, Thunder. Not yet."

"Is it just me, or is he pouting?" Becca whispers, and I look down to see the saddest expression I've ever seen on a dog. Thunder whines as his front paws tap impatiently against the hardwood floors. Poor guy. But I'm sure the pigs can smell him already, and I'd like them to acclimate a little before we have a face-to-face introduction.

"Yeah, I'd say he is," I respond as I carefully open the door. After Becca enters, I quickly move into the room, shutting the door behind me.

All six guinea pigs look at us for a moment, seemingly surprised at the new addition, before all hell breaks loose.

Lily screams her cute little head off.

Rose backs up to the side of a cage, kicking the bedding out as fast as she can.

Daffodil takes off down one of the tubes too quickly, and a piece comes unhooked, trapping her against the exit.

Bluebell is in one of the wheels peeing, and it's flying out the back to hit Daisy, who just stares at me and squeals. Daisy is the eater of the bunch. She's quite a bit bigger than the rest of the girls, and she will bum-rush them to get to food first.

And my littlest pig, Dahlia, runs around a track in one of the cages, then takes off down a section of tubes. The vet said she has anxiety, and prescribed medication.

After the third time she bit me, I gave up on the meds. So what if my guinea pig is anxious? Surrounded by this chaos, I can understand her feelings.

"Wow," Becca breathes, her eyes wide as she takes in the chaos. "This is quite the setup you've got here."

I shrug, scratching the back of my neck as I try to remain nonchalant. Hardly anyone knows about my pigs. I get it. I'm a big, tough hockey player, yet I have a room devoted to six guinea pigs. Quite the contrast. "You're probably thinking it's really weird, huh."

"No," Becca replies simply. "Honestly, I think it's cute. Have you always had guinea pigs as pets?"

"I wasn't allowed to have pets growing up," I admit sheepishly. "But I've always had a thing for guinea pigs. I only planned on getting one, but …"

"Now you have your own personal guinea pig harem," Becca jokes. "What are their names?"

I spend the next few minutes telling my wife all about my fascination with guinea pigs, how the floral names they have are not for any reason, and how I come into the room each morning to have a cup of coffee to watch them. It's oddly peaceful listening to them chirp and squeal.

"When you're on away trips, will I need to do anything specific?"

"Oh, well, uh, no?" I respond, staring at her in confusion. "I have a pet sitter."

Becca cocks her head to the side, studying me. "But if I'm here, I can take care of them. Unless you don't want me to?"

"I guess I assumed you wouldn't want to."

She turns her head back to watch as Daffodil kicks the tube back into place, successfully making her way back into one of the cages. Becca smiles softly. "I don't mind. I wasn't allowed to have pets growing up either. It's part of the reason why I was so thrilled to get Thunder. If you're okay with it, I'd like to take care of the pigs."

I nod, suddenly overcome with emotion. Becca is probably only the fifth or sixth person who knows about my pigs, and I certainly wouldn't trust anyone else with them. Somehow I know Becca will treat them exactly as I do.

"Can I — can I hold one?" she whispers hesitantly.

"Yeah, darlin'. Sit in the chair."

I grab Bluebell, since she's running back and forth in the tube, and she's the least likely to lose her shit and scare the hell out of Becca. I carefully place Bluebell into Becca's cupped hands, and watch as she studies my quietest pig. "I've honestly never held a guinea pig before, and I had no idea their fur was so soft."

"Some aren't as soft, but Bluebell's is."

Becca peers up at me, her eyes wide. "I think she just peed on me."

"Oh, fuck," I say with a wince. "I'm sorry, darlin'."

"Maybe she's marking territory. Now I'm definitely her momma," she says with a breathy giggle.

Fuck me.

This woman never ceases to amaze me.

Becca

CHAPTER 21

The following day, I headed back to work, and was immediately called into Brad's office.

"You wanted to see me?" I asked from the doorway, hesitant to step foot in the room.

"Yeah. Leave the door open," Brad says as he pulls at the neck of his shirt. Is he nervous? "Look, Becca. Clearly I overstepped with our last conversation. Looking back, I can see that I came across pretty creepy."

"You did," I admit.

"I owe you a sincere apology. You remind me a lot of my younger sister, and I think I took the role a little too far. Not only did I overstep a professional boundary, but also a physical one. I never should have placed my hand on your shoulder, and I promise it will *never* happen again."

"Thank you," I respond with a slight stammer. I did not expect the conversation to go this way at all.

"Word on the street is you're now a married woman?" he asks. "Will you be changing your name?"

"Oh," I say, surprised. "I hadn't even thought about that yet."

"Rick wanted to do a story about the marriage, but I told him no. An athlete suddenly marrying someone in Vegas is a bit of a breaking news situation, but since it involves one of our own, we won't be addressing it."

"Thank you. I appreciate that. It's been a whirlwind."

"Are you …" he trails off before looking me in the eye. "Are you okay? Happy?"

I feel a smile break across my face as I nod. "I am very happy. Jacob makes me feel so content."

Brad laughs. "You don't call him Jax?"

I shake my head. "He's never been Jax to me. I get to see the man no one else sees. The patient, caring, and peaceful man. Jax is a hockey star, but Jacob is my husband."

It's possible I bit off more than I can chew with Jacob's guinea pigs. And yes, I did mean that as a pun.

After carefully watching Jacob's routine for a week, I thought I had everything under control for his first road trip. Boy was I mistaken.

He said they liked spinach. How was I supposed to know they'd basically yank it out of my hand and then fight over it? I was accidentally bitten when I tried to separate Rose and Lily. That was after Dahlia kicked her poo onto my shirt. Daisy hides from me, and I can't coax her out from one of the huts, no matter what I try.

In an attempt to make things fun, I ordered these edible ball treats. The amount of research I did on toys for guinea pigs is pretty hysterical. The balls are good for exercise but also for their teeth. Jacob told me he occasionally lets them out of the cages.

As I nervously survey the cages, I hear a loud sigh from under the door. Thunder will not give up his desire to meet the pigs face-to-face. Thankful for that noise as a reminder, I take a towel and jam it under the door to ensure no pigs make it out of the room.

That's all I'd need to happen. "Hi, honey. How was your trip? By the way, my dog ate one of your guinea pigs."

I really don't want to have that conversation.

Alright, Becs. Put on your big girl pants and do this.

Gingerly opening the first cage, I'm able to grab Bluebell quickly. She squeaks once, then settles into my palm. Next is Rose, who side-eyes me before pooping in my hand. Lovely. Lily and Daffodil are harder to catch, but as soon as they're set on the ground, they gleefully jump around.

I had to lure Daisy out of one of the huts with a treat. Jacob said she was the eater of the bunch, and now I understand. She weighs quite a bit more than the rest.

Finally, I track down Dahlia, who nervously shakes as I carefully put her in my hand. White with black spots, she peers up at me, and I think I fall in love with her immediately. "Well, aren't you just adorable?"

I sit on the floor by the door, watching the pigs scope out the room, but Dahlia won't leave my hand. She seems content to hang with me instead of roaming around with her sisters. Are they even related? Whatever.

Yawning, I lean my head against the door. It's been a long day. Usually I'm in bed by now, but Jacob has a game in California, and I'm trying to stay up until he calls. He's called every day that he's been gone, and I find I'm missing him more than I expected.

Glancing at my phone, I see that it's almost ten o'clock. My alarm goes off at three. I really can't survive on less than five hours of sleep, so I decide to get the pigs squared away in their cages for the night so I can attempt a little bit of shut-eye. I quickly get four of them relocated, but I can't find Rose and Bluebell.

"Seriously? Where the hell could they go?" I murmur as I check the towel under the door to see if it had been moved at all. A scratching noise under the chair alerts me to Rose's location, but Bluebell is nowhere to be found. Near tears, I'm praying that I find her immediately, when my phone rings, scaring the crap out of me.

"Hey, Spitfire," Jacob's voice says warmly.

"Hi," I whisper.

"What's wrong?" His voice sharpens as he hones in on my distress quickly.

"Nothing." I don't want to admit to my husband that I lost one of his guinea pigs.

"Baby," he says softly, and my heart skips a beat, "I know when you're lying. What happened?"

"I don't want to tell you."

"Did something happen with your family? I swear, if your brother showed up there because he knew I'd be gone, I'll fly to Indiana right now and shove my fist in his mouth so fucking hard I'll have his teeth imprinted in the back of his skull," he snarls.

I can't help the giggle that bursts from my mouth. "Nothing with my family."

"You promise?" he asks warily.

"I promise."

"Something with work?"

"No."

"Whatever it is, you can tell me, darlin'."

I sigh, knowing he's right. "Promise you won't be mad?"

"I promise I'll try not to be mad."

"Fine. So I've been trying to spend time with the pigs multiple times a day so they get used to me, and tonight, I thought they'd enjoy getting out of their cages for a little bit. You had said you did that occasionally, so I thought it was fine. I even bought some special treats, and everything was going fine, but now ..."

Jacob chuckles. "Bluebell likes to climb under the recliner I have in there, and because of her coloring, she blends in with the fabric. You can't see her unless you're pointing a flashlight directly at her. Stick a piece of spinach under the chair, and she'll follow it."

"How did you know that's what I was going to say?" I ask incredulously.

"Two reasons. She's done that to me more than once."

"And the other reason?"

"Now it's your turn to promise you won't be mad," he says with an amused tone.

"Okay?"

"I have a camera in the room, baby. I saw you get everyone back in the cages but Bluebell."

I jump up, looking all over the room, finally locating a very small camera hidden at the top of a bookshelf. "This would have been nice to know a few days ago, Jacob."

"Maybe. But I've enjoyed watching you without your knowledge."

"Why do you have a camera in here?"

"Checking on the pet sitter initially. But then I found that watching them before going to bed on away trips actually relaxed me. So I kept the camera."

"Any other cameras I should know about?"

"No."

Huh. I'm weirdly disappointed in that.

Jacob lets out a loud bark of laughter. "Do you want me to put in more cameras, Spitfire?"

"What? No!"

"Becca, I literally just told you I'm watching you right now. You're pouting. What exactly would happen if there were more cameras?"

"I don't know. I'm as surprised as you are about my reaction." Just talking about this with Jacob is making me all hot and bothered. "It doesn't matter because there aren't any cameras. Anyway, I just dangle a piece of spinach under the chair and she'll come out?"

"Yeah. Go ahead and try. I'll wait."

It takes a few minutes before Bluebell takes the bait, and once she's safely back in the cage system, I let out a relieved exhale. "I don't think you have to worry about me taking them out of their cages anytime soon. That was way more stressful than I thought it would be."

"You'll get used to it. I love that you're trying, darlin'. Are you heading to bed now?" Jacob asks.

"My alarm goes off in five hours, so yes. I wanted to stay up to see how your game went."

Jacob gives me the rundown on his game as I lock up the apartment and make my way to the bedroom. After brushing my teeth, I climb into his big bed, noticing again how empty it is without him here.

"Turn on FaceTime, darlin'," Jacob commands quietly.

"What? Why?" I ask.

"If you want to be watched, I'm gonna watch while you get yourself off."

"Jacob!" I hiss, outraged as I look around the room wildly. I snort as I realize how absurd I must look, and I'm thankful there isn't a camera in here for Jacob to watch me act like a buffoon.

"You were disappointed I didn't have more cameras around the apartment. It turns you on to think about me watching you. So you're gonna put Thunder in the hallway, turn on your camera, and then you're gonna get yourself off while I tell you all the things I'd do to you if I were there right now."

Hand shaking, I force my dog outside the bedroom door, close it, then pull the phone away from my ear to press the FaceTime option. Jacob's handsome face fills the screen after one ring. Hair still damp from a shower, he's shirtless, stretched back against a hotel bed, with one arm propped behind his head. He's too pretty for his own good.

"There is something about how sexy you look in my bed. I think this is my favorite version of you. No makeup, no practiced performance that you have to put on for television. It's just you. All natural. Beautiful. Mine." His blue eyes stare intensely at me, sheer lust emanating from them in heady waves.

Holy moly. "*Jacob.*"

He groans, his eyes closing. "Fucking love when you say my name like that, Spitfire. I'm hard as a rock right now. What I wouldn't give to sink into your incredible pussy, feel you clench around me. Best fucking feeling on the planet."

Rubbing my thighs together, I relish in the friction it creates. "I wish you were here."

"Yeah?"

"Yeah."

"Touch yourself, baby. Slowly. I want you to gently circle your clit, but nothing else," he commands, his voice rough and husky as he watches.

Too far gone to care about how embarrassing it could be if anyone knew about this, I slide my hand into my panties, immediately moaning when I touch my clit. "Do you — do you want to see?"

"No," he replies gruffly. "I want to see your face when you come. I know your pussy intimately, and while I have every intention of spending quite a bit of time between your legs whenever I get the chance, it's your face that I need right now."

I gaze into his eyes, and I know I can't continue unless he joins in. "Will you touch yourself for me, please, Jacob?"

"Fuck," he hisses, his arm dropping from behind his head. "I'll do anything for you, darlin'."

Keeping his camera focused on his face, I see a shoulder shift as Jacob maneuvers into a different position. Without me asking, he tilts the camera down to show a hand wrapped around his shaft, his boxer briefs pulled down slightly so he can stroke the length comfortably. I'm completely enthralled as I watch his thumb swipe around the frenum piercing. So focused, in fact, that I've stopped touching myself, and Jacob chuckles. "If you can't stay on task, wife, I won't let you watch me."

"It's just …" I trail off.

"What?" he asks quietly.

I sigh as my middle finger resumes circling my clit. "I've never done this before. I must have assumed it was taboo, but it's not. It's incredibly erotic and sensual watching you like this. Have you ever done this?"

"No," he responds. "Never wanted to do anything like this. Until you."

"Until you," I repeat, my finger circling faster. My breathing picks up as I chase my pleasure, and I watch Jacob increase his speed. I've never had the desire to do anything like this before. At this moment, I think I'd do just about anything he asked me.

"I wish I was there," he pants, his voice strangled and thick with lust. "I'd give anything to bury myself inside you, feel you clench as you come apart. God, I fucking miss you."

"Jacob," I moan. "How many days until you're home?"

"Three."

"Fuck," I whisper.

"We're gonna circle back to the fact that you just cussed for the first time in front of me, darlin', but know that I feel the same way. Just know that I can't wait to fuck you again. When I get home, wherever you are in our apartment, just know we're doing it right there. I will not be able to wait one fucking second to be inside you. Gonna live inside you," he groans, his head falling back against the headboard as his eyes close in bliss. "Are you close, baby? Please tell me you're there. I need you to come with me."

"Jacob, I'm coming!" I shout, that last sentence the bit that does me in. He needs me to come with him. I've read it in books, and always rolled my eyes at how ridiculous it sounded. But hearing it from Jacob — from my husband — is one hell of an aphrodisiac I didn't know I needed.

"Fuck," he moans. "Me too."

A kaleidoscope of colors bursts behind my eyelids as my back arches from the bed. I let out a guttural moan louder than I think I've ever made, and I vaguely hear Thunder whining at the door. In hindsight, I'll find it humorous that my dog is concerned for my well-being, but right now, I'm too high on a wave of pleasure to care.

Aftershocks wrack my body as I come down from my orgasm, and I slow my finger to a halt. Opening one eye, I find Jacob in a similar mental space, a blissed out expression on his face as he catches his breath.

"I forgot to watch," I admit with a breathy giggle.

Jacob laughs. "I guess I did too. My eyes closed of their own volition. I'm not even sure if we were talking at all. Did I say anything interesting?"

"Yes. You promised me you'd buy me a car for every month of the year," I reply with a smile.

"Sounds about right. Done. All the same color, or an ombré rainbow?"

"Surprise me."

"Be careful what you wish for, darlin'. I think I'm gonna enjoy spoiling you."

Suddenly nervous, I backtrack. "I was just kidding. You know I don't need anything like that, right? I don't need to be spoiled. You shouldn't buy me anything, actually. That really muddies the waters, and I don't want you to think I'm only married to you for your bank account, because that's a really despicable thing, and I know there are tons of wives out there that do that kind of thing, but I'm not one of them. Actually, I should probably give you some money for rent? Or groceries? Something? This isn't an even exchange, and I want to do my part —"

"Woah," Jacob shouts, interrupting my spiral. "Relax, Becca. If I buy you anything, it's because I want to, not because I think you expect it. I know you aren't in this for my bank account. You're probably the least money-hungry person I've met in Denver, which is why I love you. And there are tons of wives that absolutely get with hockey players for the money. I'd never lump you in the same category as them. I will not, however, be taking rent or grocery money from you, so get those thoughts out of that pretty little brain of yours. You're still paying rent on your apartment. You do not need to pay anything on mine. It isn't about an even exchange. It's about me wanting to provide for you, keeping you safe, and watching you be happy. You bring me so much fucking peace, baby. You can't put a price tag on that."

Stupefied, I stare at him in complete shock.

Did he mean to say all that?

Does he realize he said he loves me?

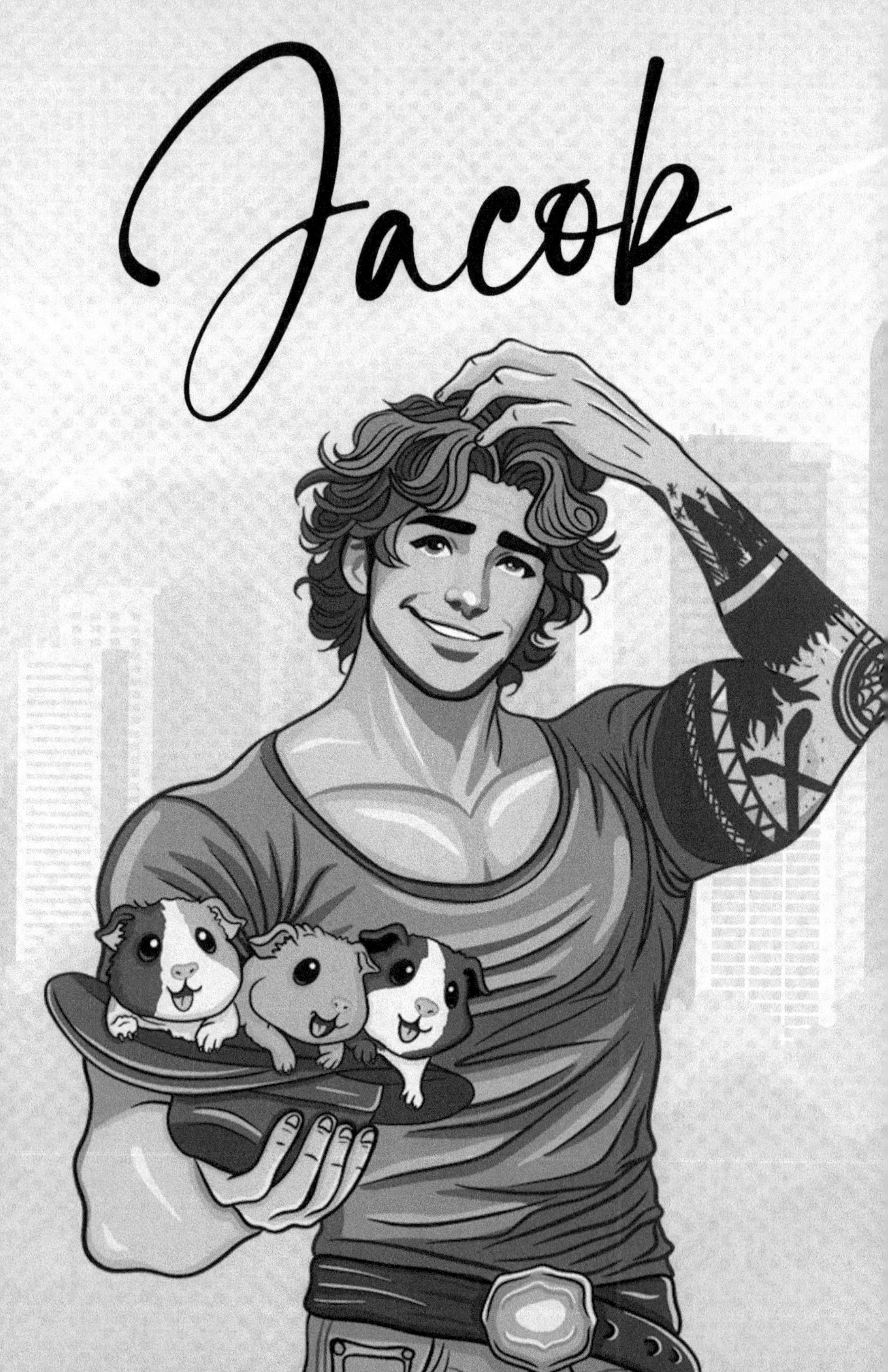
Jacob

CHAPTER 22

Why is she looking at me like that? Like she just got hit by a truck.

I try to flip through the conversation in my head, but I can't figure out what shocked the hell out of Becca. "You okay?"

"Uh-huh. Yeah, I'm great. Fabulous. Fantastic. That was an excellent FaceTime orgasm. One for the record books," she chirps, her face getting pinker as she talks. "Thunder is scratching at the door, so I need to go. Where are you headed in the morning?"

"Tampa," I murmur.

"Okay, well, safe travels. I'll talk to you tomorrow, I guess. Night!"

"Wait, can we talk —" I begin, but Becca has already ended the call.

It's at that moment I realize what I said.

"Fuuuuuck," I groan miserably. "You dumb fucking idiot."

I told her I love her.

After we essentially had phone sex, and she's talking about bank accounts and paying rent, I drop the love bomb on her.

Excellent timing, Jax.

What should I do now? Text her that it was a slip of the tongue, that I didn't mean it but really like her? Double down and say that I do love her, and I'm determined to make her love me too? Ignore it all and act like I never said anything?

Ding, ding, ding!

Option three is a definite winner. I'll play the 'I'm a dumb fucking idiot' card and act like nothing happened. I could text her and tell her that we'll talk about it when I get home, and remind her that I don't lie, but I don't want her to throw up her walls like she did when she realized I was also StickUM92. Becca needs time to wrap her head around things, and as much as I'd like to force her to communicate with me, I know I have to be patient.

Sighing, I climb out of bed. I groan as my left calf muscle locks up, and I lean down to massage it gently. The game tonight was very intense, and I pushed it more than I probably should have. As I walk into the bathroom, I decide to take advantage of the large soaker tub. We rarely get hotels on away trips that have an over-sized tub this nice, so I might as well enjoy this while I can.

While the tub fills up, I grab a washcloth. Dipping it into the tub water, I carefully wipe my release from my stomach, grimacing at how quickly I fucked it all up tonight. Had we ended our conversation right after we both came, I'd probably be happily asleep right now. God knows Becca is probably spiraling, but I can't call her back and talk her through it. Even though I want to. Fuck do I want to call her.

I remove my boxer briefs and slide into the tub, hissing as the scalding water covers my body. Leaning back, I close my eyes and relax. I can't worry about the past now. Just need to hope I can act like nothing happened … and that Becca lets me do it.

The following morning, I check Becca's location to make sure she's at work. Yeah, I follow her location, and she doesn't know it. It's

possible I'm becoming slightly unhinged about my wife. Considering she bolted when she heard the L-word, I stand by my less than trustworthy decision.

Satisfied when I see her location is at the station, I shove my phone in my pocket before climbing the outdoor boarding stairs at the airport. I do love that professional athletes get driven directly to a private hangar where we get on the plane. It's not that I hate being in an airport. I just despise going through security.

"Surprised you didn't bring the ball-and-chain with you on this trip too, Jax," our goaltending coach, Ryan McNichols, teases. "Figured she was part of the Jax package."

"Funny," I reply. "She has a job that she loves. I'd never expect her to follow me around like a lost puppy."

"Huh. That's interesting. Most women stop working once they nab themselves a hockey star."

"My wife isn't like most women."

"So it's going well?" he asks, following me past where the coaching staff normally sit. "I mean, you got married pretty quickly, didn't you? She still living by herself, or did you convince her to move in with you? Must be scary living alone in a big downtown like this. Her name's Becca, right? She's not knocked up, is she? Pretty little thing, your weather girl. Is she good in bed? Must be, to convince her to marry you that fast."

I swivel around, dropping my bags to grab Ryan by the throat. "I'm not sure what you think you're doing right now, McNichols, but keep my wife's name out of your fucking mouth."

"Jeez, man. Calm down. I was just making conversation," he says weakly, his hands up in meek surrender. I notice they're shaking slightly, and my eyes narrow.

"Who wants to know, McNichols? You aren't asking for yourself. You couldn't care less about any of our personal lives, so why now?" I squeeze his throat a bit more, and his eyes widen dramatically.

"N — no one."

"Don't lie to me," I growl. "Frankly, I know who put you up to this. I just want you to explain what your connection is and how he got to you."

"What does it matter?" he asks, and I grin wickedly. Dumbass just admitted he wasn't asking just to make conversation.

"It matters, McNichols, because this can go one of two ways. You can tell me what you know, and maybe I'll let you keep your job." I'm not. I'm going to human resources about him immediately. How Becca's brother got to him, I may never know, but clearly he can be bought, which is horrifying for our team. "Or, you can keep quiet, and I destroy you, inch by motherfucking inch, until there's nothing left of you but a few skin cells and stupid memories."

"Ry? Jax? What's going on?" Levi asks nonchalantly as he comes down the aisle. "Probably should let him go, Jax, so we can leave. Coach will have your nuts if we don't arrive in Tampa at exactly the time he marked on our itineraries."

"He's right," McNichols rasps, his face turning a little purple when I squeeze tighter.

"Fine," I growl, letting go to shove him backwards. "You think about what I said, asshole. Two choices. Make the better one."

Gasping, he nods as he turns to hustle toward the coaching staff.

"The fuck was that?" Levi asks.

"He started asking all kinds of questions about my wife, and he knew she lived alone downtown before we got married. This has her asshole brother written all over it, and I told McNichols he better tell me everything, or I'd destroy him," I explain as I shove my bag into the overhead bin.

"Uh, well, that is one violent way of threatening someone," Levi comments.

I shrug. "I make no apologies for how I choose to protect my wife."

"Very feral of you."

"Thank you."

"Wasn't a compliment, Jax," Levi says, scowling.

"Yeah, it kinda was. When you find your woman, you'll understand. Someone fucks with her, they fuck with me. And if they fuck with me, I'll finish them."

"Who are we finishing?" Gabe asks as he walks down the aisle.

"Coach McNichols asked a question about Jax's wife, so Jax threatened his life. You know, normal husband behavior," Levi says with an exaggerated eye roll.

"What did he ask?" Gabe wonders.

"Wanted to know if she'd moved in with me yet, because he knew she lives alone downtown, and how scary it must be for her. Then asked if she was knocked up."

Gabe scowls. "He knew she lived alone? Oh, yeah. I'd have gone nuts too. What the fuck was he thinking?"

Levi stares at us with his mouth hanging open in shock. "Seriously, you too? This is insanity."

"Once you have a woman, you'll understand." Gabe looks at me and nods. "Someone threatens Cassie, I'm tossing this nice guy persona and taking them out. Done. End of story."

I nod in agreement as Levi throws back his head in frustration with a growl. "This is not normal behavior, gentlemen. What the actual fuck?"

"Normal behavior?" Grant asks. "They aren't normal, but what's the issue?"

Levi quickly explains to Grant what happened, and he nods. "Oh, yeah. I can understand that. My last girlfriend … yeah, I'd have burned down the world for her if needed. What can we do, Jax? How do you need help?"

Levi groans, but I ignore him. "Clearly I'm getting McNichols fired, because he's a risk to all of us if a relative of my wife can purchase him as a lookout. Then I'll be calling my wonderful brother-in-law and letting him know that the buck stops here. Thought I made that clear the last time I spoke to the jackass, but I guess not."

"What if he still doesn't get the message?" Levi asks. "You can't fight everyone."

"Physically? No. Besides, I've got like five inches and fifty pounds on the poor bastard. That wouldn't be a fair fight." I'm not gloating. Well, not *completely* gloating. I'm stating a fact. Rodney Stephens did not get blessed in the genetics department like I did. But again, he underestimates what I'm capable of. "Sometimes you gotta fight fire with fire. He thinks he can come after me through hockey, so I'll go after him through his family's business."

On the flight to Las Vegas when Becca fell asleep on my shoulder, I'd done a deep dive into her family's money, their ties to Indiana, and what her brother would be capable of now that he controlled the empire. What started out as a car dealership morphed into Stephens Autos all over the state of Indiana and into western Ohio. That income allowed Rodney Senior to make a move into commercial real estate, where his net worth flourished. Within the past twenty years or so, he parlayed that success into a short stint in the Indiana State House of Representatives, running as a Republican, of course. After what I experienced in the short time I interacted with Becca's brother and mother, and how they expected her to dutifully do as they told her, I'm not at all surprised to find out where their political views lie.

Having been involved in a scandal with a college debutante, Rodney Senior lost his representative position quite handily to a Democrat after only two years. I found this out on Reddit, but couldn't find any actual news sources about it, which tells me the Stephens family somehow had the entire thing swept under the rug. Becca certainly didn't tell me about it, and I wonder if she even knows.

Curious to discover if there could be any skeletons in the Stephens' family closet, I fire off a text to an investigator friend I went to college with to see if he'd like to assist me in taking down

Rodney Junior and all of his minions. He's always been a fan of destroying assholes, so I'm not surprised when I get a very quick affirmative response, and I send him all the information I know about both Rodney Stephens'.

I text Becca good morning, even though I know she's at work and probably won't respond. I've texted her every morning without fail, and I'm not changing it now.

It is a long-ass flight from the west coast to Florida, crossing three time zones. By the time we land in Tampa, we go straight to the hotel for a nap, and then head to the arena for the game.

"Jax!" Coach Davenport screams. "What the fuck are you doing?"

Speaking of the game … I'm off mine. I can barely skate, I've gotten in two scuffles with Tampa Tide players, and I have zero points for the game.

"Do you need to be pulled?" Coach asks after I do an awful job of passing the puck to Daws at the start of the second period. "I don't know what's going on with you, so either get your head in the game, or tell me to pull you. Your version of amateur hour is not it."

Don't I fucking know it.

Becca never answered me, and I can't move on from it. I don't know what to do or say, and I don't even know anyone I can talk to about it.

"You know what? Pull me. Put Brown in for me," I answer bluntly. Ezekiel Brown is a rookie phenom, who will undoubtedly break records with this organization, but due to his immature attitude, he's been benched a lot.

"You serious? You want to be pulled?" Coach asks, his brow furrowed in confusion. My line heads back on the ice, and he barks out an order for Brown to go as a replacement. "Are you hurt?"

"No, but my head isn't in the game. I'm sorry, Coach. You can discipline me as you see fit. I'm not doing my best for the team, so I shouldn't be on the ice."

"We'll talk after the game," he says as he directs his attention back to the game.

A couple of hours later when we're heading to the bus to take us back to the hotel, Coach motions for me to sit with him at the front of the bus. Usually I'm way in the back, either unwinding or hanging out with the guys.

"Talk," Coach commands.

"Dang, Coach, take me to dinner first," I mutter.

"Funny. I'm guessing the issue today stems from something to do with your wife. Correct?"

"Yeah."

"And?"

"Nothing else, really. Well, something, but I'm not ready to talk about it." Ryan McNichols is sitting two rows back, undoubtedly listening to everything I say, ready to report back to Becca's brother. Which gets me thinking: Ryan has always been a really good guy. He was respected on the ice when he was our goaltender, and he's transitioned to a coach well. How on earth did Rodney Junior get to Ryan, and what could that mean for all of us?

Standing, I swivel to Ryan's seat. His eyes widen when he looks up at me, and I squat so we're closer to eye level. "What did he threaten you with?"

"I — I don't know what you're talking about," he stammers.

"Bullshit, McNichols. I've met the bastard. Blackmail is definitely in his repertoire. What did he threaten you with?"

Ryan studies me as he debates on answering. "I can't say."

I shrug. "Alright. Just know I'm going to human resources when we get home to make sure you get fired. Coaches who can be bought are kinda frowned upon, right?"

"Fuck," he breathes. "Guess it doesn't matter, because if he does what he says he'll do, I'm getting fired anyway."

"Why?" I ask, noting Coach has turned around to listen to our conversation.

"This is so embarrassing. He has a video of me with a prostitute. I'm wearing Wolves gear. If it gets out, I'm done."

"What is it with threats about inappropriate videos in this organization?" Coach yells. A prior teammate of ours, Luca Santo, was supposedly recorded on an away trip when his girl came to visit him. His girl just so happens to be Coach's niece. "For fuck's sake! Did you record yourself, McNichols?"

"No."

"So you were recorded without your consent, but happened to be wearing a Wolves shirt?"

"Yes."

"Then it's moot. You're not getting fired for that. I'd like to understand why Jax would need to go to HR, though."

Arriving at the hotel, Coach tells me and Ryan to come into his room. We explain the whole situation, including how heinous Becca's brother is, and how I assume he's doing some other illegal things in an attempt to fuck with Becca's life. In a moment of poetic timing, my phone chimes with a text. I grab it quickly, hoping it's Becca, and am only somewhat disappointed when I see it's from my private investigator. As I read the screen, my mouth drops open. "Woah."

"What?" Coach asks.

"I had an investigator look into Becca's father and brother. Turns out they aren't just nasty individuals. They're straight up criminals." Showing the phone to Coach, I watch as his eyes widen.

"Jesus. Good thing you got your girl out of that situation," he comments.

"That dude is crazy," Ryan says. "When he cornered me last weekend, I was honestly scared."

The blood chills in my body. "He cornered you? Where?"

"Outside the arena. You walked out right in front of me, and you didn't see him. The look of hate he gave you was scary enough."

Fuck. He was in Denver, and we didn't know. He could be there now. I look wildly at Coach. "What the fuck am I supposed to do? We have a game in Miami tomorrow. I won't be home for thirty-six hours. He could be there now. Becca might be in trouble."

Opening up the tracker app again, I breathe a very small sigh of relief when I see she's in our apartment.

"Do you want to go home?" Coach asks quietly.

Squeezing my eyes closed, I shake my head. "Yes and no. I want to protect her, but I also know she might feel smothered and pull away even more. I need to get things lined up so I can take him down once and for all so she's safe."

Heading back to my room, I get undressed, ready to call Becca and see how she's doing. I can play the nonchalant husband. Ask how her day was, and tell her about mine. Talk about Thunder and the pigs. But an alert pops up on my screen telling me I have every reason to be concerned. I'm close to two thousand miles away from my wife, and there's nothing I can do to protect her.

Becca

CHAPTER 23

I know I should have responded to Jacob. He's texted me every morning for weeks, and it was a relief to see that text. Nothing has changed. Except …

The L-word.

So I didn't respond. I needed time to think. To look at our situation both objectively and subjectively. I deal best with facts and numbers. Matters of the heart are neither of those things, which means I'm definitely out of my element here.

I figured I'd wait until after his game this evening and explain myself. I even made notes to help me stay on topic.

And then my stupid brother showed up.

I opened the door because I assumed it was someone in the building. How my brother managed to bypass the security team downstairs beats me. I'm not even sure how he knew where Jacob lived. But as soon as I opened the door, he barreled inside.

"Got yourself a nice one, Rebecca," he sneers.

"Why are you here, Rodney? You have to know I've blocked you. I thought you would have gotten the message by now," I answer, irritation evident in my tone. I tossed and turned all night, then snapped at poor Thunder this morning when my patience ran out. A long day at work followed, and I'm desperate to take a long bath before I collapse in bed.

"I don't think you understand how this is going to work, Rebecca. I don't care what you want or how you think. I only care about business. And you're fucking with that now, you little bitch. Now get your shoes on, because you're coming back home and doing what I tell you to do!" Spittle flies from Rodney's mouth as his face reddens with each word. I don't think I've ever seen him this angry before. Aggravated? Yes. Frustrated? Of course. But the absolute disgust emanating from him is new.

"No," I whisper, slowly sliding my foot backwards so I'm a few inches further away from him.

Rodney's eyes narrow. "What did you just say to me?"

"You heard me," I stammer, clearing my throat so my voice is louder. "I said no. I'm not marrying some crony you and Dad wanted me to marry, just to align two families. Besides, I'm already married."

"I can easily get that annulled."

"You can only annul a marriage that hasn't been consummated. Mine has," I tell him. I honestly have no idea if that's actually true, but they say it in television shows, so I'm running with it. There are probably a bunch of other reasons a marriage can be annulled, but seeing as how I've never had to research it, I really don't know.

"Just had to whore yourself out, didn't you?" he hisses.

"I'm not a whore!" I shout, outraged. How dare he! I didn't sleep with Jacob until we were already married.

"Well, you aren't telling anyone about it, alright? Ben and Dick think you're a virgin."

I stare at him incredulously. "You can't be serious. I'm thirty-three, Rodney. They have to know I've had sex."

His hand whips out before I realize, and he slaps me harshly across the cheek. Rodney immediately follows the slap with a swift punch to my abdomen, and I double over in pain as I fight to catch my breath. He's never punched me before. "If they think you're a virgin, then you agree. Understood?"

Two things happen at once. First, the doorbell rings, jarring our attention. As Rodney turns to look at the door, Thunder takes the opportunity to leap toward us, latching onto Rodney's groin. Rodney screams, but Thunder doesn't let go. "Get this thing off of me!"

Sidestepping my brother, I sprint to the door. Opening it, I find two uniformed police officers.

"Ma'am. We got a call about a man in here without consent."

I point to Rodney. "My dog has him."

The cops both wince when they see how Thunder holds Rodney in place. "Damn. Never met a truly vicious golden retriever before."

"He's not. He does protect me though, and jumped into action when *he* hit me."

"The man hit you?" I nod. "Would you like to press charges?"

I stare at my brother, writhing in pain on the floor. "Yes. Yes, I would. He punched me in the stomach, too."

"No, Rebecca. You don't understand! You have to marry Richard. We owe the Gaines Family millions, and they're only willing to forgive the debt if you marry him," Rodney blurts out.

"So I'm some kind of collateral?"

"Yes."

"How is Mom okay with this? I know I wasn't the closest with Dad, but I never thought Mom would just sell me up the river like that," I wonder aloud as I pull Thunder away from Rodney.

He cups his balls and groans. "Mom doesn't give a fuck about you. You could die and she wouldn't care."

"That's an awful thing to say about our mother!" I whisper-shout.

He gives me a vicious smile. "She's not your mother."

Three hours later, after following the police to the precinct to officially press a variety of charges against Rodney, I arrive back at Jacob's apartment in a daze. Rodney had no problem telling the officers about our family dynamic, and how I came to be. Our father had many affairs, and evidently I was the product of one of them. My birth mother was part of a housekeeping company that worked on cleaning buildings before my father listed them for sale. She didn't tell him about me until she decided to drop me at his door and run.

I was originally given to a nanny until DNA testing could confirm I was indeed another offspring. This explains my mother's cold and callous relationship with me from the get-go. I was only acceptable when I could bring success to the family. Now that my dad is dead, she has no other reason to be nice to me, especially with my refusal to marry someone they'd picked out for me.

I look around the empty apartment, and I know I'm two seconds away from a breakdown. I miss Jacob, and I desperately need him right now. With Rodney now behind bars, will he even want to stay married to me? I might lose everything.

I hear a slight squeal, and on auto pilot, I go to the fridge and grab a bag of vegetables to feed the pigs. As soon as I enter their room, their happy sounds make me even more depressed. I slowly feed them, then collapse in the chair in the corner as tears fall from my eyes. Soon I'm fully bawling, and I don't realize I never shut the door completely until Thunder jumps into my lap. I bury my face in his fur as big, gut-wrenching sobs break from my body. I've never felt so alone.

"Baby, answer your phone," I hear muffled from somewhere in the room.

"What?" I ask, sniffling as I wipe my nose with my sleeve.

"Answer your phone, darlin'."

The phone vibrates in my pocket, and upon pulling it out, I see I have ten missed calls and a bunch of unread texts, all from Jacob.

"Hi," I whisper, afraid to say anything else.

"Did he hurt you?" Jacob demands. "Why were you at the

police station? Where is the little cocksucker? I should have flown home. As soon as I got the notification he was there, I should have flown home."

"Wait. What? What notification? And how did you know I was at the police station?" I ask, pushing Thunder off my lap so I can sit up straight.

"Fuck," Jacob mutters. "The building notified me a man had been cleared to go up to our apartment by a new security trainee. Your brother said he was *my* brother, and naturally the security guy let him up. I made sure the team fired that guy, since I don't have a brother, and I have a very clear list of who is allowed up to my apartment. Honestly, I'm so fucking thankful we've got a doorbell camera, Spitfire. I about had a heart attack when I saw him get through the door."

"Okay," I answer slowly. "And the police station?"

Jacob sighs. "You're gonna hate this."

"Answer the question, Jacob."

"I track your location." It's a simple response, and one I expected when he knew where I'd been. But I'm still pissed.

"Why didn't you just ask? I would have let you follow my location. Why be dishonest about it?"

"Technically, I wasn't dishonest about it. I just wasn't honest either." I hear the remorse in his voice. "I'm sorry, darlin'. I should have told you. Does it help if I say that you can track my location too?"

"If you think I'm going to let this go because of that trivial technicality, you're mistaken," I say angrily.

"FaceTime, please. If we're going to argue, I need to see your face," Jacob says quietly. The phone beeps in my ear as he requests a video call, and I find myself growling as I accept it. His expression is murderous as he stares at me. "Fuck, Spitfire. He hit you again?"

"It doesn't matter."

"The fuck it doesn't!"

"He's in jail now, so it really doesn't matter. I pressed charges and got a restraining order. Also for him entering your apartment without my consent."

"Our."

"Huh?"

"Our apartment, darlin'. Quit saying it's only mine," Jacob says clearly.

"But it is only yours."

"No, it's not. The moment you said you'd marry me, my apartment became ours. The kiss we shared after we were declared husband and wife made it really ours. And when I finally got to bury myself between your thighs and make love to you? It's our fucking apartment, Becca. Moving on. Why was your brother there?"

"Don't you already know? I just assumed you had a hidden camera somewhere," I say snottily, but my heart beats erratically in my chest after Jacob says it's our apartment.

He sighs again, exhaustion evident on his handsome face as he rubs his eyes. "I already told you I only have the one in the pigs room. There aren't any others. All I know is he was there, and then you went to the police station. I looked up flights, trying to find something so I could get home to you, but there was nothing. I fucking hate that you dealt with this all by yourself, but I'm freaking out here, baby. Please just tell me what happened."

For a moment, I'm taken aback. I hadn't considered how this must feel from Jacob's perspective. He's so far away, and he knows my volatile brother has shown up here. That had to have scared the hell out of him. "I'm sorry, Jacob. I can't imagine how that must have made you feel."

His eyes close as he takes a deep inhale. When he opens his eyes again, the pain I see breaks my heart. "I've never been so scared, Becca. I couldn't do anything, and I was supposed to be on the ice. Coach pulled me again."

"Again?"

He nods. "I was a mess last night. I knew why you were avoiding me, and it had me completely off my game."

"You knew why I was avoiding you?" I parrot, wondering if he really does know.

He chuckles bitterly. "I told you I'm in love with you, and you had sheer panic written across your face. I figured I'd act like nothing happened, but I didn't get a chance because you avoided me."

"I'm sorry," I whisper.

He shrugs. "Nothing to be sorry for. If you don't feel the same, it's not your fault. In any case, explain what happened with your brother."

"Wait. No — that's not what I meant. You've been full speed from the moment we met, and I've been trying to catch up. I've only recently gotten my head wrapped around us being married, and then you drop the L-word. I didn't know how to process that."

He glances between my eyes, searching for something he doesn't seem to get when he sighs roughly. "Where does this leave us?"

"What do you mean?" I ask, nerves making me grip the cushion under my legs tightly.

"We got married to keep you safe from your brother. It sounds like you don't need that anymore. What do you want, Becca?"

I take a moment before responding, trying to think of how to explain my thoughts. "I want to be happy. To feel needed. To have a family that actually wants me, instead of the crappy people who were forced to deal with me all my life. I want a partner who supports me and builds me up. And I want to be with someone who is proud of me, but also someone who isn't embarrassed by me."

"Has someone ever made it blatantly obvious that they were embarrassed by you?" Jacob asks quietly.

I shrug, looking down at Thunder, who snores softly in my lap. "Other than family? No. But I'm sure a boyfriend or two would have preferred I dialed down the nerd in some situations."

"But your family did get embarrassed by you?"

"Yeah," I whisper. "I asked a lot of questions growing up. I always wanted to know the dynamics of things. How everything worked. Interpersonal communication was never a strength of mine, and it took forever for me to learn how to interact in social situations. My brother and father commented often how I'd unwittingly embarrassed them."

"You could never embarrass me, Becca," Jacob whispers, his voice somehow quiet, yet deep and clear at the same time. "Never. I'm in awe of you. You're absolutely brilliant, and I love when you talk weather to me. I hate that your family failed you, and that they never appreciated you for the exquisite person you are."

His words steal the breath from my lungs, and when I finally manage an inhale, a fresh wave of tears escapes simultaneously.

"Fuck," he mutters. "I'm sorry, baby. I didn't mean to make you cry."

"I miss you," I ramble. "I don't like being here alone. The bed is too big, and your pillow doesn't smell like you anymore. I can tell the pigs miss you too. I'm so scared, Jacob."

"Of what?" he asks softly.

"That you'll realize I'm nothing special, and you'll demand a divorce when I'm only now realizing how much you mean to me. And that's even worse, because I've always been independent. You have so much power, and I'm afraid I won't survive it when you move on."

"Becca, I'm in love with you. I love you. There is no moving on from you. I'm scared shitless you want to end this because you don't need me anymore," he confesses, his eyes covered with a sheen of tears. "I've been researching ways to take down your family all fucking day, in some weird attempt to keep you with me. I figured if I saved the day by ensuring you didn't have to marry that weirdo friend of the family, then you'd want to stay with me."

"You want to take down my family?" I ask, shock evident in my tone.

"Of course I do! Those heinous fuckers deserve what's coming to them. They've put you through hell, darlin', and I'll be damned if I just sit back and let them continue doing it."

"What exactly are you planning to do?" I can't help the smile that begins to form on my face. I've never had a man fight for me, and while I'm sure it's not very feminist of me to say, I find that I really like it. A lot.

Jacob chuckles as he runs a hand through his curls. "I have nothing to report. Yet. But I'm working on some things. Just know your brother will most likely be extradited back to Indiana for much bigger charges. He's not very smart. Did you know that? You, my lovely wife, definitely got all the brains from your parents."

"When are you coming home?" I blurt out, unwilling to acknowledge the comment about my parents. I don't even know who my mother is. The woman who 'raised' me will not get one more moment of my time.

"We have a game in Miami tomorrow night, and then I'll be home the day after tomorrow. Mid-morning, I think. Are you going to be okay?"

New tears fill my eyes. "I don't really have a choice. I'll be fine."

"Darlin' …" he says quietly. "Talk to me. Please."

I take a deep breath, closing my eyes. There are so many things I want to tell him. I need to be honest and tell him that I think I love him too. But I'm so scared. Every man in my life has scarred me emotionally. "Can I ask you a question?"

"Of course."

"If you're sure you love me, does that mean you want to stay married?"

Jacob's lips twitch as he fights a smile. "I do want to stay married to you."

"Okay," I say as I exhale in relief. "That makes me feel better."

"You were worried?" he asks.

I nod. "You wouldn't need to protect me anymore. I didn't know if you'd want the responsibility of a wife."

"Baby. You're not a responsibility. You bring things to my life that are unmatched. I haven't stopped thinking about you since we met, and I find myself wondering what you'd think about stupid shit all the time. When I'm near you, my heartbeat slows down, and

I don't feel as anxious. I'm scared shitless that you'll realize you don't need me, and I won't recover from that. You have my heart in your hands, darlin'. I don't want it back."

"Thank you," I whisper.

"For what?"

I smile sweetly. "For being you, and supporting me just as I am. I don't think I'll ever be able to verbalize how much that means to me."

"I'll always support you, Becca. No matter what."

Finally calmer, I take Thunder into the bedroom and climb into bed. Jacob and I don't talk much more, content to just be connected this way. Not ideal, as I'd much rather have him within touching distance, but still a connection I need. I fall asleep listening to his steady breathing, and wake up to find a text message from him.

JACOB

I'll spend the rest of my days loving you exactly as you need, darlin'.

With a massive smile on my face, I fire off a text to my boss, letting him know I won't be in today after the incident with my brother. Then I open up my airline app.

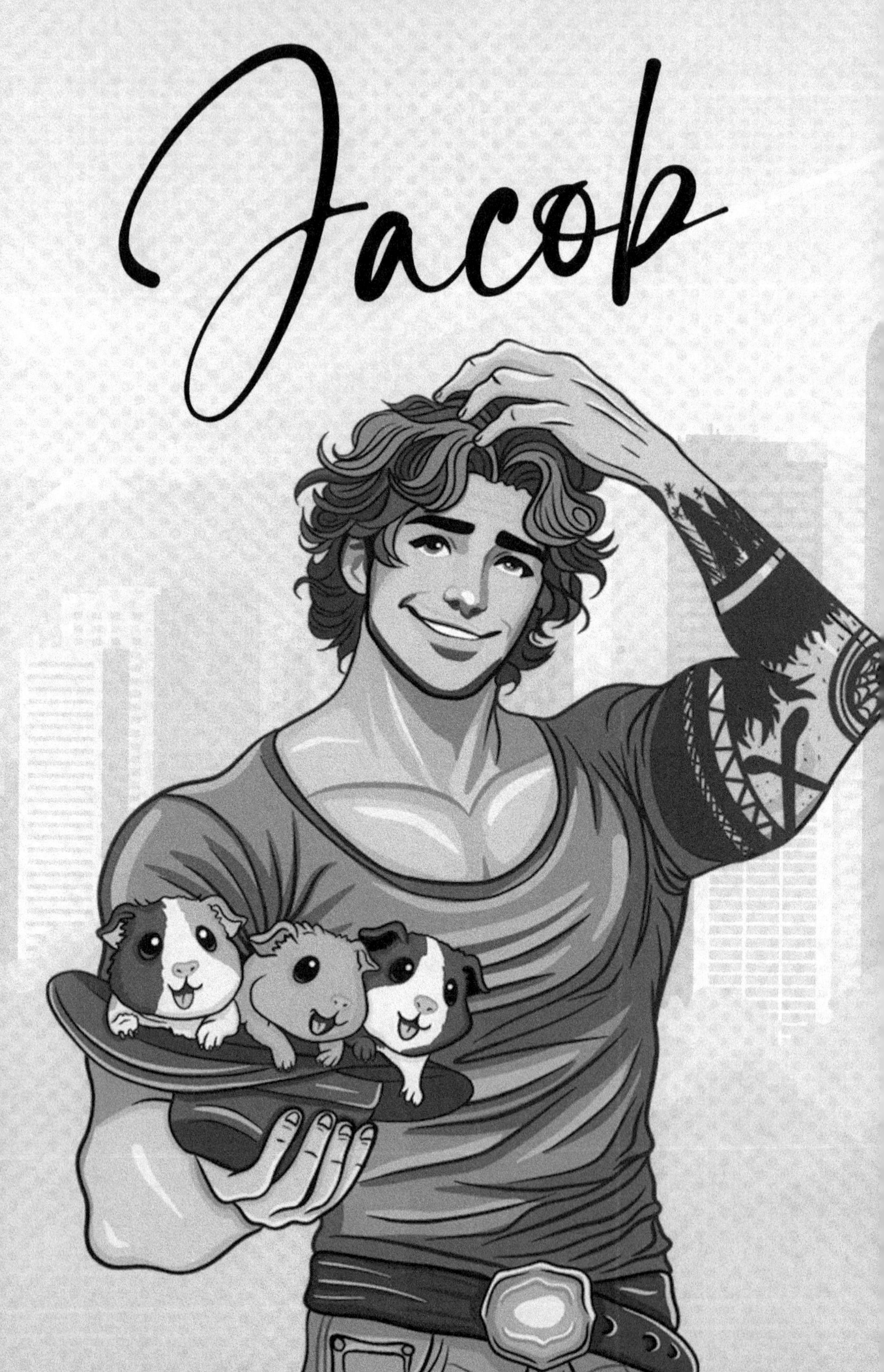

Jacob

CHAPTER 24

IT'S INCREDIBLY HARD TO TAKE A PRE-GAME NAP WHEN SOMEONE KEEPS interrupting me.

First it was Daws calling to ask about some odd recipe he wanted to try to make for Cassie when he gets home. I know I cook the most out of the guys, but I'm not Gordon Ramsey for fuck's sake. Look that shit up on the Internet, and leave me out of it.

Then my mother called to ask for more money. We got in a shouting match, and I blocked her number. I haven't spoken to her since before the birthday olives incident, and I have zero desire to deal with her again. She only wants to keep me around because I send her money, and I'm done with that now.

And now someone is knocking at my door.

"Isn't there a 'do not disturb' sign on the door?" I grumble as I throw open the door, then stare in shock as Becca giggles at me.

"There is a sign, but I figured you didn't want me hanging in the hallway," she says breathily. I don't waste a second before dragging her into my room and burying my face in her hair.

"What are you doing here?" I ask, my voice muffled. God, I can't get close enough to her. Pressing her against the nearest wall, I crowd against her body, and love feeling her arms wind tightly around my back.

"I couldn't wait until tomorrow. I needed to see you," she mumbles.

"I'm so fucking glad you're here." God, I needed this. The last thirty-six hours have been so full of nerves and anxiety that I wasn't sure how I'd make it until tomorrow. I was already thinking of asking Coach if I could take a red-eye flight back to Denver right after the game. I hate our flight schedule. It's something our previous coach implemented, and I don't know why Coach Davenport hasn't changed it. So many teams do night flights, but the Wolves have always flown early in the morning. Finishing the game here, and then having to go back to a hotel instead of flying home? Ridiculous, especially when looking at gaining time zones as we fly west.

"How did you know what room I was in?" I ask, my voice a quiet murmur against her hair.

"A friend of a friend," she replies, and I chuckle.

"Oh yeah? Any friend that I might know?"

She lifts her head to look at me, and I get lost in her beautiful green eyes. God, she brings me such peace. "I asked our sports director to contact your coach. That's how I got the room number."

"That tracks," I respond, pulling her back into my embrace and resting my head on top of hers as she burrows into my arms. "Coach was probably thrilled. He knows I've been struggling. I missed you so much it hurt."

"I missed you too, Jacob," Becca says softly, and I squeeze her harder, breathing her in.

"How are you even here? You didn't hint at this last night when we talked, or when I texted you this morning."

"I didn't know until this morning. When I got your text … I knew I needed to be here. I had to see you," she says shyly. I lift my head to look at her face, and find a pink hue coloring her cheeks.

I see her cheek, slightly puffy and red. I gently cup her face before saying, "I'm so sorry I wasn't there to protect you, darlin'. Was that all he did?"

She shakes her head, and my eyes narrow. "He punched me in the stomach, but then Thunder bit his balls."

"What?" I exclaim with a loud exhale. "The happiest dog on the planet bit your brother?"

"He saw a threat, I guess," she says with a shrug. "It's okay now. My brother got arrested, and I'm okay."

I drag my fingers along her hairline, tucking a lock of hair behind her ear. This wonderful woman has been dragged through the gauntlet, and she's here trying to calm me down. "I think I'm gonna buy the biggest dog chew I can find for my buddy Thunder. He deserves one hell of a treat for protecting you while I was gone."

Her eyebrows raise as she looks at me with surprise. "Have you been researching dog treats?"

I nod. "I know rawhide isn't good for them, so I Googled what kinds of things I can give him. Also what human foods he can't have."

"I love that you did that, Jacob," she says shyly before changing the subject. "Did I interrupt anything important? Naptime perhaps?"

"I was trying to nap," I admit. "Couldn't sleep."

"I don't want to screw with your game day preparations. I can be quiet."

My eyes dip to her mouth, and I'm suddenly not even remotely tired. Her lips part enough to make my dirty thoughts take flight. "Not thinking about sleep, darlin'."

"Oh?"

"Yeah, oh. Think I can give you at least a couple O's instead," I say huskily as my hands slide down to grip her ass. I lift her, reveling in how she automatically wraps her legs around my hips.

"I don't think you're supposed to have a workout so close to a game," she says with a giggle that turns into a moan as my lips find her collarbone.

"You're here," I murmur, dragging my tongue up her neck and into her waiting mouth. Spearmint flavor explodes on my tongue, and I groan as she bites down gently. "Trust me, Spitfire. This is gonna be the best game of my season just because I'll be performing for you."

I take a few steps toward the bed, laying her down gently, before climbing over her. I take in her delicate features, noting how her green eyes sparkle. She says, "I didn't come here for this, Jacob. I just needed to be with you."

"I know," I reply, cupping her cheek, and delighting in how she leans into my touch. "I know your heart, Becca. And I'm so fucking happy you're here. But I think you do need this, just as much as I do. Please let me make love to you. I know there's nothing better in the world than being connected to you this way."

"Jacob," she whispers as a tear slips from the corner of her eye. I gently wipe it away, then lean down to kiss her, but her words stop me in my tracks. "I love you."

Time stops.

I think I can hear traffic ten stories below, and I definitely hear the unmistakable cackle of Gabe across the hall. My heart pounds so severely I wonder if Becca can feel it.

"Say that again," I rasp, emotion clogging my throat.

Becca smiles softly, cupping my face in both hands. "I love you. I think I've been in love with you for much longer than I realized. No one has ever supported me the way you do, or been as patient as you. You bring me peace. You've become my home, and I'm so thankful I ran into you months ago because I don't know where I'd be if it weren't for you. You meet me where I am, no matter the circumstances."

"Thank fuck," I blurt out. "You can't take it back now, darlin'. You're mine, and I'm not ever letting you go."

"Promise?" she replies cheekily. A wide grin spreads across my face as I stand up, pulling her to sit up. Lunging toward my suitcase, I grab the cowboy hat I've worn on this trip, and place it on her head.

Becca inhales sharply as her hands reach up to touch the brim.

"With every breath I take," I answer. "You remember the significance of a woman wearing a man's cowboy hat?

She nods shakily. "I do."

"I've never allowed a woman to wear mine. Never wanted a woman to wear it. This is the first, and the last, time I'm giving my hat to someone. You're it for me, Spitfire," I tell her quietly, before taking her lips in a drugging kiss. "Now let me love you, baby."

"By all means, have your way with me."

Yes, ma'am.

I press off Becca, standing to rip off my shirt. I yank down my shorts and boxers, then grab her hand to pull her up. I make quick work of her clothes, finding it hard to focus as Becca touches every piece of my skin she can reach. Once she's naked, I push her back onto the mattress before climbing on top of her. Our kisses are chaotic and maddening. Full of lust and laughter. Filling my heart with more love than I could ever imagine. We roll until Becca is atop, her body stretched out on mine perfectly.

When Becca sits up, her knees on either side of me, I raise a brow at her. "You got some plans, Mrs. Mitchell?"

She beams at the name as she nods. "I do. And I can't have you overexerting yourself. I need my husband to perform well on the ice tonight."

"Fuck I love it when you call me your husband," I groan.

Becca grabs my cock, positioning it at her entrance before slowly sinking down. "Do you like it better when I call you my husband, or when I call you mine?"

Fuck. "The latter, actually."

Becca surprises the hell out of me when she bends over to grab my cowboy hat, placing it gently on her head. She then leans down so her mouth is next to my ear and whispers, "Mine."

Jesus. I'm two seconds away from coming, and my wife hasn't even moved yet.

My wife.

I hope that never gets old.

Becca begins a tortuously slow pace as my hands stroke across her soft skin. Eyes closed with her head thrown back, she is exquisite as she rides me. Her pussy flutters around me the closer she gets to her orgasm, and I'm fighting tooth and nail not to come myself. I want her to come while I watch, and then I want her to come again, but with me.

"You're so fucking beautiful like this," I grate out. "You're glowing."

"I thought only pregnant women were supposed to glow," she pants, and fuck me, but the thought of her pregnant with my baby is so hot I almost lose my load right there.

"Fuck," I hiss.

Becca's eyes open, and she studies me. "What? You should share your thoughts, Jacob."

Oh, she wants me to share? Alright.

I flick the hat off her head, then grab her by the waist, flipping us. The move keeps her legs wrapped around me. "You want to know what I'm thinking?"

"Yes. Always."

Leaning down, I kiss her hard, then whisper against her lips, "I'm thinking about you. Pregnant. Glowing. You riding me while our child grows inside your belly. Watching how it changes your body. It makes me wonder how sensitive your tits will be, and if I'll be able to get you off by just playing with them. Sucking on them. Owning you."

"Holy hell, Jacob," Becca sucks in rapidly, her eyes so blown out with lust I can barely see any of the iris. I feel her pussy tightening, and I slip a hand in between our bodies to find her clit. Pushing down, I witness Becca's eyes roll back as she comes. As much as I try to fight it, I follow her over the cliff.

After cleaning us up, I drag Becca under the sheets.

"Was that just the sex talking? Or were you really talking about babies?" she asks quietly. I look down to find her chewing nervously on her bottom lip.

"I guess I was really talking about babies. We haven't really had that conversation yet. Do you want kids?" I ask.

"If you'd have asked me six months ago, I would have said no. Growing up the way that I did, I was fearful of bringing another person into life. I worried I wouldn't be a good mother, that I didn't have the right skill set for it. But then I met you," she smiles, "and you had an equally shitty upbringing. Yet you don't have the same outlook. You see the world differently, and you've shown me how patient you can be. You're going to be an amazing dad, Jacob. And that gives me hope that maybe, someday, I'll be a good mom."

"I think you aren't giving yourself enough credit, Becs. I see how you are with Thunder. He's basically your first baby. Just because you have a shitty family doesn't mean you're destined to be a bad parent. We've had the best examples for what *not* to do. Now we get to parent the way we wanted our parents to be. That's a pretty nice set of circumstances if you ask me."

"Can I be honest with you?" she asks.

"Always."

"I don't think I could handle being pregnant, or having a baby, with your schedule. I couldn't wait twenty-four more hours to see you. I can't imagine how difficult it would be with a baby."

"I figure I only have a year or two left before I retire," I confess, telling her something I've barely said out loud to myself. I've only spoken to Coach about my contract, but I'm glad to be bringing this up to my wife now. Her input is critical for my plans, because she's my family. We're a team now. "I'm tired. My body isn't recovering like it did in my twenties. And while I will always love this sport, I'm seeing the light at the end of the tunnel. Whether a baby comes this year, or five years from now, don't worry about me. I know my future is you. I just want us."

"My biological clock isn't necessarily ticking," she says with a laugh, "but a baby will happen before five years are up. I don't want to wait that long."

"Okay, darlin'," I reply with a chuckle. "You're the baker. You make the decision about when we start trying."

Becca bursts into laughter. "The baker?"

"It would be a bun in the oven, so that makes you the baker."

"What are you then?"

"A distributor? Supplier? I provide the necessary ingredient."

"The distributor. Has a nice ring to it," she says with a snicker. "But I think you're actually the baker, and I'm the oven."

"I think I'll go with baker, because calling me the distributor means I either sound like an insurance company, or a weird vigilante who doles out penances for crimes that slide past authorities."

Becca's loud cackles blur the sound of my alarm going off. "Damn. I've got thirty minutes until I need to be on the team bus."

She frowns. "Gosh, that went by faster than I thought it would. When will you be back tonight?"

I nudge her chin with my thumb. "I was hoping you'd come to the game."

"Really?" she asks as a beautiful smile breaks across her face.

"Yeah, baby. You haven't seen me skate yet. I'd like you to come."

She nods enthusiastically, and I'm so fucking happy I shout with glee. "Jacob! Everyone probably heard that!"

"Good," I mumble as I cover her body with mine and nuzzle her neck. "Then everyone knows you're spoken for."

Three hours later, I'm on the ice, my eyes on my wife instead of the puck, and I couldn't care less.

"Jax! Get the fuck off the ice if you aren't gonna do your fucking job!" Coach bellows at me. I skate toward the bench, massive smile on my face. He stops me before I step off the ice, his eyes narrowing. "I take it everything worked out with your wife? Did she find you okay?"

Using my stick, I point to Becca. She's right behind our bench, exactly where I want her to be. "Sure did. You could have warned me she was coming, you know."

"Yeah, I could have, but I bet you enjoyed the surprise." Coach turns to see her, but she doesn't notice him. Her eyes are solely focused on me. "Tell her to wait at the visitor's locker room. I didn't have enough time to chat with her when I met her in Cleveland, and I left you two in your own little bubble on the way back to Denver."

"I'll make sure she's there," I answer.

"And Jax," Coach says, snapping his fingers in front of my face, "Don't pull that shit again on the ice. This is your job, so be here, and do the fucking work."

I nod as I sit beside Daws, and he leans toward me. "The fuck was that, man? You got your head in the clouds out there."

I struggle to withhold the shit-eating grin that breaks across my face. My cheeks actually hurt from smiling so much since Becca showed up. "I know, but I'm good now. My girl loves me, and she's here, so now I can focus."

Gabe rolls his eyes as he chuckles, but I know he understands. He and Cassie had a similar experience at the first game she attended as his. He got hurt, went into the locker room, and came out with the focus of a gnat. Apparently Cassie had visited him during that time and professed her love for him, and he was understandably distracted after that. Now I get it. "I gave you shit after that first game with Cassie, but damn. Now I know how you felt. I could walk away right now and not care."

"I know what you mean. I haven't publicized it yet, but I'm retiring at the end of the season. My contract is up, and I don't think my body can take much more. I'd be willing to think about a one-year contract with the Wolves, but I won't be traded. We're happy in Denver," Gabe says quietly.

"Second line!" Coach shouts.

My mind whirls as I take in Gabe's words, but I shove them to the side as we get a breakaway with the puck. Gabe has a shot all lined up, but at the last second, he passes it to me. I'm closer to the goal, but a Miami defender sits between me and the goalie. Doing some relatively fancy footwork I probably couldn't repeat if I tried, I fake to the right, switch my stick, and shoot from my left side, watching as the puck sails over the goalie's right shoulder.

The boys crowd me in celebration of my goal, and I look at Gabe in confusion. "Why didn't you take the shot?"

He shrugs and gives me a smile. "Your girl is here. Trust me, Jax. If she's anything like Cassie, she'll be *really* excited to celebrate when you get back to the hotel."

I laugh as I shake my head, but as soon as I lock eyes with Becca behind the bench, I know what Gabe says is true. She's looking at me like she's never seen anything hotter.

After a blowout win where I scored two goals and had two assists, Becca meets me by the locker room entrance. She's downright quivering with sexual tension, and I'm not sure if she'll make it back to the hotel before she combusts.

"Jacob, I — what — I mean, wow," she stammers.

I'm still in my uniform, only having removed my skates, and I lean down to whisper in her ear. "You okay, darlin'? You seem a little tense."

I hear her whimper. "Why was that so hot?"

"The goal?"

"No," she moans. "The whole thing. The goal was hot. You getting in that other guy's face. Did you wink at me at one point? I've never come in public before, Jacob, so I don't know how I might act, but that almost made me find out."

"Never in public?"

"I mean, not in front of other people, no."

"But you've come in public before?" I ask, lowering my voice so only she hears. No one is in the periphery, but this conversation is clearly meant for only me and my wife.

"Define public," she whispers.

"Well, if I were to take you into a room down the hall right now, and have my way with you, would you come? And would that be considered public?"

"Good Lord," she moans. "Maybe? I don't know. How long until you're ready? Do you have to ride the bus? Jacob, I'm *aching*."

Fuck. "You need me to take care of that ache, baby?"

"Yes. Please."

Taking her hand, I drag her down the hallway. I don't know where I'm going, but I'm determined to find a private area. If my wife needs me to take care of that ache, I'm fucking doing it.

Becca

CHAPTER 25

Old Becca would be embarrassed, or mortified, to be discussing sex and orgasms in public.

New Becca just wants — no, *needs* — to get off, consequences be damned.

I jog behind Jacob as he strides down a darkened hallway. At this point, I'm so turned on I wouldn't say no to him doing me against the wall right now.

"I like where your mind is, Spitfire, but no one sees your body, or your orgasm, but me," he says over his shoulder.

"Did I say that out loud?" I wonder.

"You did."

"I'm not apologizing," I respond, making him laugh. He tries two doors before he finds one unlocked, and unceremoniously drags me into what appears to be a large room with shelves of cleaning supplies. He shuts the door, and I hear the lock engage as I'm pushed against the wall.

"This is gonna be quick, darlin'. I don't know how long we have until someone comes along, and Coach will have my ass if he realizes I'm not where I'm supposed to be."

"You don't have to do this," I whisper. "I can wait."

Jacob cups my face between his hands. "I told you I'd make you happy. And if you think I'm going to turn down a chance to get you on my tongue, you're sorely mistaken."

I've barely digested his words before Jacob is on his knees, my leggings and panties around my ankles, and his mouth covers my pussy. I let out a loud moan before covering my mouth with my hands. His tongue slides against my clit with a quick flick, flick, flick, and he pushes one finger into my channel, finding my G-spot and pressing against it. The combination, along with how turned on I was to begin with, brings me to the brink immediately. When he catches my clit between his teeth, I bow off the wall in an extremely intense orgasm. But he doesn't stop. I come twice more before Jacob finally sits back.

"I can't feel my legs," I blurt out, looking down to find him dragging the back of his hand across his mouth. He gives me a devious smile as he pulls my clothes up.

"I'm not apologizing," he parrots back at me, making me laugh this time.

"I should have thought about this. How am I supposed to walk? I don't know if I can get in and out of a rideshare or not."

"You won't be. You'll ride the bus with me," Jacob says simply.

"Won't that get you in trouble?" I ask.

"I doubt it. They may ask that you get on the bus before the team. Sooner or later, a reporter is going to connect the dots that you rode the bus in Cleveland, and I don't want someone to make a big stink about it."

"A teammate?"

"No, the media. People are dumb, and they focus on stupid shit. That'll be the focus instead of a guy getting a DUI, or someone being under investigation for tax fraud. I don't want to bring any unnecessary duress to you than absolutely needed."

"I'm honestly surprised we haven't been more of a focus in the news," I comment. "I know my boss promised he wouldn't allow any coverage on our marriage, but I expected everyone else to be salivating at the news."

"No one really knows yet, darlin'. Our PR department has done a great job of redirecting everyone, and even the pictures someone took of us in Vegas never saw the light of day." Jacob rises, leaning in to peck my lips quickly. Crowding me against the wall, I feel so treasured. Sheltered. Loved. "I promised to protect you, and I'll do everything in my power to do so. Plus, I kinda like being in this little honeymoon bubble with you."

"I love you," I whisper, so overcome with emotion and adoration for this man that I can't go another second without gushing about it.

"Never gonna get old hearing that from you," he says quietly. "I love you. As much as I would love to stand here with you, I have to get back."

"Go," I say, laughing. "I think I need a minute more."

He kisses me again, before opening the door to sprint toward the locker room. I take a long exhale, my body still vibrating from the orgasms, but I jump when my phone buzzes with an incoming call. It's marked as a private number, and against my better judgment, I answer.

"This is the thanks I get for raising you?" My mother screams. "You have my only child arrested? I have never been so disgusted with you in my entire life!"

"You didn't raise me," I fire back. "You put up with me. At least now I know why. It wasn't my fault your husband cheated, but you still treated me like trash."

"That's because you are trash! You're no better than your actual mother. Trash that thought she'd made it big when she got pregnant with you. Honestly I wasn't surprised when she dumped you on our doorstep and ran."

"She ran?" I whisper, tears filling my eyes. I hoped my brother was lying. That maybe my birth mother was out there somewhere, even though I knew the truth in my gut. I'd already assumed I'd never find her, because she'd have reached out already if she wanted to be found.

"Of course she ran. Your father wouldn't give her the money

she wanted. He only gave her items you'd actually need. Once she realized you weren't the cash cow she thought she had, she was gone." The sheer gloating oozing out of my mother's voice is making me nauseous. Until yesterday, I thought I'd just been a disappointment to her. I never could have imagined she actually despised me.

"Do you even know her name?" I ask somewhat belligerently.

"Drop the charges against my son, and I'll tell you," she answers.

My mouth drops open in disbelief. Bartering for my birth mother's name? Certainly didn't have that on my bingo card for the week. "No, *Margaret*. I'm not trading Rodney's release for a woman's name."

"Then I hope you burn in hell, you ungrateful little bitch," she hisses, and I hear the telltale sign of the call ending. Removing the phone from my ear, my hand shakes as I look at the screen. Adrenaline courses through my veins, but not in a bad way. For once, I'm proud of myself. I may not have gotten the last word, but I stood up to the woman who raised me. Or at least pretended to raise me. Old Becca would have bent over backwards, trying to appease my family. New Becca recognizes how toxic my family is, and wants no part of it.

"Becca?" I hear, and when my head raises, I see a man in his late thirties smiling at me. "Bennett Davenport, Jax's coach. I'm not sure if you remember meeting me in Cleveland."

"Oh, hi," I rush out in an exhale of relief. "I do remember you. I only saw the back of your head during the game, and the one time I rode the bus I didn't see you after you yelled at everyone to be respectful. I'm glad we can talk now."

He laughs. "You did see me, but you and Jax were a little preoccupied. I'm assuming the same preoccupation is what brought him into the locker room late this evening as well."

Heat flares up my neck and onto my face. "Well, umm ..."

Coach Davenport waves a hand nonchalantly. "I think it's a rite of passage with this organization to have some preoccupied fun here and there. My wife and I … well, I almost got fired for what we did, and my niece apparently convinced her husband to try out the Zamboni during a power outage."

"That thing that mows the ice?" I wonder aloud. Jacob told me the name, but I couldn't remember it.

"You really need to meet my niece and her husband. She called the Zamboni an 'ice lawnmower' for the longest time," he says, laughing while using air quotes. "Her husband retired a year ago. Are you hoping for Jax to retire sooner rather than later?"

"Oh," I blurt out, surprised. "We haven't talked about it in depth. I'd never ask him to retire. He's obviously quite happy playing hockey."

Coach Davenport tilts his head to the side, studying me. "He's not. He won't admit that, though. At least not to me. I think he's ready to be done, but wants to be sure he has the support of his friends and family. It's an incredibly difficult decision, choosing between what your heart wants and your body needs."

"I won't tell him to retire. That's not my decision," I state firmly. I'm flabbergasted at how quickly the conversation with Jacob's coach got serious. I don't know this man, yet he's giving me his opinion on Jacob's career. "It almost sounds like you want me to convince him to retire, and that is not my place. Honestly, it's incredibly disrespectful for you to assume Jacob can't make his own career decisions. He's spoken so highly of you, but I'm finding you to be a big disappointment."

Coach Davenport's grin widens as he throws back his head in raucous laughter. "I'm not trying to convince you to do anything. I did want to see if you'd fight for Jax, though. He's had a shitty hand of cards dealt to him in regards to family members, and I wanted to be sure his wife would be his champion. You're one hell of a fighter, Mrs. Mitchell."

"Not cool, man," Jacob says from behind me as he pulls me into his arms. The scent of his body wash floats over me, and I immediately relax into his embrace. "I don't appreciate you trying to trick her."

Coach Davenport shrugs. "I'm sick of seeing my guys get suckered into situations with puck bunnies, or relationships with women who only want them for their bank accounts. If they're in it for the wrong reasons, they'll agree with everything I say. But, just like the case with Becca here, when they're truly happy and in love, they'll argue back. You've got a strong woman in your corner, Jax."

"I know I do," Jacob replies proudly. Coach Davenport nods at us before walking back toward the locker room. "You okay, darlin'?"

I nod. "That was a very strange conversation. I didn't like what he was insinuating."

"I only caught the tail end. What was his argument?"

"Basically that you needed me to convince you to retire, and I said I wouldn't do that."

"Why?" he asks as he grabs my hand and begins walking behind his coach.

"Because I trust you to talk to me about it first, and if you wanted to continue playing, I'd support that. I'd never make that kind of decision for you, and I think you'd end up resenting me if you decided to retire based solely on my opinion."

"I'd never retire just because of you, but I'd want your opinion. We're a team now, Spitfire."

"So," I begin as we walk outside into the muggy Miami air, "what are your thoughts on retirement? I know we talked about how you can tell your body isn't the same as it was in your twenties. But is your heart still in it? I'll support whatever you want, Jacob. I'm here to be a sounding board whenever you need me."

"Well, I'm thirty-four. I have another year after this on my contract. I'm already one of the old guys in the locker room, and across the league, there aren't too many guys older than me. Really only a handful. I feel like I'm skating on borrowed time here," he confesses as he motions for me to climb on the bus. Multiple guys call out to us when they see me, making me feel weirdly happy to be part of this family.

"What would make you keep skating?" I ask as we get settled in a row.

"A lot of things," he says, his voice lowering. "A no-trade clause for starters. I'm having difficulty thinking about leaving you for away games, so I can't wrap my head around the possibility of us living in different cities."

"Is money a concern?"

Jacob gives me a lopsided grin. "No, baby. Money is not a concern. Trust me when I say we're good."

"I didn't mean it like that!" I protest with a laugh. "What if they offered you a contract for a lot less than you make now?"

"Hmm. I don't know. I'd have to think about it. Usually a contracted amount directly correlates to how valuable the team thinks you are, so if they offered me something significantly less, I'd assume they also didn't feel I would bring anything to the team."

"I think this is where I'd really give my opinion," I state firmly. "If you don't feel like an asset, you won't enjoy the time with the team. I just want you to find joy."

He gives me a sweet smile. "I know you do, darlin'. I'm pretty damn lucky that you bring me more joy than I can handle."

My phone vibrates in my pocket, jarring me out of our conversation. Seeing another private number, I turn the phone completely off and throw it into my bag.

"What was that?" Jacob asks, surprise evident in his tone.

"Oh, probably my mother calling with another guilt trip about my brother. Oh, I guess that's not accurate. She's my step-mother."

"What the fuck?" Jacob seethes. "What have I missed here?"

I quickly explain what my brother said yesterday, and then the phone call with my mother only a few minutes ago. "In hindsight, this explains so much. I always felt like she didn't truly love me, but I couldn't understand why. Here she was, tasked with raising a child that her husband created out of wedlock. I can't imagine that was easy for her."

"Becca, I swear to ever loving God, you better not give that woman even one ounce of sympathy. Her husband cheating on her was not your fault. The fact that she took it out on you is ridiculous. She treated a *child* like shit because she was mad at her husband."

"It doesn't matter now. I told her I wouldn't trade any favors for my birth mother's name, and that was that. As long as she and Rodney leave me alone, I'm happy to move on."

"Oh, I'm gonna guarantee they leave you alone," Jacob says as we pull into the porte cochère in front of the hotel. "I'll call the investigator tomorrow to get an update."

"It's such a surreal thing to have your husband hire a PI to research your family," I muse with a shake of my head.

"I'm sure it is, darlin'. Your dad and brother were into some shady shit. With your dad being gone, everything is gonna fall on your brother. He's going away for a long time, baby."

"What were they involved in?"

"So far, my PI has found bribery, falsifying documents, forgery, tax evasion, some kind of prostitution ring, and insider trading."

"Prostitution?" I shout.

"That's what you picked out of that sentence? I thought you'd have questioned the insider trading. That one involves your mom — I mean, step-mother — so she might go to prison too."

I pause, thinking about the uppity woman and how appalled she'd be in gen pop of a women's prison. "I really love this for her."

He smirks. "I figured you would."

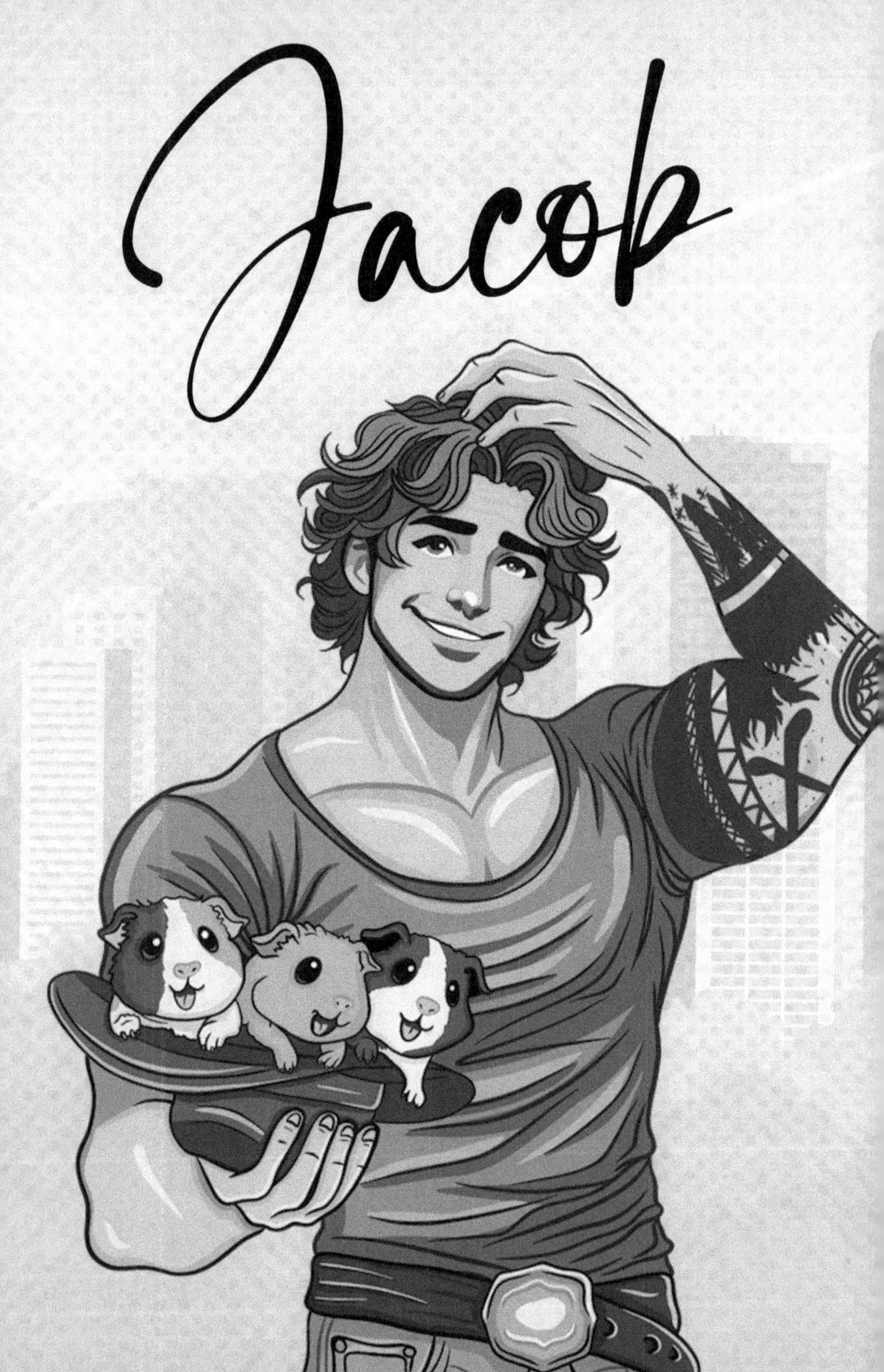
Jacob

EPILOGUE

My private investigator made his money's worth with Becca's family. Some white collar criminals are impressive with how they cover their tracks. Then there are people like her family, who left one hell of a paper trail for every illegal thing they did. By the time all was said and done, Rodney Junior received a sentence of fifteen to thirty years in prison, while his dear mother received ten to twenty years.

I only know of their sentences because I kept up with their trials. My wife wrote them off the moment we left Miami, and never mentioned them again. She made peace with her lack of biological family. Only after my investigator found her original birth certificate were we able to piece together the first few months of her life.

Becca's mother, Tina, struggled immensely attempting to raise Becca on her own. Contrary to what Becca's step-mother suggested, Tina did not ask for money. She had loved Rodney Senior, and innocently hoped Rodney would come to his senses and leave his wife for her and Becca. When that didn't happen, Tina fell into a deep depression. She lost her job, was evicted from her apartment, and could no longer afford any of the necessities of raising an infant. In a moment of intense despair, she left Becca on Rodney's doorstep, and intended to return for Becca once she established herself again.

Unfortunately, Tina never returned. The PI tracked her to Detroit, where she seemed to disappear. A death record showed Tina passed away from complications due to breast cancer when Becca was around fifteen.

Becca mourned the mother she never knew, but found peace knowing Tina was no longer suffering in any way. It took some time, however, and I worry what I'm about to tell her will set her back again.

"Baby?" I call as I enter our apartment. It's been two years since I met Becca Stephens, and not a day goes by that I'm not thanking God for putting me in Becca's path.

"With the pigs!" she shouts. We lost Rose and Daffodil to guinea pig old age, and I find Becca, more often than not, hanging with the remaining four. I never knew how traumatizing an animal dying would be, and I certainly never knew the average lifespan of a guinea pig was so damn short.

"Hey," I tell her as I stride into the room. Thunder now has a large dog bed in the corner, content to watch the pigs. All it took was Dahlia biting him once and he never chased another pig again. Placing a brief kiss on Becca's forehead, I squat next to her, pulling a small rodent box from behind my back. "I have a present for you."

"Oh!" she squeals. "Did you get us another guinea pig?"

"Yes ..." I answer hesitantly as she carefully opens the lid. "Technically I got two. You know I have a thing for even numbers."

"They are so adorable," she gushes quietly. Looking at me, she asks, "have you already named them?"

"Well, I've named one. I wanted you to name the other one. The brown and black one needs a name, but the all white one, I've named —"

"Hyacinth," she interrupts. "I know you. You named her Hyacinth."

I do fucking love how this woman knows me, inside and out. "Her name is Hyacinth."

To this day, I get Becca bouquets of white hyacinths fairly often, and she never tells me to stop.

"I think the brown and black one should be called Tulip," Becca says. "I hope the rest of the girls are nice to them."

"We'll work on introducing everyone slowly, but for now, we'll put the two newbies in their own cage."

"That makes sense." She looks up at me again, love shining in her eyes. "I don't know why you decided to get me guinea pigs today, but thank you. I love them."

I hesitate briefly before explaining what I *really* need to tell her. "I have something else I need to give you, and I'll admit I'm a little freaked out about how you're going to handle it."

"Okay?" she responds with a light laugh. "You're not going to unretire, are you?"

"No," I chuckle. Our conversation in Miami made me acutely aware of my career, and whether or not I felt I'd achieved everything I'd set out to do. I realized quickly that I was pleased with what I'd done. I made the decision to retire at the end of that season, and I haven't regretted it once. "My PI reached out to me. I never told you, but he continued to investigate your birth mother. He finally found some family of hers."

"What?" she breathes, and I wince slightly as her eyes fill with tears. Fuck, I hate it when my wife cries.

"Yeah. She had a baby book for you, darlin'. She kept track of everything, even journaling a few times she saw you in public after she took you to your dad's."

"Oh my God," Becca whispers as I pull the book out from behind my back. She reverently takes it from me, tracing the hand-written 'Rebecca' on the front. I watch as she carefully flips through the book, full of Polaroid pictures and tidbits about her newborn life.

"There's something else, baby," I tell her quietly, waiting until her eyes meet mine. "You have a sister."

"What?" Tears cascade down her cheeks as she digests the information. "She had another baby?"

"A couple years after you were born. She just turned thirty-three. Her name is Emma, and she wants to meet you."

"Really? She wants to meet me?"

"She does."

"Does she still live in Detroit? Is she married? Does she have kids?" Becca peppers me with questions.

"She moved to Chicago. She is married, and I believe she's currently pregnant with her first child," I answer, but I'm surprised when Becca cries harder. "What's going on in that head of yours? I didn't think you'd be more upset."

"I'm just so happy," she cries. "Because it's something I'll get to share with her."

"What?"

She gives me a watery smile as she places something in my hand. "Pregnancy."

I stare down at the digital pregnancy test, the word 'pregnant' big and bold across the screen, and I forget how to breathe. "Pregnant? Really? We weren't even really trying."

She nods. "I'm as surprised as you. The OBGYN said it might take a while because of my age. I didn't even realize my period was late until I got sick outside the station this morning. The food trucks didn't smell good to the baby, I guess."

I reach forward and tenderly touch her stomach. "There's a baby in there."

Becca nods again. "It's surreal, isn't it? I'm making a human."

We spent the first eighteen months of our marriage enjoying each other's company. We weren't actively trying to get pregnant, but we weren't opposed to it either. Becca's OBGYN explained the concept of a geriatric pregnancy, which is a bullshit way to say

Becca's reproductive system is getting older. The doctor also encouraged us to be patient and to enjoy the 'trying' process of making a baby. I always enjoy sex with my wife, but I could tell Becca was going to stress herself out with negative thoughts.

Two months with two negative pregnancy tests were heartbreaking, but it never occurred to me that she'd get a positive this quickly.

"I wonder how far along my sister is," Becca says quietly, a smile blooming on her face as she says the word 'sister.' "She really wants to meet me?"

"She does. In fact, the private investigator gave her my phone number. I wasn't completely confident that you'd be excited about this information, so I figured it was better to dole out my number instead of yours. Emma should be calling in about an hour."

Becca sniffles, wiping her nose with the corner of her shirt. "This is a lot to process in an hour's time."

"A sister, a niece or nephew, and a son or daughter? Yeah, I'd say it's been a big afternoon," I laugh.

Becca's eyes widen. "A niece or nephew! I never thought of that! How old is your information? Maybe she already had the baby. I should get a gift just in case. Oh! What if she decides she wants to do a FaceTime call instead? I look like crap. Should I shower? I have to make a good first impression, don't I?"

"God, I love you," I tell her, grinning widely. "You are so fucking amazing. And no, you don't need to shower. You look spectacular."

She rolls her eyes. "You just want to get lucky."

I cock an eyebrow at her. "So? We have a whole hour. Might as well take your mind off everything with a couple of orgasms."

"Oh, I guess. If you insist," she says sweetly as she grabs my face and brings it to hers. Becca attempts to deepen the kiss, but I pull away. "What's wrong?"

I nod toward the guinea pig cages. "Not in front of the kids."

Standing, I swoop Becca up into my arms, bridal style, and carry my laughing wife all the way to our bedroom. She doesn't complain with her orgasm, or the three others I give her, before I follow her into bliss myself. What a way to celebrate the best day of my life so far.

The only day that tops it is nine months later, when Becca gives birth to our son, Jackson James Mitchell.

I couldn't have predicted the happiness I'd find when I ran into my little Spitfire years ago, or the peace and contentment she'd bring just by being near me. I guess our forecast calls for beautiful days, filled with Colorado blue skies, and I'm pretty damn happy about it.

Preorder the next book in the Mile High Sports Series starring Colorado Coyotes quarterback Jamie here:

If you can't get enough of Jacob and Becca, I've got a special bonus scene just for you! Our pair is headed out to do a little summer storm chasing as they look for another white tornado. Get it here:

Want to keep up with updates, news, and other Jen-related thoughts? Sign up for my newsletter here:

And join my Facebook group here!

Acknowledgements

In another life, I know in my heart I was a meteorologist. Weather never ceases to amaze me. How quickly things change, how every cloud is unique, and how a single storm cell can bring drastically different precipitation within the same county (in fact, in 2015, I was under a tornado warning, and the northern part of my county was under a winter storm warning!).

I'd like to thank my fellow weather lover, Valerie, for fact-checking all the weather details, and confirming I've done a suitable job.

My PA, Morgan, for attempting to keep me in line and on task.

To my beta team for correcting all of my mistakes and reminding me to actually try to remember details (nice try, ladies, but it's a lost cause at this point).

To KB Barrett and S. Renea for delivering the best dang covers I've ever seen, not only bringing Jax to life, but also his perfect pigs. I'm absolutely in love with the covers for this series!

To Tamara, Catie, Becky, and AJ: I'm so thankful for you all and your friendship. Our author zooms are sometimes off the rails, but I wouldn't have it any other way.

To Luna Literary Management, thank you for your ridiculously phenomenal creativity with graphics and pulling in tons of new readers to my world.

And finally, to my husband and kids: thank you for putting up with me, especially when I procrastinate and have zero time-management skills, thus becoming a hot mess when I'm up against a deadline. I'd say I'll do better for the next book, but just like I said to the beta team, it's a lost cause. Procrastination is my jam.

Also by
JENNIFER J. WILLIAMS

Jennifer was born and raised in Ohio, but currently calls Colorado home. A lifelong lover of romance books, Jen felt pulled to write stories with older characters, because "old farts" deserve love too. Jen prides herself on delivering realistic characters that struggle with normal problems. She spends most of her free time within her zoo: two kids, two dogs, and two cats...and a new puppy! When not containing the chaos, Jen can be found lounging on her covered porch devouring books on her Kindle.